DIAL P FOR POISON

MOVIE CLUB MYSTERIES, BOOK 1

ZARA KEANE

BEAVERSTONE PRESS LLC

DIAL P FOR POISON
(Movie Club Mysteries, Book 1)

You can take the girl out of the force, but you can't keep her away from the action...

Maggie Doyle moves to Ireland to escape her cheating ex and crumbling career in the San Francisco PD. When the most hated woman on Whisper Island is poisoned at her aunt's Movie Theater Café, Maggie and her rock-hard muffins are hurled into the murder investigation.

With the help of her UFO-enthusiast friend, a nun, and a feral puppy, Maggie is determined to clear her aunt's name. Can she catch the murderer before they strike again? Or will her terrible baking skills burn down the café first?

Join my mailing list and get news, giveaways, and an exclusive FREE Movie Club Mystery serial!

http://zarakeane.com/newsletter2

A NOTE ON GAELIC TERMS

Certain Gaelic terms appear in this book. I have tried to use them sparingly and in contexts that should make their meaning clear to international readers. However, a couple of words require clarification.

The official name for the Irish police force is *An Garda Síochána* ("the Guardian of the Peace"). Police are *Gardaí* (plural) and *Garda* (singular). Irish police are commonly referred to as "the guards".

The official rank of a police officer such as Sergeant O'Shea is Garda Sergeant O'Shea. As the Irish frequently shorten this to Sergeant, I've chosen to use this version for all but the initial introduction to the character.

The official name for the Whisper Island police station would be Whisper Island Garda Station, but Maggie, being American, rarely thinks of it as such.

The Irish police do not, as a rule, carry firearms. Permission to carry a gun is reserved to detectives and specialist units, such as the Emergency Response Unit. The police on Whisper Island would not have been issued with firearms.

Although this book follows American spelling conventions, I've chosen to use the common Irish spelling for proper names such as Carraig Harbour and the Whisper Island Medical Centre.

1

Whisper Island, Ireland

My career in the San Francisco PD ended the day I had to arrest my husband. Okay, so maybe I shouldn't have punched him…twice. And kicked him in the groin. But seriously, what would you do if you'd discovered your husband was sleeping with his paralegal, and adding to your humiliation with a boozy post-screw drive down a busy freeway? He knew how I felt about fidelity, and he knew my thoughts on drunk driving. It was both our misfortune that I'd happened to be the cop who'd pulled him over.

Thanks to my temper, four weeks after my marriage and my career had imploded, I found myself five thousand miles away from home, clinging to the side of a rocking boat and hurling the last of my dignity into the waves below.

"I hate boats," I muttered, pressing a napkin to my mouth. "And I hate storms."

A flash of lightning zigzagged across the sky as if to illuminate my point. Despite my nausea, I drew in a breath at the magnificence of the jagged coastline looming in the distance. The sheer cliffs towered over the rough sea, just as hauntingly beautiful as I remembered from childhood summers. I hadn't been to Whisper Island in over ten years, but I recalled every tree, cave, and hill of the island where my father had been born.

The ferry rocked into the harbor at midnight, an hour behind schedule. Shivering in the icy wind, I limped down the pedestrian gangplank, dragging my two rolling suitcases behind me. The suitcases contained the remains of my life. I'd sold all but two of my evening gowns to a friend's used dress store and had listed most of my shoe collection on eBay. I'd have sold my jewelry, but it apparently belonged to Joe's mother, courtesy of some fancy legal wheeling and dealing he'd done to ensure I couldn't claim more than a pittance if we ever split up. My nostrils flared. Never trust a lawyer, especially one you marry.

On the pier, I paused and scanned my surroundings. Several fishing boats bobbed in the water, straining at their moorings. No tourist yachts were in sight, but I'd never been to the island in winter. Apart from the bitter January wind, the pier was just as I remembered it: an old-fashioned wooden affair with a ferry terminal at one end and the red-and-white facade of the yacht club built into the side of the cliff. After the foot passengers had disembarked, the cars would exit the ferry and be transported up the cliff by means of a car elevator. I shuddered at the prospect of being enclosed in such a tight space and felt grateful I was on foot. I inhaled the sea air, relishing the salty taste on my tongue. It was good to be back.

"Maggie? Is that you, love?" A woman's voice boomed into my ear, making my heart leap in my chest. In the next instant, a small woman roughly the shape of a soccer ball tackled me in a bear hug.

"Aunt Noreen? Have you been waiting all this time? We're more than an hour late."

She waved her hand in a dismissive gesture. "The ferry is always late this time of year. I asked old Tom up in the ferry office to give me a call when he spotted the boat. My house is only a fifteen-minute drive away." My aunt looked me up and down before squeezing me in another bear hug. "It's lovely to see you, Maggie. It's been too long."

Four years to be precise. My aunt had grown older and plumper since the last time I'd seen her, which had been at my wedding. She wrested my suitcases from my grasp, and I found myself hauled down the pier in her determined wake. She marched me past the ticket office and toward an ancient elevator, already packed with ferry passengers. Those who'd arrived in vehicles watched dubiously as they were loaded, one by one, into a special cage and hoisted up the cliff.

"I prefer the harbor in Smuggler's Cove," my aunt said, following the direction of my gaze, "but Carraig is the one closest to the mainland, and it's the only one the ferry stops at during the winter months."

"I guess there aren't enough passengers to warrant making the trip all the way to the other side of the island."

"Exactly. As of May, it's a whole different story." My aunt gestured for me to step into the rickety elevator. "Let's get you home. It's freezing out here tonight."

I dug my frozen hands into my jacket's pockets. "I, uh, think I'll take the stairs."

My aunt frowned at me. "Are you sure? It's a long way up."

"I could do with the exercise. Can you take my luggage?"

"Sure. See you at the top." Noreen dragged my suitcases into the elevator, oblivious to the wince of pain from the elderly man she rolled over. She gave me a cheery wave before the doors slid shut and the elevator began its shuddering ascent.

I took a deep breath and contemplated the steps that led from the pier to the top of the cliff. It had to be several floors high, but a rickety metal staircase was preferable to an enclosed space. Or so I told myself until I reached the hundredth step, panting for breath. Man, I was out of shape. After a month spent at the bottom of a bag of Doritos, what could I expect? Groaning, I hauled myself up the steps and breathed a sigh of relief when I reached the top. Tomorrow, I'd go running. I might even go wild and eat a salad.

Noreen and my suitcases were waiting for me in the parking lot near the elevator exit, standing beside a dilapidated Ford Fiesta that bore traces of its original green paint among the rust.

"Well now," my aunt said, giving me a critical once-over. "Would you look at the state of you? Sure, you're nothing but skin and bones."

The skin-and-bones part was far from the truth. I didn't need to stand on the scales to know I was the most out of shape I'd been my whole adult life. During my post-crisis slump, I'd comfort eaten my way up a dress size.

Noreen beamed up at me, and I braced myself for another rib-crushing hug. She didn't disappoint. When my aunt released me from her viselike clutches, she opened the trunk of the car and hurled my suitcase in among an array of fishing rods, hockey sticks, and golf clubs. Despite my aunt's girth, she was a formidable sportswoman and a terror on the hockey pitch. "Let's get you home and fed, love."

"Thanks," I said as I slid into the passenger seat, gingerly removing a golf ball from under my backside, "but I have no appetite. I spent most of the trip over from the mainland being sick over the side of the boat."

Noreen gave a derisive snort. "Nonsense. You've been through a traumatic time. You need feeding."

"Trust me, I've been doing plenty of feeding," I

said with a wry smile. "Tomorrow, I promise I'll finish all twenty-three meals you put in front of me. Right now, all I want is sleep."

"All right," she grunted, clearly unhappy at my reluctance to chow down on an enormous meal served at midnight. "Now, how do you feel about cats?"

The question came out of left field. "I...have no particular opinion about them." In truth, I was ambivalent about animals. My only childhood pet had been a goldfish, and my contact with pets since had been fending off rabid dogs while arresting their owners.

"Excellent," Noreen said as though I'd just informed her she'd won the lottery. "I have eight."

"Eight...cats?" My eyebrows shot up in alarm. I hadn't visited my aunt's house on Whisper Island since I was a teenager, but I recalled her cottage as being on the snug side of small. "Where do they all sleep?"

"Oh, you know." She waved a hand vaguely as her car shot out of the parking lot at breakneck speed and turned onto a winding cliffside road. "Wherever they feel like it. I'm putting you in Roly and Poly's room. Don't worry, love," she added, seeing my expression of horror. "Just shoo them off the bed if they're bothering you."

Visions of a cat-infested house danced before my eyes. I peered out the window and saw how close we were to the edge of the cliff. Swallowing hard, I hunched back in my seat and let my aunt prattle on about islanders I'd never met. Had I made a massive mistake in accepting her offer of a home and a job? After all, what did I know about cafés? What did I know about living in Ireland?

"All you'll need to do while I'm in the hospital," Noreen had said on the phone two weeks after I'd lost my job and filed for divorce, "is serve a few cups of coffee. The change of scene will do you good. Fresh air and exercise are what you need. There's no point in moping. You're better off without that buffoon, and if those eejits in the San Francisco Police Department don't realize they're losing a gem, you're better off without them, too."

At the time, I'd been veering between drunken and tearful rants to my long-suffering best friend, Selena, and reliving the joy of shoving a handcuffed and bloody Joe into the ambulance after the crash. Had there been any true justice, Joe would have lost his attorney's license along with his driver's license, but money and connections rule, and Joe had an abundance of both. Instead, I'd found myself suspended, and I'd chosen to resign rather than allow my superiors to sentence me to a career as a pen pusher.

The irony of snubbing an admin job in favor of a lowly position as a waitress on a remote Irish island wasn't lost on me, but at least I was living life on my terms. As Noreen had said, the fresh air and distance from my life in San Francisco would do me good. It was only for a couple of months. Long enough for me to get my head together and give me a chance to decide what I wanted to do with the rest of my life.

I regretted my complacency the moment we screeched to a halt outside my aunt's ramshackle cottage. I got out of the car, clutching my neck as a whiplash victim would, and gaped in mounting horror at the sight before me. Inside a fenced enclosure, a large animal roamed. "Is that an alpaca?" I asked in a voice barely above a whisper.

"Yes, that's Horace." Noreen beamed. "Didn't I tell you about my side job? I run a petting zoo."

2

When I dragged my groggy body out of bed at six o'clock the next morning, I was spared the indignity of feeding my aunt's menagerie, but not her panic attack-inducing driving.

"Sorry about the early start, love," Noreen yelled over the roar of the engine as she accelerated past the alpaca and through the gate that separated her plot of land from the road. "I need to open the café in time to catch the breakfast trade."

"No problem." I pulled my woolen hat over my red curls and clutched at my seat belt, braced for another hair-raising drive. Noreen kept the car just over the legal speed limit, but the combo of her jerky driving style and the lack of suspension in her ancient vehicle made for a bouncy ride. To add to my discomfort, I wasn't used to driving on the left side of the road, and I kept trying to hit the brakes. After I'd assured myself that my aunt wasn't about to drive us over the edge of a cliff, I began to relax and enjoy the view.

In stark contrast to last night's dark and stormy welcome, the sky was clear and the moon shone brightly. At this time of the year, the sun wouldn't rise for another couple of hours, but the gentle glow of the moonlight illuminated the landscape. I soaked up the familiar sights of rolling hills and rugged coastline. My heart clenched when I spotted the woods where I'd played as a child during summer vacations spent with my aunt. Although I couldn't see it, the memory of the lake on the far side of the woods loomed large.

"What's the island's original name? I've forgotten the Gaelic term."

"Gaelic is called Irish around here, my girl. Your cousin, Julie, runs Irish language evening classes at the school. You should sign up for one."

"I won't be here long enough to make it worthwhile."

My aunt grinned at me. "We'll see about that. To answer your question, Whisper Island is Inis na Cogar."

"In-Ish-Na-Cougar?"

Noreen laughed. "Not quite, but near enough."

"Where does the island get its name?"

"The shape of the cliffs in certain parts of the island produces a sound like voices whispering when the wind blows."

"Very poetic." To my ears, the sound I'd heard

getting off the ferry last night had more in common with a plane engine, especially when the waves crashed against the rocks, but whatever.

"Whisper Island hasn't changed much since you were here last," Noreen said as if reading my thoughts. "The young people come and go, of course, but old fogies like me stay on."

"Do you still get an influx of tourists in the summer?" I asked, staring out at the smattering of farms that dotted the landscape.

"That we do. If it weren't for the annual invasion, I'd be in dire financial straits." She grimaced. "Okay, *worse* financial straits than I'm already in."

"That bad?" My forehead creased. "I had no idea. Mom said you were doing well."

"I am…in the summer." Noreen shook her improbable black curls. "Like most of the businesses on the island, I rely on the tourist trade. This time of year is hard. I'm experimenting with ways to bring in a little extra during the winter months to take the pressure off."

I grinned. "Hence the petting zoo?"

"Exactly. I also offer the café and the room at the back of the building to local clubs and societies that are too small to qualify for space in the town hall. In return for using my place free of charge, the clubs' members agree to buy drinks and snacks from the café."

"That's a brilliant idea."

"The downside is needing to work late, but it's

saved my bacon this winter." She scowled. "I can only hope it lasts. Sandra Walker keeps petitioning the town council to revoke my Special Restaurant License. Without it, I won't be allowed to serve alcohol on the premises."

I snorted. "Sandra hasn't changed. Lemme guess: she's seen you come up with a creative way to make some extra cash during the low season, and she wants to divert that business to her daughter's restaurant."

"Exactly—a restaurant that no one wants to go to. It's not a case of Sandra wanting a piece of the pie. She wants the whole cake. For months, I've had to deal with surprise visits from pest control, health and safety, and rumors about my café not being sanitary."

"Ugh. I'm sorry, Noreen. No one with a lick of sense will believe it."

"I hope not. I can't afford to lose any more customers, especially this time of year." Noreen's lips twisted into a wry smile. "You know the most annoying part? I know Sandra is trying to get my license to serve alcohol revoked, but I can't prove she's behind the smear campaign. And because this is a small community, I have to grin and bear it when she swans into my place to attend a club meeting."

"All the while making snide remarks about you and your café?" I shook my head. "Like mother, like daughter. Melanie's a pain, but she didn't stand a chance with a mother like Sandra."

My aunt shot me a quick glance. "You're bound to

run into Melanie and Paul while you're on Whisper Island. Are you okay with that?"

To my disgust, the pain of Paul Greer's betrayal still nagged at me. Not as deep or sharp as Joe's, but the hurt—or the memory of that hurt—lingered. First loves left their mark.

"I'm okay with seeing Paul again." I hoped this was true. "I'm less thrilled with the idea of encountering Melanie, but I'll deal."

Melanie had been my childhood nemesis. The fact that Paul had picked her to cheat on me with had made the situation worse, but we'd all been kids. Had Paul and I not had the added frisson of a long-distance relationship with three passionate summers spent together, we'd have fizzled out pretty quickly. Beyond his undeniable good looks and charm, Paul and I hadn't had all that much in common. I was the American girl who'd spent summers on the island, and he was the handsome and wealthy local boy who'd swept me off my feet. I'd spent our long months apart pining for him and convinced we were destined to be together forever. He, apparently, had used my absences as an excuse to move on to the next available girl. Melanie just happened to be the one he'd gotten pregnant.

"I didn't think Paul and Melanie's marriage would last," my aunt mused, "but ten years and four kids later, they're still together."

"Which is more than can be said for my marriage." I fingered the dent left by the wedding and engagement rings I'd removed the night my marriage had ended.

My aunt reached across and patted my arm. "Don't worry, love. We'll fatten you up and find you a good Irishman. I have a few candidates in mind."

"Oh, no." I straightened in my seat, alarm bells sounding in my mind. "Please, no matchmaking. I am so not in the mood for a man right now."

"Maybe it's a little soon," Noreen conceded, "but give it a few months, and I'll hook you up with a nice fella."

"I'm only staying on Whisper Island two months."

Noreen snorted and waved a hand in a dismissive gesture. "So you say. Let's talk about that in a few weeks, eh?"

I opened my mouth to protest the point but closed it again without saying a word. Arguing with Noreen was pointless. When she got an idea into her head, she clung to it with ferocious tenacity. Besides, after two months of having a houseguest, she'd be thrilled to be rid of me.

"Oh, before I forget…open the glove compartment, will you? There's an old mobile phone in there that you can use while you're on the island."

I opened the glove compartment and slid out a battered cell phone that looked several years old. My heart swelled at my aunt's thoughtfulness. "Thank you so much, Noreen."

"It's a pay-as-you-go deal, so you'll need to keep it

topped up with credits. And it doesn't have any of the bells and whistles of a modern phone."

"As long as it works, I'm happy. I'm reluctant to use my U.S. phone over here in case I rack up crazy charges."

My aunt swung the car to the left and took the road toward Smuggler's Cove, the town that over half of the island's five thousand residents called home.

"Tell me about your café," I prompted, keen to divert the course of the conversation away from my checkered love life. "You were vague on the phone."

Noreen laughed. "I wasn't vague. You weren't listening."

She was probably right. I'd been hung over the afternoon she'd called me with the job offer and surrounded by boxes that contained the remnants of my married life. "Yeah...I'm sorry about that."

"Don't be. You were going through a tough time. We've all been there, love."

A lump formed in my throat. My immediate family—mother, father, and siblings—hadn't understood why I'd quit the police department as well as my marriage. When Noreen had called and offered me the chance of a time-out from my life, the soothing lilt of her Irish accent had comforted me, and I'd agreed to come to Whisper Island on a whim.

"The day you called, I'd just moved the last of my stuff out of our—out of Joe's—house. I wasn't in good shape." I bit my lip and blinked back hot tears that I was determined not to shed. Joe Maitland wasn't worth the loss of moisture.

"You're welcome to stay with me as long as you like. Who knows? Maybe you'll grow to love the island so much that you'll never leave." She flashed me a sly grin. "I'll even teach you to cook."

"I'll happily take you up on the cooking lessons, but this is a temporary stop for me. I'm a city girl at heart." Thanks to my Dad, I qualified for an Irish passport and didn't need to worry about an employment permit.

"Sure, what does a city have to offer that we don't? Apart from pollution, traffic congestion, and crime? Any interest or hobby you have, the likelihood is that we've got a club for it. And if there isn't one, start one. That's what I did."

I suppressed a smile. While my father had left Whisper Island the instant he'd finished school, Noreen had never left. Their sister, Philomena, had lived on the mainland while getting her college degree, but she'd moved back a few years later with her young family in tow.

"How are Aunt Philomena and Uncle John? And Julie and the boys?" I'd been close to my cousin when we were kids. To my regret, we hadn't kept in touch. I'd invited her to my wedding, but she'd been backpacking in Australia and hadn't been able to make it.

"Philomena is the very same." Noreen rolled her eyes. "Still bossing people around, both at the library and the various clubs she's involved in. John's

construction business hasn't done well since the property boom ended, but he's hanging in there. Both Jack
and Luke are living in Dublin. As for Julie, she's back
on the island, teaching at the primary school and, as I
mentioned before, teaching Irish language evening
classes. She said she's looking forward to catching up
with you."

"That'll be nice." My heart swelled at the thought
of reconnecting with my cousin. I could do with a
friend, assuming we still had as much in common as
we'd had as kids.

Through the car window, the rolling hills and
winding road gave way to straight streets and a
marked increase in buildings. We entered the town of
Smuggler's Cove a moment later and drove down the
main street past a variety of shops, restaurants, and
businesses, their signs bathed in the light of the street-
lamps. Many of the names were familiar to me, but
there had been changes over the years. I scanned the
storefronts as we drove past. "Which one is
your café?"

"That's it to your right," Noreen said with a note
of pride in her voice, "wedged between the news
agency and the greengrocer's."

I peered out the window and sucked in a breath.
A hand-painted sign proclaimed The Movie Theater
Café. "Oh my goodness," I gasped. "You renovated
the old cinema? I always *loved* that place."

My aunt pulled into the free parking space outside
the café and killed the engine. "When I told your

mother about my plans, she commissioned the sign." She chuckled. "I didn't have the heart to tell her we call movies 'films' in Ireland, but I don't think my customers care. In fact, much of the summer crowd is American tourists. They find the name charming."

"It is charming. I remember thinking it was such a shame that the building was derelict." I unbuckled my seat belt and got out of the car, taking in the sight of the old-fashioned billboard under the café's sign. It read, *Showing this week: The Breakfast Club 07:30 to 11:00.*

"Clever," I said, nodding toward the billboard. "I guess breakfast includes a traditional Irish fry-up?"

"Of course. We also cater to those with smaller appetites, though. We serve a variety of muffins, scones, croissants, and granola, as well as sweet treats galore." My aunt extracted a key from her voluminous purse and opened the door of the café. We stepped inside.

"Oh, wow." I sucked in a breath and soaked in the details. The café was housed in the foyer of the movie theater. The accordion doors had been replaced with one door to the left and a row of floor-to-ceiling windows that stretched to the other wall. The concession stand now served as a bar, and sported an impressive Italian coffee machine as its centerpiece. Comfortable-looking leather chairs surrounded wooden tables that were each named after a vintage movie star. The box office appeared to be the place where people paid for their food and drinks, as well as collected information on upcoming island club events. I turned to my aunt. "You've done a fantastic job with the renovations."

"Thanks." My aunt grinned at me. "You used to play make-believe in here with Paul when you were kids, remember?"

My cheeks grew warm. I'd done a lot more than play in the movie theater with Paul Greer the last summer I'd been on Whisper Island. And look how that had ended... I shoved away the memory of my naive eighteen-year-old self and flexed my shoulders. "Will you give me the grand tour before you put me to work?"

Noreen's smile stretched wide. "With pleasure. As you can see, this is the café itself. The kitchen is back here." She led me through a door behind the concession stand and into a small but well-equipped kitchen and gestured for me to take a look around. "I cook traditional Irish breakfasts all morning. My lunchtime menu is limited in the winter—just sandwiches, soup, and a hot meal of the day. You'll be well able to handle the cooking when I'm getting my wisdom teeth out tomorrow."

I jerked up from the cabinet full of mysterious utensils I'd been examining, banging my head in the process. "Um, you know I was serious about burning water, right? Waiting tables, I can handle."

"I'll soon teach you to cook, love," Noreen said with a confidence that I didn't share. "We have a whole day before I leave for the mainland."

Oh, boy. One day to transform me from Queen of the Microwaved Ready Meal to Baking Goddess? My aunt had no idea what she was up against. "Speaking of your trip to the hospital, who's looking after the petting zoo while you're gone? Because much as I love you, I draw the line at shoveling animal excrement."

Noreen's crackle of laughter was infectious. "You're off the hook. I've asked Paddy Driscoll to feed and water the pigs, the goats, and the alpaca. All you'll need to do is open a few tins of cat food and feed the dog."

"The dog is no problem, but I'm not sure the cats like me." Roly and Poly had made their disdain for me clear the moment I'd thrown them off the bed last night. I hadn't met the rest of Noreen's cats yet, but I anticipated a mutually lukewarm reaction.

"Oh, they'll get used to you." My aunt beamed at me. "Poly is expecting, but you probably won't need to deal with her kittens."

My jaw dropped. "Wait a sec…you're leaving me in charge of a pregnant cat? Labor and delivery are not my areas of expertise."

"Don't worry. Poly's not due for another couple of weeks. Now, let's look at the part of The Movie Theater Café that I know you'll love." My aunt took my arm and dragged me out of the kitchen, moving at a surprising speed for a woman of her size.

Noreen stopped outside the door of the movie theater. When she threw open the door, I sighed with pleasure. The theater looked like a photo out of one of my aunt's vintage movie magazines. The red velvet seats had been restored to their former glory, as had the curtains that framed the stage. A chandelier hung suspended from the ceiling, adding to the old-world vibe.

"What a great place for clubs to meet." I ran a hand over the plush red velvet upholstery. "They have seating, a stage, and a big screen. Which clubs use it?"

"Now let me see…" A crease formed on my aunt's forehead as she rattled off the clubs' names. "There's the Whisper Island Knitting Society on Mondays; the Quilting Queens on Tuesdays; the Historical Society on Wednesdays; their enemies, the Detectorists, share Thursdays with the Unplugged Gamers; and the Golden Age Movie Club and the Vintage Mystery Book Club share Fridays." Noreen beamed. "No prizes for guessing that I'm the founder and president of the Movie Club, and Philomena is the president of the book club."

"Both the movie and the vintage mystery clubs sound amazing. Do you watch old movies together and discuss them after?"

My aunt bobbed her head. "We watch a film once every month, but some of us choose to meet more often to chat, take care of club admin, and just have fun. When many of our film discussions touched on the books that the films were based on, Philomena suggested we add a mystery novel book club to complement the Movie Club. So now we watch a film on the second Friday of the month, and we hold a book discussion on the last Friday of the month."

I picked up a flyer from a table by the entrance. "What do the Unplugged Gamers do?"

"They play board games. I guess the name is to differentiate them from video game fans." My aunt tapped on a name at the head of the flyer I'd picked up. "Do you remember Lenny Logan? You might have met him with Julie."

I scrunched up my forehead. "The name sounds familiar." A memory stirred. "Wait a sec…the stoned guy? The one with the mullet and the *Star Trek* T-shirts?"

Noreen threw back her head and roared with laughter. "That's him. Lenny's lost the mullet, but he's otherwise unchanged."

The bell over the entrance door chimed. I replaced the flyer where I'd found it. "Sounds like our first customer of the day has arrived."

"It'll be someone looking for a take-out coffee or a full Irish breakfast." My aunt raised an eyebrow and threw me a look of challenge. "Want your first cooking lesson?"

"Want, no. Need, yes." I gave her a mock salute. "I'm yours to command."

Laughing, my aunt bustled out of the movie theater and back into the café. Before I followed her, I cast another look around the gorgeous room, and my heart swelled. Maybe life on Whisper Island wouldn't be boring after all.

3

My first day at the café passed in a haze of burned sausages (me) and freshly baked scones (Noreen). By six o'clock, my feet and my back ached, and I was looking forward to shooing my aunt's cats out of her bathtub and enjoying a long soak. I loaded the latest pile of dirty dishes into the dishwasher, wiped my sweaty palms down the front of my red apron, and switched on the machine. Voices floated into the kitchen from the café, including my aunt's hearty laugh.

A pang of guilt gnawed at my stomach. A day to learn to cook was not going to cut it, and I didn't want to let my aunt down. Noreen's kindness in offering me a refuge to recharge and reassess my life had been a godsend. The least I could do was give her the reassurance that her café was in good hands while she was in the hospital. At the rate I was going, I'd have the local fire department on speed dial.

When I rejoined my aunt behind the food and drinks counter, she was chatting to a dark-haired wiry guy in a hooded sweatshirt, who was chewing on a toothpick. He turned to face me, and his bony face split into a grin. "Hey, Maggie. What's up?"

"Maggie and I were just talking about you earlier," Noreen said, although I didn't need her hint to identify the man. The scraggly beard was new and the mullet was gone, but I'd have recognized Lenny Logan anywhere.

"Hey, Lenny. Long time no see." I stretched out my hand, and Lenny pumped it with more strength than I'd given him credit for.

"Julie told me you were coming back to the island." Lenny moved his toothpick from one side of his mouth to the other. "You planning on staying long?"

"For as long as she likes," my aunt said.

"For a couple of months," I corrected.

"Awesome," Lenny drawled. If Fillmore from the movie *Cars* had had an Irish accent, he'd have sounded just like Lenny. "You gotta come to one of our club meetings."

"For your Unplugged Gamers?" I grinned. "The last time I played *Monopoly*, I went bankrupt. And if I recall correctly, it was a game lost to you."

"Yeah, you were a terrible player," Lenny said, matter-of-factly, "but you might prefer one of our strategy games. Ever tried *The Settlers of Catan*?"

"Nope."

"That's a good one for beginner gamers. Wanna join us next Thursday evening?"

"I'd love to, but…" I glanced at my aunt. "Am I scheduled to work then?"

Noreen shoved her glasses into place and consulted a printout next to the cash register. "Yes, but as long as you're willing to serve Lenny and his friends food and drinks, I have no problem with you joining their game."

"In that case, I'll see you then, Lenny. Thanks for the invitation."

"Hey, no problem. We meet here two Thursdays a month, and the other weeks we hunt aliens. You're welcome to join us."

"I…" I stared at him open-mouthed. "Lenny, I don't know what to do with that information. You hunt *aliens*?"

"Well, kinda." His pale blue eyes grew serious. "Me and Mack—do you remember Mack McConnell?—we take our stargazing equipment into the hills and look for UFOs or any sign of extraterrestrial life."

"Every found any?"

"Just the odd UFO," he said, his expression earnest, "but no landings."

"Lenny," I said, struggling not to giggle. "When you guys go alien hunting, is there any smoking funny stuff going on in those hills?"

His gaze shifted to Noreen, and then back to me. "Um…maybe?"

"And you don't see any connection between that and seeing UFOs?"

Lenny stared at me balefully. "No. Hey, any time you want to come out with us, lemme know. We can show you our equipment."

"If any other man said he and his friend would show me their equipment, I'd interpret it a whole different way."

"Eh?" Lenny looked genuinely baffled. "Well, maybe the game nights are more your thing."

My lips twitched. "Probably. I'll see you next Thursday."

"I'll see you before then." Lenny indicated the coffee cup in his hand. "I buy a take-out decaf every evening after work, along with one of Noreen's vegan scones."

"You'll meet Maggie at the Movie Club as well," Noreen added. "She won't want to miss that."

"You're a member?" I asked Lenny. "I guess I shouldn't be surprised. You made me and Julie sit through old Vincent Price films, remember?"

He grinned. "Those were good times. Yeah, I'm a member of a lot of clubs. There's not much else to do on Whisper Island in the evenings."

Except hunt aliens, apparently. I swallowed a giggle.

"When does your Movie Club have its next meeting?" I asked my aunt. "You said it rotated weeks with the book club."

"We're meeting tomorrow," Noreen replied. "I'd

like you to be there to serve cocktails and snacks, just in case I can't make it back to the island in time. And don't forget to wear a nice evening gown. We don't dress up for every meeting, but we try to make an effort on film nights, usually an outfit that reflects something about the film or the era it's from."

"Dressing up sounds like fun, but what did you mean when you said you might not make it back to the island on time? First, I thought you said you'd only be at the hospital for one day, and second, no way should you be attending a club meeting right after having surgery."

"What a fuss pot you are, love. If everything goes well, I'll be home tomorrow evening, but general anesthetics are unpredictable. The doctors might keep me overnight." She addressed Lenny's questioning look. "I'm getting my wisdom teeth out tomorrow. Unfortunately, the dentist says they're the stubborn kind. They need to be removed at the hospital, so it's off to the mainland for me."

"Are you going alone?" Lenny asked.

"No. Sister Pauline is coming with me, and Maggie is looking after the café."

Or trying to…

"If you need help serving drinks at the Movie Club meeting, let me know," Lenny said to me. "Film nights attract a lot of people."

"That's sweet of you," I said, trying and failing to keep the relief out of my voice. "I enjoy mixing drinks, but it's been a while since I needed to make cocktails for a crowd."

Lenny's easy smile was infectious. "No worries. I'm happy to help."

"What movie are you guys planning to watch?"

"We're doing a series of Hitchcock films. This month's pick is *Dial M for Murder*."

"Seriously?" My smile widened. "That's one of my favorites."

Lenny picked up the paper bag containing his scone. "I gotta make tracks. I'm supposed to repair Colonel Richardson's computer this evening, and Sandra Walker has been hounding me to install a new RAM chip in hers."

"A what?"

"It'll upgrade the memory on her laptop."

"Are you a computer repair guy?" I asked, recalling the mountain of tech equipment Lenny had kept in his room as a teenager.

He shrugged. "Kind of. I work a few doors down at my parents' electronics shop, but I do some repair work on the side. My main side gig at the moment is helping your aunt Philomena digitize the island's library catalog." He laughed at my aghast expression. "Yeah, we're way behind the times on Whisper Island."

Lenny waved goodbye and ambled out of the café with the same easy lope he'd had as a kid. A lot had changed on the island since my last visit, but Lenny Logan had not.

I served tea and toasted sandwiches to old ladies named Miss Flynn and Miss Murphy, both of whom I recalled from childhood summers and neither of whom I could tell apart. Both ladies wore their iron-gray hair pulled back into tight buns and favored tweed twinsets offset by pearl necklaces. I doubt they realized how much they characterized the stereotype of the elderly spinster.

"It's lovely to see you again, Maggie," the one in the green tweeds said.

"You've turned into a pretty young woman," her friend in pink added in a tone of surprise.

I suppressed a grin. "Yeah, I was an awkward teen."

"You were tall and gangly and hadn't grown into yourself yet," said Joan Sweetman from the next table, where she was enjoying an after-work coffee with her fellow golf club captain. Joan, a local gallery owner, was an elegant woman in her early fifties and the widow of Smuggler's Cove's former mayor. Her companion, Cormac Tate, was the principal of the island's elementary school. I'd met both Joan and Cormac when I was a teenager and had vague but warm memories of both.

"Thanks, Mrs. Sweetman. You're looking well." Apart from a smattering of wrinkles, Joan's good looks were unaltered.

Joan's lips twisted into a wry smile. "Good makeup cleverly applied hides a multitude of sins."

I laughed. "Can I get either of you another coffee?"

Joan shook her head. "One is enough for me."

"I'll take a second cappuccino," Cormac said, "but go easy on the froth."

"Got it." I carried a tray laden with used plates and cutlery back to the counter.

The bell above the door jangled, and I glanced over my shoulder. Sandra Walker sailed in, wearing a pantsuit that had been fashionable back in the Eighties. A tense silence descended over the café. Sandra surveyed the crowd and fixed her pale blue eyes on me. "Well, well. So you're working here now, Maggie? That's a comedown, isn't it? Didn't your wealthy husband pay you a decent divorce settlement?"

I clenched my teeth and tightened my grip on the tray. "I know divorce takes a few years in Ireland, Mrs. Walker, but it's not lightning fast in most U.S. states. Mine won't be finalized for another few months."

Sandra cocked her head to the side and gave me a slow once-over. Her smug smile indicated she wasn't impressed by what she saw. "You've filled out since I last saw you, but then, you did join the police. Is it true that American cops eat donuts all day?"

For crying out loud. Couldn't Sandra at least show originality in her choice of snide remarks? "Oh, yeah," I replied, deadpan. "Forget the war on drugs. We're fighting the war on fast food. It's our duty to get donuts off the streets, one box at a time."

Before the baffled Mrs. Walker could formulate a response, my aunt cut in. "Are you here to collect the donation box for the Whisper Island Runathon, Sandra? I told Mary I'd send it over to her this evening."

Sandra collected herself, pulled her padded shoulders back, and sauntered over to the counter. "Yes, so she said." Sandra Walker's smug smirk slid back into place. "But as treasurer, it's *my* responsibility to make sure that all local business owners are doing their bit to raise money for the event, and it was my idea to conduct a preliminary count."

Noreen rolled her eyes. "I have a poster about the Runathon on the door of the café and sign-up forms on the counter and by the cash register. The collection box is right here on the counter. I'm doing *my bit*, as you put it, to raise awareness, but I'm not prepared to shake a box under my customers' noses. If they decide to participate in the Runathon, they'll pay an entry fee. Surely that should be enough to cover expenses. Why do we need to collect extra money?"

Sandra Walker's sneer froze, and a flash of anger burned in her eyes. "We've been over this before, Noreen. The extra money is for charity."

"A charity you have yet to specify. If you want people to cough up donations, you need to be crystal clear on which charity you're raising money for."

Mrs. Walker's nose twitched. "As I told you last time you brought this up, the committee is still debating which charity we'll choose this year. We'll let people know in due course."

"When you do, I'm sure the people of Whisper Island will be more willing to donate." My aunt shook the box. The faint rattle of coins indicated it didn't contain many. "There's no need for you to count the money. Two people have donated so far this week, and they both dropped in a two-euro coin."

"Either you're not making much of an effort to persuade your customers to donate—" a wicked glint appeared in Mrs. Walker's eyes, "—or you don't have many customers. Given how queasy I felt after your chicken and mushroom soup last week, I'm not surprised."

With this parting shot, Sandra Walker sauntered out of the café.

I whistled. "What a cow. Is it my imagination, or has she gotten worse?"

"It's The Change," Joan Sweetman said, making Cormac blush to the roots of his receding hairline. "It hit her hard."

The spinster in the green tweed twinset addressed my aunt. "Ignore her, Noreen. Your soups are delicious. Sandra loves to stir up trouble."

"Much as I wish she'd keep her snide remarks to herself," her pink-clad companion said, "I find her odious gossip column far worse."

"Whoa." I gawked at them. "Sandra is *paid* to shovel dirt?"

My aunt gave a disdainful sniff. "We suspect the

local rag hired her to write a gossip column. Officially, Sandra covers island social events and club meetings for the paper. Apart from the odd dig, those pieces are fairly harmless."

"Why do I sense an all-caps '*but*' coming?" I asked dryly.

Noreen laughed. "*BUT* there's also a monthly blind gossip column in the paper, and some of those pieces are vicious. I've complained to Sean Clough, the *Whisper Island Gazette's* editor, but he says the weeks they include the blind gossip column are the paper's best-selling editions."

"I never read that column," Cormac Tate announced in a wholly unconvincing manner. "Absolute rot."

My aunt shrugged. "Rot or not, those blind items have generated plenty of ridiculous rumors and caused hurt feelings."

"Is there any truth in them?" I asked, my brow furrowed. "Even if Sandra invents most of the stories, she's bound to hit close to the truth every once in a while."

Cormac Tate's already ruddy complexion turned purple. "It's all nonsense," he roared, apparently forgetting his insistence that he never read the column. "Inventions of Sandra Walker's sick imagination. She ought to be outed and sued for slander."

"Libel," Joan corrected gently. "Slander is oral defamation, not written."

I exchanged a loaded look with my aunt. What

had Sandra written about Cormac to produce such a violent reaction from him? I shifted my weight from one foot to the other. Sandra sure knew how to stir up trouble wherever she went. She'd only been in the café a few minutes, but the tense atmosphere she'd generated lasted well after she'd left. "Right," I said with determined cheer and picked up a plate of sweet treats. "Anyone want a muffin?"

4

On Friday morning, Noreen headed for the mainland, leaving me with the keys to her car and the café, and as much prepared food as possible. Her faith in my ability to run the café in her absence gave me a much-needed confidence boost. I could do this. With the dough for the scones and bread already made, all I needed to do was put them in the oven. The soup of the day—leek and potato—required reheating, leaving me with just the full Irish breakfasts to cook from scratch. Surely even I couldn't screw up a few fry-ups? My newfound self-assurance lasted until the moment I set off every smoke alarm in the building.

Ten minutes after he'd come to my rescue, Tom Ahearn, the chief of Smuggler's Cove's volunteer fire department, removed his helmet. Amusement twinkled in his eyes. "Well, the fire's out, but it'll take a while for the smoke to clear."

I shifted my weight from one foot to the other and pushed a stray curl out of my face. "Thanks. How did you get to the café so fast, anyway? Did one of the customers call you?"

"If the smoke alarms in the café aren't switched off immediately, they trigger an alarm at the fire station. When I got the call, all I had to do was run across the road—I own the sporting goods shop farther down Main Street." Tom gestured at the blackened frying pan, which was currently soaking in the sink. "What were you trying to cook?"

"Eggs à la inferno," I quipped.

Tom's bushy eyebrows shot up. "You managed to set scrambled eggs on fire?"

"It's a talent of mine." I crossed my arms over my chest and stared at my scuffed boots. "Are you going to tell my aunt about this?"

"No need," Tom said cheerfully. "Some helpful soul will have texted her by now."

I swore beneath my breath. The fireman was right. Between the people who'd been in the café at the time the fire broke out, and the crowd that had gathered outside on the pavement in the aftermath, somebody was bound to contact my aunt. "Thanks for your help," I said through gritted teeth, wishing Tom didn't find the situation as amusing as he apparently did. "I'll try not to cause any more fires before Noreen gets back."

"No problem. All part of the job." He leaned over to examine a batch of scones that I'd removed from the oven before the fire. "Can I take a couple with me?" he asked, hand poised to grab a few. "I've always been partial to Noreen's scones."

"Sure. Just make sure you take one from the middle of the tray. The ones on the outside could be marketed as weapons of mass destruction."

Tom blinked and pulled back his arm. "Uh, thanks, Maggie. Maybe I'll pass."

I nodded sagely. "Probably wise."

"I'll see you around. My wife wants to catch up with you while you're on the island. Maybe you remember her. Rita Clooney? She's a friend of Julie's."

"Yeah, I remember Rita." Unless things had changed, calling Rita Julie's "friend" was a stretch. The Rita I remembered was a spiteful telltale, but perhaps she'd matured since the summer I'd turned eighteen.

"Well, good luck," Tom said, giving me a mock salute before he left the café.

I surveyed the mess in the kitchen and swallowed a sigh. Then I flexed my shoulders and grabbed a basket of scones. I strategically hid the singed ones at the bottom. Time to do some damage limitation. Plastering a smile on my face, I went into the café. Even with the door wide open, it still stank of smoke, and only a few stalwart regulars remained. "Anyone want a scone?" I asked. "They're on the house."

"I'd love one," said the tweed-clad spinsters in unison.

I flashed Miss Flynn and Miss Murphy a smile of gratitude and deposited four of the most edible scones on their plates, along with a ramekin filled with clotted cream and another containing Noreen's home-made strawberry jam. (I'd made the grave error of referring to it as "jelly" on my first day at the café, and the customers' expressions of horror had taught me my lesson.)

The Spinsters were seated at their preferred table, Bette Davis. Beside them, two elderly gentlemen were seated at Cary Grant. They resembled Statler and Waldorf, the grumpy old dudes in *The Muppet Show*. According to my aunt, both men were called a variation of the name Gerald and were known as the Two Gerries in consequence, especially because they tended to travel as a team.

"Would you like a scone?" I held the tray aloft, angled to display the unburned offerings.

Gerry Two eyed me with distaste. "Harrumph," he said, imbuing the exclamation with a wealth of meaning. "Am I likely to break my dentures? The one you served yesterday nearly killed me."

"Do you call this tea?" Gerry One frowned into his cup, and his bristly white mustache quivered. "Do you not drink real tea in America?"

"Fine," I said, shoving a stray curl behind my ear. "My scones suck, my cooking's worse, and I can't make a decent cup of tea. But I'm willing to learn, and I want to try to keep this place going for the twenty-four hours my aunt isn't here. You're the customers. How can I salvage this situation?"

"For a start," Miss Flynn said, "you can learn how to make tea with tea leaves. You've only used tea bags before, haven't you, dear? I can always tell."

"Yeah," I admitted. "And only for guests. I'm not a tea drinker." I regarded them hopefully. "You guys want a coffee? I make a mean espresso."

Four pairs of eyes stared back at me balefully.

I sighed. "Okay, then. Tea from tea leaves it is."

Miss Murphy shuffled to her feet and followed me behind the counter. "Let me give you a lesson in proper tea preparation."

"Is this an act of self-preservation?" I asked.

She gave me a wry smile. "Let's just say I'm picky about my tea, and I'm fond of Noreen. I'd like her still to have customers by the end of the day."

I grinned. "In that case, I'll gratefully accept a lesson in the fine art of tea making."

Thanks to Miss Murphy's 101 in Tea Prep, and Miss O'Flynn's advice on the correct temperature to bake scones, the café remained a fire- and disaster-free zone. Sister Pauline had kindly sent a text to say that my aunt was well after her operation and that they were catching the six o'clock ferry in the hope of making it to the Movie Club on time.

At seven o'clock, the café closed for the day, and I

started setting up for the Movie Club meeting. I was putting the finishing touches to my killer punch mix when Julie arrived, armed with two trays of home-made cookies.

I hadn't seen my cousin in years, but I'd have recognized her anywhere. She was a couple of inches shorter than me, and curvier, with auburn hair, hazel eyes, and a heart-shaped face that made her look younger than her twenty-eight years. Her face lit up with a warm smile when she saw me. "Hey, Maggie. I told Noreen I'd stop by and help you set up for the Movie Club. Let me dump these trays and give you a hug."

Julie's embrace was gentler than Noreen's but equally heartfelt. "It's good to see you," I said. "It's been way too long."

"Tell me about it. It was a shame I couldn't make it to your wedding."

My lips twitched. "That's okay. You might make it to the next one."

Julie scrunched up her nose. "I'm sorry your marriage didn't work out, Maggie. For what it's worth, I'm glad you came back to Whisper Island, even if the circumstances aren't ideal."

"I'm glad, too. I needed a change of scene, and you can't get much different from San Francisco than Whisper Island."

"My enthusiasm for your visit isn't entirely altruistic." Julie grinned. "I have a favor to ask of you."

I grabbed a damp cloth and cleaning spray from

the counter. "As long as you don't mind me wiping down tables while you talk, shoot."

"If you have a second cloth, I'll help."

I tossed her one, and we got to work.

"Noreen mentioned that you jog regularly," Julie said.

I grimaced. "I haven't done it as often as I should have lately, but yeah. I like running."

"Brilliant." Julie practically bounced on the spot. "I want to participate in this year's Runathon, and I need a running partner. Without someone to hold me accountable, I'll never motivate myself to lace up on cold winter mornings."

"I saw a poster about the Runathon. When is it being held?"

"Saint Patrick's Day. That gives me exactly eight weeks to train."

I strode over to a poster featuring a gorgeous landscape view of the island and a smaller photo of a running team. "It says here there are 5K and 10K events. Which one are you aiming for?"

"The 5K. I'm pretty sure the 10K would kill me."

I took a closer look at the photo and started to laugh. "Let me guess...would Mr. Handsome here have anything to do with your sudden desire to run?"

My cousin blushed to the roots of her auburn hair. "Oisin Tate teaches sport at the school."

I checked out the handsome features and slick smile. A little cocky, but who was I to judge? I'd already proven that I had the world's worst taste in men. "Not bad. I can see why you have a crush on him."

"Me and half the female staff," Julie said gloomily. "I doubt I stand a chance. It's tough finding any man to go out with on the island, and a looker like Oisin Tate is hot property."

"Tate," I mused. "Any relation to Cormac Tate, the school principal?"

"Yeah. Oisin is his son."

I tackled another table, polishing the inlay of James Stewart's face until it shone. "And you want to impress him with your running prowess?"

Julie laughed. "Hardly. If I can manage the 5K without dying, I'm calling it a win. No, I was looking for an excuse to spend time with Oisin outside the school staffroom, so I volunteered to help organize the run. Unfortunately, volunteering is synonymous with participating."

I moved to Bette Davis and treated her to the same vigorous polish I'd given to James Stewart. "If you're new to running, I suggest we train three times a week, leaving a rest day between each run."

"Sounds good to me," my cousin said. "That's what the plan I downloaded from the internet recommends."

"Want to start tomorrow? The student who helps on Saturdays is opening the café in the morning, and I don't need to show up before eleven."

"Okay. How about meeting at nine? I could drive to Noreen's, and we can follow a route from there."

"It's a plan." I tossed the dirty cloth over the side of the sink and washed my hands. "Thanks for bringing cookies. I couldn't face baking after this morning's fiasco."

It was Julie's turn to grin. "I heard about the fire."

I rolled my eyes. "I'm sure the whole town's heard by now."

"What fire?"

I whipped around at the sound of my aunt's voice. Noreen walked into the café, accompanied by Sister Pauline and Lenny Logan.

"Noreen," I exclaimed. "You should be at home in bed."

"That's what I told her," Sister Pauline said, shaking her head. "But she wouldn't listen."

"Nonsense," my aunt replied. "I'm in pain and crotchety. What I need is a distraction. Watching a film sounds like the perfect way to spend the evening."

"She's drugged," Lenny said in his stoner drawl. "She's on those super-high-dosage codeine pills that people buy on the black market."

"Only mine were legally prescribed." Noreen sniffed the air. "I smell smoke. Tell me about this fire you mentioned, Maggie. What happened while I was away?"

I scratched the back of my neck, and a guilty flush warmed my cheeks. "There was an incident earlier today involving eggs and the smoke detectors."

A laugh broke through Noreen's stern expression. "So that's why Pauline didn't want me to check my messages when we were on the ferry. Was any serious damage done?"

I hung my head. "Only to my pride."

"Dude, I hear you've learned to make some killer scones." Lenny's bony face stretched into a wicked grin. "And Granddad says your muffins are to die for —literally."

"Hey, I didn't kill anyone, okay? The scones and muffins weren't as good as when Noreen makes them, but they were edible." Some had been, at least. "What are you doing here this early, Lenny? I thought you said you'd be here at eight."

"I'm not staying. I met your aunt and Sister Pauline down at the harbor and offered to give them a lift, but I have to drop a laptop off to a friend and collect another before the Movie Club meeting starts. I'll be back in time to help you make the cocktails."

"Thanks, Lenny. I appreciate it." I checked my to-do list. "Right. Should we divide and conquer, Julie? I'll make sure I have everything ready for the cocktails."

"And I'll set out the snacks and non-alcoholic drinks," my cousin said.

Noreen placed her hands on her ample hips. "What am I supposed to do while you two are running the show?"

"You are going to sit down and relax." I pointed to a seat.

My aunt grunted but sat.

Sister Pauline patted her on the arm. "I'll make you a nice cup of tea, Noreen."

"Could you bring me a glass of water to swallow my painkillers?" My aunt stifled a yawn. She was more tired than she was admitting.

"You shouldn't take them again for another hour." Sister Pauline turned to me. "She's supposed to take two pills of Solpodol no more than four times a day for the next three days. The hospital gave her the exact number of pills to last her until she sees the dentist on Monday for a post-op checkup. Can you make sure she takes the painkillers at the correct intervals?"

"Sure," I said and reached for the container.

"I'm not a child," my aunt snapped. "I can manage my own medicine, thank you very much."

Sister Pauline and I exchanged an oh-well-we-tried glance, and I handed the container back to my aunt. "Just make sure you don't OD. That's a crazy-high dose of codeine."

Lenny consulted his watch. "I'd better make tracks. I'll be back in half an hour to set up the film equipment and help Maggie."

"Lenny is responsible for the tech side of things," Noreen explained after Lenny left. "If it weren't for his technical expertise, I'd be lost."

"I'm looking forward to the movie. Your Movie Club idea is genius." After the stress of burning scones and making bad tea, unwinding in front of an old movie sounded like bliss.

"Ah, well," Noreen said. "Not much exciting happens on the island, so we try to make our own fun."

"I'm perfectly happy to roll with the easy rhythm of life on Whisper Island."

Noreen nodded, clearly satisfied with my answer. "Excellent. I was worried you might get bored."

"Oh, no. After the emotional roller coaster of the last few weeks, Whisper Island's lack of drama is what I need." I surveyed the café and nodded in satisfaction. Julie and I had done a good job getting the place ready for our guests. I held up an empty cocktail glass and grinned. "Who wants to be the first to try one of my cocktails?"

5

——————

Before the club members started to arrive, Julie and I went into the café's restroom, slipped into our evening gowns, and did our hair and makeup. Hanging out with my cousin was just like old times. We hadn't kept in touch as much as I'd have liked, but we slipped right back into our easy friendship.

I applied a final coating of scarlet lipstick and stood back to examine my figure in the mirror. Not too bad, if I did say so myself. The red sequined gown was one of the two I couldn't bear to part with when I'd had to sell my clothes after the breakup. It brought out the rich red of my long curly hair and offset my blue eyes. In addition to the dress, I'd salvaged a matching clutch purse and a pair of sparkly stilettos that Joe had hated me wearing because they made me taller than him. Judging by the tightness in the waist area, I needed to lose a few pounds, but the extra weight had the advantage of increasing my cleavage.

"You look gorgeous, Maggie."

I turned my attention to my cousin. Her tawny-colored dress brought out the auburn in her hair. "Same back at you." I glanced at my watch. "I guess I'd better get out there and start shaking cocktails."

By eight o'clock, my arms were ready to fall off from all the cocktails I'd shaken. My aunt was drowsy after her surgery, but noticeably less grumpy than she'd been when she'd arrived back on the island. At fifteen minutes past eight, Lenny burst into the café, wearing a harassed expression and wrangling a box full of gadgets. Sandra Walker followed smugly on his heels.

"Sorry I'm late," Lenny said to me, keeping his voice low. "Sandra waylaid me outside my dad's shop and insisted on me giving her a lift back to her house to collect her laptop. I don't know why she's making such a fuss. You'd swear she had state secrets on that thing."

"Sandra likes drama," I said, "her own and other people's."

"Crying out loud. All she needs is a new RAM chip. I said I'd get to it tomorrow." Lenny slipped off his frayed denim jacket, revealing a tux underneath.

"Looking good, Lenny."

He gave me a quick appraisal that was purely platonic. "You're not looking too bad yourself, Maggie."

I beamed. "Thank you." Although I preferred casual wear, having an excuse to dress up was fun.

Lenny scanned the pile of chopped fruit and liquor bottles. "Okay. I need instructions. What are we making?"

I handed him the cocktail menu. "In keeping with the Fifties theme, I went with three authentic Fifties-style cocktails and one cheat. We have a Sidecar, a Tom Collins, a Pink Squirrel, and my personal fave, a Peppermint Cream."

"Whoa," Lenny said. "Lots of crème de something ingredients on this list. I've heard of the first three, but the Peppermint Cream is new to me."

"Trust me, it's delicious." I'd started making Peppermint Creams for Joe's cocktail parties with his attorney friends, and they'd always proved to be a hit.

Julie carried a tray of clean cocktail glasses to the counter. "What's in the peppermint cocktail? I'm thinking of trying one."

"A dash of milk, crème de menthe, white crème de cacao, hazelnut cream liqueur, and Baileys Irish Cream."

My cousin's eyes widened, and she handed me a cocktail glass. "Sold."

I laughed. "Coming right up."

"I'd like a Peppermint Cream as well," Sandra Walker said, bustling over to the counter. "And Sister Pauline wants a Tom Collins."

Lenny reached for a cocktail shaker. "You mix the

peppermint drinks, Maggie, and I'll take care of the others."

Lenny and I mixed drink after drink, while Julie made sure everyone was supplied with mineral water, sandwiches, and snacks. My gaze drifted over the crowd. Philomena, Julie's mother, waved to me from the corner, where she was wedged between the Spinsters and the Two Gerries. Joan Sweetman chatted with a sporty-looking woman in her fifties, who I recognized as Lenny's mother, Linda Logan. Cormac Tate, Julie's boss, was talking golf with James Greer, Paul's father. More faces drifted past, some familiar, others strangers. The fireman, Tom Ahearn, ordered drinks for himself and his sour-faced wife, Rita. A chatty woman with freckles introduced herself as Brid and insisted we'd played together as children. Maybe we had. I'd have to ask Julie. The attendee who stood out was a disheveled blond guy wearing a battered German Army jacket and military boots. If this was his costume for the night, he'd dressed up for the wrong movie.

Uncle John, Philomena's husband, appeared at the counter, a grin stretched across his broad face. He had less hair than I remembered but otherwise looked the very same. John shook my hand heartily, crushing it so hard I thought it would break. "Great to see you again, Maggie. Julie is delighted to have someone her own age to hang out with. There aren't many young people left on the island."

"It's good to be here," I said, and meant it. "It's been too long. Can I get you a drink?"

After I'd served my uncle a Tom Collins and a Peppermint Cream, I flexed my aching shoulders and turned to Lenny. "You weren't joking when you said the Movie Club nights were busy. I expected maybe ten people, but there's more like thirty tonight."

"They don't all show up to every meeting," Lenny replied, "but film nights attract a crowd. The Hitchcock series we've been running is pretty popular."

"I'm relieved for my aunt. She said business is slow in the winter."

Lenny poured a Sidecar into a glass frosted with sugar. "Business is slow everywhere on Whisper Island this time of year. It is what it is, and some businesses are more affected than others. My parents' electronics shop does a steady trade all year. If they feel the pinch, it's because of online shopping, not the lack of tourists."

The bell above the door jangled. I glanced up and sucked in a breath. Paul Greer strode in, looking dapper in a three-piece suit. His fair hair was slicked back from his forehead, emphasizing his movie star good looks. My gaze moved to the woman on his arm. Despite my best intentions, a surge of pure jealousy rushed through my veins. The years had been kind to Melanie. My spiteful side had pictured her plump and haggard after bearing four children, but she was slim and elegant on Paul's arm, and just as beautiful as she'd been when Paul had cheated on me with her.

Lenny removed the Peppermint Cream cocktail I'd just placed on a tray and shoved it my way. "This one's for you. You look like you need it."

"Thanks, but I'm driving."

He raised an eyebrow. "So only drink half of it."

"One mouthful." I took a sip, and the frothy goodness temporarily distracted me from dwelling on all that I hadn't accomplished in the decade since I'd last encountered Paul and Melanie. After all, why should I care what they thought of me? Why should it matter that Paul hadn't developed a beer gut, and Melanie hadn't turned into a hag?

"Maggie." Sandra Walker's high-pitched tone sliced through my reverie with cutting edge precision. She staggered over to the counter and waved her empty cocktail glass in front of my face. "I'll have another of those mint thingies. You'll have to give me the recipe. I'm sure I can improve it."

Lenny choked back a laugh. I struggled to keep a straight face but took Sandra's cocktail glass. Judging by the woman's glassy eyes and the slight slur in her voice, she was drunk—or well on her way to achieving that state.

I mixed her a fresh Peppermint Cream and handed her back her glass. "Slow down on these. They're stronger than they taste."

Sandra swayed on the spot. "I can handle my drink," she said, enunciating every syllable. "Unlike some people I could mention." With a spiteful sneer at the crowd, Sandra staggered in the direction of her daughter and son-in-law.

I exchanged a glance with Lenny. "She's drunk."

"I don't remember seeing Sandra drunk before," Lenny said cheerfully. "It's kind of fun watching her struggle to stand straight."

Noreen bustled over to the bar, a tray of dirty glasses in her arms. "I'll bring these through to the kitchen."

"You should be taking it easy," I admonished, removing the tray from her clutches.

"I like to keep busy," she replied in a sulky tone. "Besides, it's time for me to take my next dose of painkillers. I want to get them down before the film starts."

"I'll deal with the dirty glasses." Lenny took the tray and disappeared into the kitchen.

I poured my aunt a glass of water and slid it across the counter.

As she rummaged in her purse, a crease formed between her brows. "I could have sworn I had more pills in this container the last time I looked." She shook her head and dropped two onto her palm. "That last dose must have hit me harder than I thought."

"If you need me to drive you home early, just say the word," I said. "I've only had half a cocktail."

"I'll be fine, love." Noreen swallowed her medicine and drained her water glass. "I'm looking forward to watching the film. Speaking of which, it's time for me to ring the bell and get everyone into the movie theater."

~

ALTHOUGH THIS WAS my third or fourth time watching *Dial M for Murder*, the experience of watching it in an old movie theater enhanced both the Fifties setting and the atmosphere of suspense. Once the credits rolled, the satisfied audience filed out of the theater, bringing their empty cocktail glasses with them. Noreen caught up with me at the doors, where I was thanking club members for attending. Her face was pale and drawn, and she looked every day of her fifty-six years. "Want me to drive you home?" I asked her. "I can come back and clean up after."

My aunt shook her head. "I'll be fine. I've hung on this long. Another half hour won't kill me. Can you check to see if everyone is out of the theater?"

"Sure."

Now that the movie was over, I turned the dimmer switch. Warm, yellow light flooded the theater, robbing it of some of its mystique. At the far end of the third row, someone wearing a green dress had fallen asleep. A couple of women had worn green tonight, and neither was the type to go for a snooze during a movie. Then again, Sandra Walker had been pretty drunk when I'd served her the second cocktail. "Hey," I called. "Movie's over. Time to go home."

No response.

Jeez. Sandra—or was it Brid?—must be out for the count. Not that I could blame them. I glanced at my watch. Eleven twenty-five. I was ready to collapse into my cat-infested bed the instant I got back to Noreen's place. I stifled a yawn and picked my way down the steps. When I neared the third row, I recognized Sandra Walker's slumped form. A prickle of unease snaked down my spine. Sandra *had* been pretty drunk the last time I'd spoken to her, but surely two cocktails hadn't made her pass out?

"Mrs. Walker?" I sidled down the row toward her seat and then reached out my hand to touch her arm. I recoiled, breathing hard. Her skin was cool to the touch. Yes, it was a cold January night, but the heat in the packed movie theater had made me sweat. Sandra's skin shouldn't be this chilly. My heart thumping against my ribs, I felt for a pulse. There was none.

My breath caught in my throat. Briskly, I collapsed the armrest of the neighboring seat and went through the motions of CPR, even though I knew it was too late. "Help," I shouted between blows. "Call emergency services."

"Maggie?" Julie appeared at the entrance to the movie theater. "What's wrong?"

"Call a doctor," I repeated. "And the police. Sandra Walker is dead."

6

"Dead? Are you sure?" Under her freckles, Julie turned pale.

"Yes," I said with a touch of impatience. "No doubt about it." I took my phone from my pocket and hit the button for emergency services.

While I rattled off the essential details to the dispatcher, faces appeared in the doorway to the movie theater. "Unless one of you is a medical professional," I said coolly, slipping my phone back into my pocket, "you can take a hike."

A man with a wild head of wiry curls pushed his way through the crowd and took the steps down to the third row two at a time. "Dr. Thomas Reilly," he said by way of introduction. "I run the Whisper Island Medical Centre."

I moved aside, and Dr. Reilly leaned over to examine Sandra Walker. In truth, I was glad to leave the handling of the body to an expert. I'd seen dead bodies before. Plenty of them. But death's cold finality never failed to give me the shivers.

After he'd checked Sandra for a pulse, the doctor's eyes met mine and his mouth tightened. "I'd say she's been dead at least an hour, but I'll need to examine her more closely to give a more accurate estimate."

The sick sensation that had been building in my stomach since I'd first seen the slumped figure in the seat sent a surge of bile up my throat. I swallowed past it and took a deep breath. Now was not the moment to lose my cool. "I've called an ambulance," I said. "And the police."

The doctor frowned. "The guards are hardly necessary."

I fixed him with an icy stare. "Sandra Walker seemed fine when she arrived at the café, yet now she's dead. I'd say that warrants at least a cursory examination by the police, the guards, or whatever you call them in Ireland."

"I understand you used to be in the American police force." Dr. Reilly treated me to a condescending smile. "Perhaps you're too used to violence to recognize death by natural causes."

"You're very quick to make that call. You haven't even examined her properly yet."

Dr. Reilly's smug smile vanished. "And you, Ms. Doyle, are very quick to suspect foul play. You're letting the atmosphere of *Dial M for Murder* cloud your judgment."

"I'm not saying Sandra Walker was murdered," I

said with as much patience as I could muster. "I just think we need to keep an open mind and look at all the possibilities."

The doctor's nostrils flared. "*We* need to do nothing, Ms. Doyle. You jumped the gun by calling the guards. Sergeant O'Shea won't be pleased to have his time wasted."

I crossed my arms over my chest. "Sandra Walker wasn't popular, and she appeared to be in perfect health when she arrived this evening. I don't think calling out the police is overkill, no pun intended."

The doctor rubbed the back of his neck and said in a weary tone, "Sandra Walker probably died of a heart attack."

"Were you her family practitioner?" I demanded. "Did she have heart issues?"

"Yes, she was a patient of mine. And no, I wasn't aware of any heart problem." The concession caused Dr. Reilly's self-assurance to falter for a moment, but he soon rallied. "However, Sandra was fifty-six. It's hardly unheard of for people her age to die of a sudden heart attack."

"Hmm." I stared at Sandra's prone form and rubbed the back of my neck. The doctor was most likely correct in his assessment of Sandra's cause of death, but I couldn't shake the sensation that something was wrong. Was I paranoid? I'd come to Ireland to regroup after a bad marriage and a lackluster career. Why look for trouble where there was probably none? My gaze lingered on Sandra's cocktail glass, still half full with Peppermint Cream cocktail. A lingering doubt nagged at me.

After a tense few minutes, during which the doctor and I ignored each other and I avoided looking at Sandra Walker's body, Julie opened the doors to the movie theater and approached the third row, accompanied by the island's most senior police officer, Garda Sergeant O'Shea. O'Shea was dressed in civilian clothing and wore a disgruntled expression on his craggy face that matched the impatience apparent in his every movement.

"What's all this about a dead body?" he demanded and surveyed the scene. He blanched when he saw Sandra's corpse.

"Sandra Walker is dead," I said. "I thought a police officer should examine her body."

"And I disagreed, but she'd already placed the call." Dr. Reilly regarded me with a dislike that was mutual. "I suspect the shock of discovering the body rattled Ms. Doyle's senses."

Sergeant O'Shea's nostrils flared. "Do you mean to tell me you've dragged me away from a golf club dinner because you overreacted?"

"A woman you knew is dead, and you're upset about missing your dinner?" I glared at him. "At the very least, you should track down her family. Her daughter and son-in-law were at the movie, but they might have gone home already."

"They're out in the café." Julie bit her lip. "I told them a white lie. Everyone is aware that Dr. Reilly is in here with you, and I said you weren't feeling well to avoid panic."

"Have Paul and Melanie noticed Sandra's missing?" I asked.

My cousin fiddled with her necklace. "Yes. Melanie thinks Sandra went home."

"They all saw me come in. We can assume half the island knows by now that something dodgy happened in The Movie Theater Café." Sergeant O'Shea's ruddy complexion turned purple, and he glared at me accusingly. "Poor Melanie will be very upset that you called the guards."

"It's your job to be here," I snapped. "Why aren't you taking notes? You're not even pretending to examine the scene."

O'Shea glared at me. "There's no scene to examine, Ms. Doyle. We're in a movie theater, sure, but this here is real life. Real life on *Whisper Island*. If Dr. Reilly thinks one of his patients died of a heart attack, then that's all I need to know."

I crossed my arms over my chest and stared him down. "You could at least inform her family of her death."

"She's right. We should fetch Melanie," Dr. Reilly said gloomily. "Better she hears the bad news from us than let the rumor spread."

Julie nodded. "I'll get her and Paul."

A few seconds later, Melanie announced her presence with a hysterical screech. "Mummy? Oh, Mummy." Melanie flew down the steps and threw herself on her mother's body, sobbing, and almost sent the cocktail glass flying.

Paul followed his wife at a more sedate pace. He scanned the room before fixing his attention on me. When our eyes met for the first time in ten years, I felt a stirring of mild dislike, but no stronger emotion.

"Hello, Maggie," Paul said, his tone as bland as his expression.

I nodded curtly. "Paul."

I'd avoided Paul and Melanie earlier, or rather, they'd avoided me by ordering their drinks through other Movie Club members. Up close, Paul's handsome face bore the puffiness of a man who drank more than was healthy.

"What happened to her?" Melanie wailed. "She was fine earlier."

"She was drunk," I amended, "but she seemed okay apart from that."

Melanie narrowed her eyes and rounded on me. "Nonsense. Mummy never gets drunk."

"She was knocking back cocktails this evening," I said before casting my mind back to Sandra's final order. Unless she'd ordered another drink from Lenny and I hadn't noticed, I'd only made two Peppermint Creams for her, and the glass beside Sandra's seat was half full. Why had I said she'd been knocking them back? I frowned. Sandra had appeared to be very drunk when she'd placed the second order. The Peppermint Creams were strong, but surely she wouldn't have been that drunk from one?

"Perhaps she was feeling unwell, and that made you think she was drunk," Dr. Reilly said as if reading my mind.

My gaze moved toward Sandra's body and the cocktail glass beside her seat. "Shouldn't we hang on to Sandra's glass? Maybe get it analyzed?"

The others stared at me as though I'd just spouted Shakespeare.

"Seriously," I added. "Maybe someone spiked her drink."

"Don't be absurd," Sergeant O'Shea snapped. "If I were a betting man, I'd say *you* were the one who drank too many cocktails, not Sandra."

My nails bit into my palms. It took every ounce of self-control I possessed not to lose my temper. "Not that it's any of your business, but I've had half a cocktail this evening. I'm not drunk, and I'm not inventing a mystery where there is none. Even if you and Dr. Reilly are convinced that Sandra died of heart failure, the least you could do is examine the contents of her cocktail glass."

O'Shea's nostrils flared. "We don't have a forensics lab on the island, and I'm not wasting tax payers' money having it sent to the mainland."

"Melanie?" I turned to my erstwhile nemesis, and her expression hardened. "She's your mother. Do you want the glass examined?"

"What I'd like," Melanie said through gritted teeth, "is for you to leave us alone. I don't want you spreading nasty rumors about Mummy drinking too much." Her lips tightened, and she dabbed at her eyes delicately with a cloth handkerchief.

I slow-blinked. Melanie's mother had just died, and she was playing for her audience.

"Probably best you join your aunts and the others, Maggie." Paul forced an unconvincing smile.

"Yes, leave. And tell Noreen to come in here," ordered the sergeant. "We'll arrange for the body to be removed by the fire exit."

They turned their backs on me as if to emphasize the point that my presence wasn't wanted. Frustrated but not defeated, I cast a last glance at Sandra's prone form. On impulse, I removed a tissue from my purse and used it to pick up the cocktail glass.

"What are you doing?" Sergeant O'Shea demanded.

"You said you weren't interested in Sandra's glass," I said smoothly, "so I'm tidying it up."

Before he could utter a protest, I marched up the steps and out of the movie theater. I shoved past the curious crowd out in the café and battled my way to the kitchen. I leaned against the fridge and released the breath I hadn't realized I'd been holding. The situation stank. Why did no one else see it but me? My eyes dropped to the cocktail glass in my hand, and my resolve hardened. Sergeant O'Shea and Dr. Reilly could take a flying leap. I'd save both the contents and the glass, just in case. What harm would that do?

I'd just finished pouring the remnants of Sandra's final cocktail into a plastic screw-top bottle when

Lenny barged in, wearing a harried expression. "Is it true that Sandra Walker's dead?"

"Yeah. Say, you didn't make her a cocktail, did you?"

Lenny's eyes widened. "Do you think it was something she ate or drank? The rumor going around is a heart attack."

"As far as I can recall, I made Sandra two cocktails, and she didn't finish the second. I remember thinking she was drunk when she ordered the second Peppermint Cream. Did you make her a different cocktail at any point?"

Lenny considered this for a moment before shaking his head. "No. Sandra wasn't much of a drinker, and I was making the gin and whiskey-based cocktails. The sweet Peppermint Creams would have been more her style."

A thought occurred to me. "You gave Sandra a ride tonight."

"Yeah." He grimaced. "She insisted on me collecting her laptop. I guess she won't be needing that new RAM chip after all."

"So you have her laptop?" I prompted. "A laptop that could well contain a folder with her gossip columns and blind items about people on Whisper Island?"

Comprehension dawned on Lenny's face. "Yeah. Want to take a look at it?"

"I do. I'll just finish bagging this cocktail glass first."

After I'd put Sandra Walker's cocktail glass in a makeshift evidence bag, I followed Lenny out of the café and down the street to where he'd parked his VW van. We'd just reached Lenny's vehicle when an ambulance pulled into the lane that led to the movie theater's exit.

I exchanged a glance with Lenny. "I guess we'll have to go back inside and give the laptop to Melanie."

"Sure." Lenny gave me a wink. "But not before I take a look at those gossip columns of hers first." His smile faded when he opened the back of the van. "That's weird. I was sure I'd locked it."

The prickle of unease I'd experienced earlier returned in full force, and my heart rate kicked up a notch. "Has anything been stolen? Is Sandra's laptop still there?"

Lenny rooted around in the mountain of cables and gadgets that filled the back of his van. "It's here." He held up a battered-looking Samsung laptop. "I guess I must have forgotten to lock the van after I went back and forth with equipment."

"Maggie?" A woman's voice made me whirl around. Sister Pauline stood in the doorway to the café. "Noreen is looking for you," the nun said. "She's rather upset."

I imagined that "rather upset" was an understatement. "I'll be right in," I said, and Sister Pauline nodded and went back inside the café. I turned to Lenny. "Do you want to meet tomorrow to take a look at the laptop? I'm assuming you can hack through whatever password Sandra used?"

"No need to hack. Sandra gave it to me."

"Of course. You were going to install a new RAM chip for her. Okay, I'll call you tomorrow morning. In the meantime," I added with a grimace, "I'd better see how Noreen is coping."

After Lenny had driven away, I retraced my steps to the café. The uneasy sensation I'd had since I'd found the body worried me. I tried to shove my doubts aside, but I couldn't shake the feeling that something wasn't right about Sandra's death. My instincts were rarely wrong and had served me well as a police officer. However, without evidence, I had nothing to compel either the doctor or Sergeant O'Shea to listen to me. Maybe the laptop would shed some light on Sandra's death.

7

The night after I discovered Sandra's body, I slept badly. Dreams of poisoned cocktail glasses haunted me, and I woke up shivering. In the dark, two pairs of feline eyes glowed. Roly, the cat with the white patch on his nose, meowed and rubbed against me. I stroked his soft fur and pulled him close. Soon, Poly joined us, her pregnant belly wobbling, and we snuggled under the quilt until my alarm went off for the second time. Groaning, I blinked at the display. Eight forty-five. *Ugh.* I was going to be late. I swung my legs over the side of the bed, stood, and stretched. "Running is good for me," I said to Roly and Poly. "Right?"

Their only response was to stare back at me, unblinking.

I sighed and pulled on my running gear. I'd promised my cousin I'd be her running partner, and I wouldn't let her down. Out in the hallway, my aunt's bedroom door was closed. After the drama yesterday evening, not to mention her surgery, she must be exhausted. I tiptoed to the front door and just missed tripping over Bran, the only one of Noreen's other animals that the cats allowed into the house.

Bran, a border collie-Labrador mix, looked up at me with pleading eyes. He whined and licked my hand.

I leaned down and stroked his fur. "Smart dog. You recognize a sucker when you see one. Want to come for a run with me?"

Bran panted and pawed at the front door.

"I'll take that as a yes." I clipped the dog's leash into place and opened the cottage door. Bran took off like a shot, dragging me in his wake. "Whoa, big guy. Slow down. I'm supposed to be taking you for a walk, not the other way around."

Julie leaned against the gate, a mischievous grin on her face. "If we're taking Bran, we're not going to manage the walk part of the walk-run intervals my program recommends."

"If we don't take him, he'll howl the place down and wake Noreen. I've only been here a couple of days, but I've figured out how Bran operates." I shot past my cousin, struggling to keep up with the dog. "Consider this our warm-up," I shouted over my shoulder.

Laughing, Julie closed the gate and jogged to catch up with me. "You look like I feel this morning, Maggie. Rough night?"

I grimaced. "It was hard to sleep after what happened."

"You must have stumbled across a few dead bodies during your time with the police."

"True, but never anyone I knew. Even at a shoot-out where a fellow police officer was killed, I hadn't known the guy. Discovering Sandra's body was a shock, especially finding her on Noreen's premises."

"Maggie..." Julie trailed off, as if unsure how to phrase what she wanted to say. "Lenny told me you saved the contents of Sandra's cocktail glass. Surely you don't think there was something wrong with the cocktail? I mean, everyone was saying she'd died of a heart attack."

"She probably did. I bagged the glass and its contents on autopilot. It's what I would have done had I been a police officer on the scene, and that idiot O'Shea was showing no interest in what Sandra ate and drank before she died. Crazy as it sounds, I need you to convince me that I'm paranoid."

Julie exhaled audibly. "That's assuming I can breathe once we start running. We could go back to Noreen's and chat over coffee."

I grinned at my cousin. "Don't sound so hopeful. You asked me if I'd train with you, and I agreed. Let's go do this thing."

Julie pulled a face. "All right. I apologize in advance for my super-slow pace. I have a feeling that you and Bran are going to be way ahead of me."

"No need to apologize. Go as slow as you need to,

and I'll try to get Bran to cooperate." "Try" being the operative word. The dog tugged on his leash, impatient to increase his speed.

We reached the end of the lane that separated Noreen's land from her neighbor's. I led the way to a trail I'd spotted when I was scouting the area for potential jogging routes. "I've been looking forward to our run. I haven't had a chance to explore the island in daylight since I arrived. It's even more beautiful than I remembered."

The frost-tinged fields rolled before us, stretching all the way down to the cliffs. In summer, the fields would be a lush green and dotted with sheep and cows. In the cold of January, the animals were nowhere to be seen. A group of modern cottages broke the monotony of the rolling hills, and a farm was located beyond them.

"We get so few hours of light this time of year," Julie said, huffing and puffing in her effort to keep up with Bran and me. "I leave for work in the dark and come home in the dark. And yeah, it's gorgeous here. It's one reason I decided to return after I got my teaching qualification. The drawback is a shortage of eligible men, at least among the permanent population."

"How's the men situation during tourist season?"

Julie winked at me. "Much better, but they leave at the end of summer. What about you, Maggie? Are you ready to start the dating game again?"

"Ugh," I said with a shudder. "Definitely not. If

I've learned one thing over the last few weeks, it's that I have lousy taste in men."

"You've been unlucky," Julie conceded, "but that doesn't mean you'll never find a good man to settle down with."

"You sound like Noreen. She's determined to hook me up with an Irishman."

Julie laughed. "Of course she is. She's plotting ways to convince you to stay. She loves having family on the island."

"That's sweet, but this is a temporary stop for me. I want to use my time on Whisper Island to do some thinking and decide what I want to do with the rest of my life."

"And then you go and stumble over a dead body a couple of days into your holiday. That sucks."

"It sucks even more for Sandra Walker," I said dryly. "Come on, let's take the path to the left."

We took the winding trail that led from my aunt's property to an area of woodland. Reluctant to make Julie run through woods where she'd have to navigate branches and slippery leaves, I skirted the trees and followed the path past a neighboring farmer's wall. It was the old kind constructed out of stacked stones. As a kid, I'd been afraid to walk next to those walls in case they collapsed, but they were sturdier than they appeared.

Bran spotted something of interest further along the track and strained at his leash.

"Are you ready to sprint for a couple of minutes?" I asked. "If so, I'll set the timer for our intervals."

"No," Julie puffed, "but I'll do it."

"Okay. Ready, set…go."

I let my cousin set the pace, and deliberately slowed down to make sure she didn't try to run faster than she should. After two minutes, my timer beeped, and we slowed to a walk.

"Well done," I said. "We'll walk it out for a couple of minutes and then try another sprint."

"Ugh," Julie said with a groan. "What possessed me to sign up for the Runathon? I must have been insane."

"A sexy guy you have a crush on," I reminded her. "Just think how good you'll feel when this is over."

My cousin blew out her cheeks. "By the time this is over, I'll be auditioning for the cast of *The Running Dead*."

I laughed. "You're not that bad. Now quick before our next running interval—what do you think happened to Sandra? Am I crazy for questioning the doctor's assumption that she died of a heart attack?"

"Can you identify why you have doubts?" Julie asked. "Would you feel the same if one of the other Movie Club members had died under the same circumstances?"

I frowned and considered my cousin's questions. "No, I don't think I'd have jumped on the idea of foul play as quickly if someone else had died last night. Sandra had a talent for upsetting people. And another thing: both Melanie and Lenny insisted that Sandra wasn't much of a drinker, yet I could have sworn she was drunk when she ordered the second cocktail from me."

"Wait, Sandra ordered two cocktails last night? For herself?" Julie's brow creased. "That doesn't sound right. Sandra always boasted about never having more than one drink when she was out, and I never saw her drunk."

"Did she have a drinking problem? Maybe she fell off the wagon."

"By having two drinks as opposed to one?" Julie cocked her head to the side, and then shook her head. "Sorry, I don't buy it."

Neither did I. The timer beeped, indicating the need for speed. During our next running interval, Julie concentrated on breathing, while I turned the Sandra Walker conundrum over in my mind. Far from convincing me I was paranoid, Julie's confirmation about Sandra's drinking habits had turned up the alarm bells in my head.

"Okay," I said when we slowed down to a brisk walk beside a lake on the far side of the woods. "Let me go over this again. Sandra didn't tend to drink more than one alcoholic beverage a night, yet she appeared to be drunk when she ordered the second cocktail from me. Could she have been ill, and the symptoms mirrored a drunken person's behavior? Or was she on medication that interacted badly with alcohol?"

"I can think of a number of choice adjectives to describe Sandra Walker's character," Julie said dryly, "but 'stupid' isn't among them. I can't see her mixing meds and cocktails. The most likely explanation is what you mentioned before: Sandra was unwell, probably from the onset of her heart attack, and you mistook her slurred speech and unsteady walk as the effects of alcohol."

"It's possible, but I have this nagging doubt that I can't shake." I rubbed my achy forehead. "Maybe I'm paranoid and seeing suspicious circumstances where there are none."

The timer beeped, indicating our next running interval. Julie squeezed my arm. "Come on. Put Sandra Walker out of your mind, and let's finish our run. The sooner we get through this, the sooner we get showers and coffee."

We completed four more alternating run-walk intervals and circled back to Noreen's.

Julie leaned against her car and gave Bran a final pet. "Thanks for coming with me, Maggie."

"No problem. Want to meet again next week?"

"Sure. How does Monday morning sound? It would need to be early, though."

"I can do early. Wanna say five-thirty?"

"Sounds good. If I don't see you before then, please don't worry about Sandra. I'm sure it was as the doctor said—a heart attack and nothing sinister."

I forced a smile. "Sure. I'm going to put it out of my mind for the rest of the weekend."

"That's a smart idea." Julie's expression turned serious. "Listen, I have a stack of self-help books if you're interested. You said you wanted to do some thinking about what to do with your life. Maybe they'll give you some guidance."

I loathed self-help books and scoffed at every form of pop psychology, but Julie's offer was kindly meant. "I'm good for reading material at the moment," I said diplomatically, "but thanks."

"Well, if you change your mind, just let me know." My cousin waved goodbye and got into her car.

After Julie's car had disappeared down the road, Bran and I trudged up the path to the cottage. I was more than ready for a shower and coffee, and Bran was doing his I'm-hungry-style whine.

Before I went into the house, I found Bran's supply of dog food in the barn and filled both his food and water bowls. He treated me to an enthusiastic lick, and I stroked his fur. "You love having someone to drag around at breakneck speeds, don't you? Just don't get used to it. I won't be here for long, and poor Noreen definitely doesn't want to take you for a run."

Bran gave me one last lick before turning his full attention to his food. I went into the cottage and washed my hands. Time for that shower I'd been craving.

When I entered the kitchen, my aunt was sitting at the table, rummaging through her purse. "Should you be up, Noreen? There's no need for you to go to the café today. I can handle it."

My aunt gave a crack of laughter. "I'm sure you can. With a little help from the fire brigade."

I bit my lip. "Yesterday was unfortunate, but I'll have it all under control today." And if I didn't, hopefully, Kelly—the girl who helped out on Saturdays—would be capable of avoiding fire. "Seriously, go back to bed. You look exhausted."

"Don't worry, love. I'm on my way back to bed. I just got up to take my medicine." Noreen extracted her container of pills from her purse and shoved her glasses into place. As she stared at the container, frown lines appeared on her forehead. "That's odd. There are only a few pills left."

8

I sucked in a breath, and the wheels turned in my mind faster than I could speak. "Are you sure? Did you miscount?"

"Maybe the lid came unscrewed. This has to be a mistake." My aunt searched her purse before sitting back and shaking her head. "No stray pills fell into my purse." She examined the container for the second time, and then poured its contents into the palm of her hand and counted the pills. Her mouth grew tight. "An entire day's worth of pills is missing, Maggie. I know I was tired yesterday, but I certainly didn't take double the prescribed amount."

"Sister Pauline said you had twenty-four Solpodol to be taken over the next three days."

"Exactly. I've taken two doses of two pills each since I left the hospital yesterday. There should be twenty pills left, not ten." Uncertainty crossed over my aunt's face. "Do you think the hospital pharmacy counted them incorrectly?"

"And gave you fourteen instead of twenty-four?" I examined the container. "Was it full when you got it yesterday?"

Noreen nodded. "To the brim."

"Looking at the size of these pills, the container wouldn't have been full with only fourteen pills in it."

"I'll have to phone Dr. Reilly to see if he'll write me a prescription for more." My aunt sighed. "I hope I can get hold of him on a Saturday."

A memory nagged at me, something to do with the pills… "Wait a sec. When you came over to get a glass of water before the movie started, you commented on the number of pills in your pill container. You said something along the lines of there being more pills in the container the last time you'd looked. That implies that the pills went missing before the movie began."

My aunt frowned. "I was groggy last night, but now that you mention it, I remember saying something like that." Her expression brightened. "If I was that tired, I *must* have dropped the pills somewhere. Maybe they spilled in the café."

"I didn't notice any when I was cleaning up last night."

"But you'd just discovered Sandra's body. You were distracted."

"True," I said doubtfully, "but Julie didn't mention finding pills anywhere, and she helped me clean up."

A thought occurred to me, unwelcome but logical. "When we were kids, Lenny had a reputation as a stoner. You don't think he took them?"

"No," my aunt said emphatically. "Lenny isn't a drug addict. He might smoke the odd joint, but I doubt it goes farther than that these days."

The weight that had been pressing on my shoulders lightened. I liked Lenny. I didn't want to think of him stealing prescription drugs. "All right, but you can understand why I asked you about him." I leaned over and gave my aunt a kiss on the cheek. "I'll go get ready to leave for the café. Don't worry about the pills. I'll stop by the pharmacy and see what they can do."

But first, I thought grimly, I'd pay a visit to Sergeant O'Shea.

When I arrived at Whisper Island's police station, the front door was locked. I pressed the bell for the second time, but no one appeared on the other side of the frosted glass door.

An old man walking an equally elderly terrier stopped on the pavement before me. "If you're looking for Sergeant O'Shea, he's getting in a last few rounds of golf before the snow comes."

My nose twitched. "You've got to be kidding me. Who's in charge of maintaining law and order on the island while he's working on his handicap?"

The old man shrugged. "Ah sure, there's not much to do this time of year. He has a couple of reserves to help him, but they're both eejits."

"A ringing endorsement," I said dryly. "Is the golf club still attached to the hotel?"

The man inclined his head a fraction. "Yes. The clubhouse is on one side of the course, and the hotel is on the other."

"Thanks for the info." I got back into Noreen's car and drummed the steering wheel. O'Shea was going to lose his cool if I showed up and interrupted his game. Did I care? Heck no. I was looking forward to winding up the arrogant police sergeant. With a sigh of satisfaction, I fired up the engine.

I found Sergeant O'Shea lining up a shot on the sixteenth hole, a cigar clamped between his teeth. He looked ridiculous in his tweed golfing cap and matching pants, teamed up with an incongruously puffy winter jacket. The policeman was with a group of friends—all male, natch—and a sour-faced caddy.

The sergeant swore fluently when he caught sight of me and narrowed his beady eyes. "What do you want, Ms. Doyle? Did you find another corpse in your aunt's café and decide there's a serial killer on the loose on Whisper Island?"

O'Shea's golfing cronies guffawed with laughter.

I ignored them and focused my attention on the police sergeant. "I preserved Sandra Walker's cocktail glass and its contents. I'd like you to have it tested."

The sergeant stared at me for a long moment, his

beady eyes bulging. Then he forced another hearty guffaw. "Are you still on about that? The idea that someone spiked Sandra's glass is preposterous."

"Is it?" I asked, keeping my tone calm and cool. "No one knew anything about Sandra having a heart condition, including the doctor, and she wasn't exactly Ms. Popularity."

"But *murder*?" The sergeant's walrus mustache twitched. "That's absurd. We don't have *murders* on Whisper Island."

One of Sergeant O'Shea's golfing buddies cleared his throat. "Well, there was that Australian who threw his wife off their yacht a few years ago and tried to make it look like an accident."

The policeman rounded on him. "They were *tourists*, Dick. Permanent residents don't do things like that."

I rolled my eyes. Was the guy seriously that naive? If Sergeant O'Shea was what passed for law enforcement around here, Sandra Walker didn't stand a chance at having her death properly investigated. I changed tack. "Even if Sandra wasn't murdered, did it occur to you that she might have spiked her own drink?"

The sergeant's bushy eyebrows drew together to form a hairy V. "Suicide, you mean? Out of the question. Sandra wasn't the suicidal type."

On that point, we were in agreement, but I pressed on. "It makes sense to have Sandra's glass tested by a toxicology lab."

Sergeant O'Shea's grip on his golf club was so tight that his knuckles were turning white. His ruddy complexion, in contrast, was beet red. "If I thought for one second that there was anything unnatural about Sandra's death, I'd have called in the forensics team. But I don't, so I didn't. For heaven's sake, woman. The district superintendent would have my hide if I wasted our limited budget on every islander who died of a heart attack."

If I'd suspected Sandra had taken her own life, I'd be less inclined to press the issue, but we couldn't rule out the possibility that she had been murdered. "All you need to do is—"

"Enough," O'Shea bellowed. "Go back to burning scones, Ms. Doyle, and let me continue my game."

I sighed. I wasn't going to get anywhere with this lazy lump of lard. "Please at least consider testing the contents of Sandra's glass. Tests are standard procedure in the U.S., and I can't imagine your system is different in Ireland."

Judging by the sergeant's furious expression, I'd said the wrong thing. "In case it's escaped your notice, we're not in the U.S.. We're not even on the Irish mainland. You have no experience policing a small community, and no jurisdiction here. Don't tell me how to do my job."

I let my gaze drift to his golf club, which was still clutched in one of his meaty hands. "I'll let you get back to doing your *job*, Sergeant. Nice outfit, by the way."

With this parting shot, I trudged back to the parking lot, fuming at the policeman's blatant disinterest in getting off his behind and doing his job. When I reached the car, I paused before opening the door and let my gaze drift over the impressive facade of the Whisper Island Hotel. Maybe I could go in and talk to Paul and Melanie. If they pushed for tests, Sergeant O'Shea would have to relent. My stomach churned at the thought of facing them, but it had been ten years after all. What did I care about a broken heart that had healed long ago? My feet felt like lead. Maybe I cared too much. I squared my shoulders and forced my legs into motion.

The hotel lobby was deserted, save for a lone receptionist seated behind a polished wood counter. "Good morning," she said when I approached. "How may I help you?"

I gave her a sunny smile that didn't match my mood. "My name is Maggie Doyle. I'd like to speak to Paul or Melanie Greer. Both if they're available."

The receptionist's expression froze for a millisecond before resuming its professional friendliness. "I'm not sure today is a good time, but I'll ask. One moment, please." She picked up the phone and hit a button. "There's a Ms. Doyle here to see you, Paul. Should I send her through? Yes. Thanks." She put down the phone and glanced up at me. "Mr. Greer will see you in his office." She stood up and led me to a door behind the reception desk. After a perfunctory knock, the receptionist opened the door and gestured for me to go in.

Paul sat behind a large mahogany desk, and Melanie perched on the edge. They both looked pale and drawn beneath their professionally applied fake tans.

Melanie stared at me dully. "What do you want, Maggie?" she asked in a tired voice. "If your aunt is worried about us suing her, we don't plan to."

"Why would you sue my aunt? It's not her fault your mother died." It was the wrong thing to say, and I realized my mistake the instant the words left my mouth.

Melanie's mouth tightened. Paul stood and squeezed his wife's shoulder. "How can we help you, Maggie? I guess this isn't a social call."

"No." I shifted my weight from one leg to the other, awkward and aware that they hadn't offered me a seat. "I spoke to Sergeant O'Shea on the golf course. I mentioned that I'd taken the precaution of saving Sandra's cocktail glass."

Paul's eyes widened. "Why would you do that? Sergeant O'Shea said it wasn't necessary. Surely you don't think the cocktail caused her heart attack?"

"They were rather strong," Melanie added, shooting me a look of pure venom. "Mummy wasn't used to hard drinks."

"I urge you to ask the police to send the glass and

its contents for tests. As a precaution," I added, seeing their matching expressions of horror.

Paul gave a stiff laugh. "This is absurd. You're acting like someone poisoned my mother-in-law's drink."

"All I'm saying is that it would be wise to get it tested in a lab," I replied, choosing my words with care.

"You're insane." Melanie's voice raised a notch, and her hand fluttered to her expensive necklace. "Everyone loved Mummy. No one would want to harm her."

I resisted the urge to roll my eyes. Was Melanie genuinely clueless as to her mother's true nature, or deliberately obtuse? "If you're convinced no one would hurt your mother, there's no reason to fear the lab results, is there? Getting the glass tested is standard procedure." But not on Whisper Island, according to that idiot, Sergeant O'Shea. My hands balled into fists. The man was an incompetent fool.

Melanie, breathing hard, rounded on me. "This is your suggestion, not Sergeant O'Shea's. *He* didn't mention any suspicions that Mummy's death wasn't from natural causes. In fact, no one has mentioned it apart from you."

"Sergeant O'Shea is an idiot," I said, forgetting my vow to remain calm and diplomatic. "He doesn't want tests done because he's lazy. If the test results cast the heart attack theory into doubt, he'd be expected to put down his golf club and do some work for a change."

Paul's lips twitched, but Melanie's mouth trembled. She twisted the rings on her fingers and paced back and forth in front of the desk. "How dare you insinuate there's something suspicious about my mother's death? Don't you think it's bad enough knowing she's gone without you spreading malicious rumors?"

"From what I've heard, spreading malicious rumors was more your mother's area of expertise than mine."

Melanie's sharp intake of breath was audible. Okay, so a career in diplomacy wasn't in my future, but I'd said what everyone else thought.

Melanie's face contorted with rage. "You've been back on the island for five minutes and you think you're an expert? Get out of our hotel. And if I hear you've been smearing my mother's name, you'll be hearing from my solicitor." She turned to her husband. "Make her leave, Paul."

"Come on, Maggie." Paul took my arm and dragged me to the door. "You're upsetting my wife."

"At least consider what I've said," I pleaded when we reached the door. "I'm sorry I upset Melanie, but I don't understand why she wouldn't want to get the glass tested. If it were my mother, I'd make sure I'd done everything within my power to determine the exact cause of death."

Paul fixed me with a hard stare, and a shiver went

down my spine. "Some questions don't need to be answered, Maggie. Go home and stop causing trouble." He spun on his heels and marched in the direction of his office.

I stared at his retreating back for a long time. Granted, I'd never make it onto their list of favorite people, but Paul and Melanie were mighty keen not to have the cocktail glass tested. Did Paul have something to hide? Or did his wife?

9

I spent the afternoon at the café fielding questions about my discovery of Sandra's body and trying not to burn muffins. By the time Kelly finished her shift at four, I was bone-tired and hoarse from dealing with curious customers. I'd also managed to create a flood involving coffee and milk foam.

When Lenny ambled in just before closing time, I was mopping up the mess. "Hey, Maggie. How's it hanging?"

"To the left," I quipped, "but going downhill fast. How about you?"

"I'm pretty good." He hesitated and looked around the café. Apart from the Spinsters and the Two Gerries, everyone had gone home. "Can I have a word with you? About the laptop?"

"Sure." I lowered my voice. "Did you find anything?"

Lenny frowned and shook his head. "Sandra

wanted a new RAM chip, but she should have been looking for a new computer. That laptop is fried."

I blinked. "Is it beyond repair?"

"Looks like it." Lenny's gloomy expression matched his tone. "I worked on it all morning, but no luck. I dropped it over to the hotel before I came here. Paul said he'd get their tech guy to take another look at the laptop, but in my opinion, it's only fit for salvage."

I frowned, sifting through the info I'd stored in my head. "Sandra didn't mention it was broken when she asked you to put in the RAM chip?"

"No, but she didn't have a clue about computers. Maybe she thought it just needed a new RAM chip and would magically resurrect itself."

"Maybe. It's strange, though."

"Yeah, but not much stranger than her turning up dead at the Movie Club." Lenny scratched his beard. "You know, I've been thinking. Did you see that weird green light hovering over the screen while we were watching *Dial M for Murder?*"

"No, Lenny." Oh, boy. If he was going to mention extraterrestrial involvement in Sandra's death, I hadn't had enough coffee to deal with it.

"Because maybe aliens beamed Sandra up during the film, stole her soul, and tossed her body back to earth." Lenny peered at me earnestly. "It happens."

"Sure it does—in sci-fi movies."

"Just think about it for a second. It would totally

explain why she suddenly keeled over. She was fine when you served her the cocktails."

I sighed. "You know, Lenny, we were having a totally sane conversation until you tossed E.T. into the mix. Leaving alien involvement out of the equation, remember I saved Sandra's cocktail glass last night?"

He nodded. "Yeah. You bagged it and put it in the fridge like a pro."

"I spent the morning trying to convince Sergeant O'Shea and Melanie to get it tested for substances that could have caused her death."

Lenny drew his brows together. "Do you seriously think Sandra was murdered?"

"I don't know what to think. I just find it frustrating that Sergeant O'Shea refuses to have the glass checked."

"What's his excuse?"

I raised an eyebrow. "A surgical attachment to his golf club? I figured the suggestion of murder wouldn't fly with him, but I thought he'd at least consider the possibility of suicide and get the glass tested."

"No way," Lenny said. "I don't see Sandra killing herself, especially not in public."

"I agree it's unlikely, but everyone seems to think my murder theory is far-fetched."

Lenny's brow furrowed. "Do you know Mack McConnell? We hung out with him a couple of times when you were over that last summer."

"Vaguely. He had long red hair and a wannabe goatee, right?"

Lenny grinned. "That's him. Mack looks the very same today. He's a pharmacist who works here on the island at his family's pharmacy. We could ask him to test the contents of the glass. Any idea what substance we're looking for?"

My thoughts leaped to Noreen's missing codeine pills, and I swallowed past the lump in my throat. "Nothing in particular." My gaze dropped to my scuffed boots. "If he agrees to look at the cocktail, could I have a word with him first?"

Lenny eyed me thoughtfully. "Sure. I'll give him a call now. He usually works at the pharmacy on Saturdays."

"Thanks. I appreciate it."

Lenny went outside the café to make the phone call and returned a minute later. "Mack finishes work in ten minutes. He said he'd check the glass in their lab if you bring it over now."

I glanced at my watch. "The café closes in ten minutes. Would you mind staying and serving any last-minute customers? I'll come right back after I drop the stuff over to Mack."

"Sure. No problem." Lenny slipped off his jacket and slid behind the counter. "Do you know where Mack's pharmacy is?"

"I think so. There's a McConnell's Pharmacy farther down this street. Is that the one?"

"Yeah. Mack said to knock if he's already locked up."

"Okay. I'll get the cocktail stuff and go straight over."

I went into the kitchen and removed the two makeshift evidence bags from the café's refrigerator. I wasn't sure Mack would need the cocktail glass in addition to the liquid I'd saved from it, but I figured it wouldn't hurt to bring it just in case. Once I had everything concealed in a large shopping bag, I put on my jacket and stepped outside.

In the hours I'd been inside the café, daylight had given way to darkness. When I passed Sandra Walker's news agency, I shivered inside my jacket and hurried down the street toward McConnell's Pharmacy. Mack was at the door when I arrived, about to lock up for the night. He smiled at me through the glass window and opened the door to let me in.

"Hey, Maggie. Great to see you again." Mack pumped my hand and bounced back on the balls of his feet. Like Lenny, he was tall and gangly, but that was where the resemblance ended. In contrast to Lenny's short dark hair and casual clothing, Mack had freckles and long ginger hair and looked like he lived in a lab coat.

"It's good to see you, too. Thanks for agreeing to look at the cocktail glass."

"No problem." He glanced through the large display window. "Come through to the back. People are nosy around here."

I laughed. "Tell me about it."

Mack led me through to a back room that was

furnished with a desk, books, and lab equipment. "You do realize that it could make it hard to submit the glass as evidence if there is a trial?" he asked after he'd closed the door.

"Yeah, I'm aware of that, but given that Sergeant O'Shea has no intention of sending it to a forensics lab for testing, it's a chance I'm willing to take." I opened the shopping bag and extracted the container with the remnants of Sandra's final cocktail. "I brought both the glass and the leftover cocktail."

Mack laughed. "An ex-cop never dies."

I grinned. "I guess not. Do you need the glass as well?"

"Nah. Might be smarter to leave it untouched, just in case we do find a suspicious substance in the cocktail. Any idea what we're looking for?"

My stomach sank and I nodded. "Check for Solpodol."

Mack whistled. "Do you think Sandra Walker died of a codeine-paracetamol overdose?"

"It's possible. Could that cause a person to die suddenly and quietly?"

Mack considered the question for a moment. "Yeah, I think so. The symptoms include drowsiness, dizziness, dilated pupils, shallow breathing, sweating, and nausea."

"She appeared to be drunk, but everyone says that's highly unlikely."

"The symptoms of a codeine overdose could be

mistaken for intoxication," Mack said. "Did Sandra throw up at all?"

"Not that I'm aware of. I saw no signs of it when I found her dead in the movie theater." I shuddered at the memory. "Her skin was cold and clammy."

"That ties in with an overdose of Solpodol." Mack examined the makeshift evidence bag. "The test will take a while to complete, and I'm going to want to run it twice, just to be sure. Where can I reach you when I have the results?"

I scribbled down my cell phone number on a piece of notepaper and handed it to him. "Call me any time, day or night."

"Will do." Mack shoved his glasses up from the bridge of his nose and stared at the container with an expression of intent. "Enjoy your evening, Maggie."

I looked at the bag in his hands. "I'm sorry you won't be enjoying yours."

Mack's grin was wide. "Oh, I will. I love this stuff. I wanted to be a forensic pharmacologist."

"What stopped you?"

"Not enough jobs in Ireland." He shrugged. "So I gave in to parental pressure and stuck with pharmacy."

I understood all about parental pressure, both the giving-in-to-it part and the defying it. "In that case, have fun."

After dropping off the cocktail glass to Mack, I walked back to the café. Lenny had locked up and started clearing the tables.

"Thanks," I said. "I can take it from here."

"Okay." Lenny shrugged into his jacket. "Let me know what Mack says. Ten to one says he'll find nothing and you can relax."

I forced a smile. "I hope so. Enjoy your weekend."

For the next half hour, I scrubbed tables and put up the chairs for the cleaning lady who'd come by in the morning. I'd just finished loading the dishwasher when Mack called. "Hey," I said, my heart pounding. "That was quick."

"Yes. The test I used is one employed by paramedics and law enforcement. It gives fast and accurate results, but they still need to be confirmed in a lab to be considered conclusive." Mack's tone was clipped and formal, a far cry from the easy camaraderie we'd shared thirty minutes ago.

My hands grew clammy around my phone. "And?"

"And Sandra Walker's cocktail contained codeine. I ran the test twice before I called you."

I swore beneath my breath. "Thanks, Mack. Please hold onto the remnants of the cocktail until I've had a chance to talk to Sergeant O'Shea."

"You'd better be quick," Mack said. "I saw him pull up at the station a couple of minutes ago. Want me to join you there?"

"Yes, please." I was already pulling on my jacket. "I'll be there in five." Three if I sprinted.

∼

When Mack and I entered the station, Sergeant O'Shea was leafing through a filing cabinet. The slick smile he bestowed on Mack froze the instant he registered my presence. "Not you again," he said in a thunderous voice. "I told you to stop wasting police time."

I crossed my arms over my chest and glared at him. "Since when does a round of golf count as police time?"

The veins in Sergeant O'Shea's neck bulged.

"Maggie asked me to examine the contents of Sandra Walker's cocktail glass," Mack interjected.

The policeman's beady eyes swiveled in the pharmacist's direction. "She did what? I told her to keep out of it."

"And it was just as well she asked me to run tests," Mack continued, deliberately ignoring the sergeant's truculent manner. "The cocktail tested positive for codeine."

"See?" I placed my hands on my hips and stared the sergeant down. "Sandra Walker *was* poisoned."

"Now slow down a minute, young lady. Even if the cocktail contained codeine, are you sure it was Sandra's glass?"

"I showed you the glass when you came to look at Sandra's body."

"Ah," he said in a triumphant tone, "but how do I know that the cocktail Mack McConnell tested was Sandra's? I only have your word for it."

I rolled my eyes and tapped my foot. "If you'd

done your job and bagged the evidence, you wouldn't need to rely on my word. Besides, a lab can test for saliva and match the DNA to Sandra."

The sergeant's purple face turned puce. "I—"

"Fact is," I continued, "the contents of Sandra's glass tested positive for codeine. Either Sandra put the codeine into her drink, by accident or design, or someone spiked her cocktail. I checked the sign-in sheet, and twenty-eight people attended the Movie Club evening, including Sandra. We can assume Sandra's drink was spiked by one of them, so that narrows down the list of suspects."

"Suspects. Poison." Sergeant O'Shea was on the defensive. "You're jumping the gun here, Ms. Doyle."

"Am I? I don't think so. You need to send the rest of the cocktail to a forensics lab for further tests, and you should order an autopsy on Sandra's body."

The sergeant's nostrils flared, but he knew I was right. He opened and closed his mouth several times, but only a squawk came out. "Fine," he snapped, pinning me in place with his hostility. "If you're so keen for me to question the *suspects*, as you call them, let's start with you."

10

I f Sergeant O'Shea was under the impression that the idea of a police interrogation would intimidate me, he was a greater fool than I'd thought.

"Of course," I said smoothly. "I made Sandra's drink, after all. If you're interested in seeing last night's guest list, I took a photo of it with my phone."

The police officer's face contorted, and his hammy hands balled into fists. "It seems you're well prepared, Ms. Doyle. Seeing as you're so keen to be questioned, let's make this a formal interview and record it."

I regarded him with intense dislike. "Naturally, but we'll need to wait for my lawyer to get here first."

Sergeant O'Shea let out a roar of indignation. As I'd suspected, he had no intention of wasting his Saturday evening waiting for a lawyer to show up. "Fine. Let's make it informal."

I nodded. "Mack, would you mind staying? I'd like an impartial witness present at my 'informal' interview."

"Sure. First, I'll text my sister. She's a barrister in Cork, and she's staying with my parents for the weekend. We'll have her come by and wait outside."

"Okay, fine." The sergeant held up a hand. "No interview, formal or otherwise. Just give me the list of people at the film last night."

After a few minutes of the sergeant fumbling with his cell phone, he received a copy of the guest list. "Have you filled any prescriptions for codeine recently, Mack?"

"Not in the last few days." The pharmacist glanced at me. "I checked when the test on the cocktail came out positive. If you get a warrant, I'll have a list of all prescriptions containing codeine that we filled in the last six months waiting for you. Of course, a black market source is always a possibility."

"All right," the policeman grunted. "We need to find out where the codeine came from."

Oh, boy. I hadn't been looking forward to this moment, but I'd known it was inevitable the instant Mack had called with the test result. "I have an idea where the codeine could have come from, but not who put it into Sandra's glass."

Both Mack and Sergeant O'Shea stared at me.

I cleared my throat. "Noreen had her wisdom teeth removed yesterday morning in a hospital on the mainland. They prescribed Solpodol pills for her."

"Solpodol?" Sergeant O'Shea addressed Mack. "Is that like those Solpadeine soluble thingies my wife takes for her migraines?"

Mack nodded. "Solpadeine and Solpodol are both painkillers containing a codeine phosphate and parac-etamol mix, but the dosage of codeine is much higher in Solpodol. Therefore, it's available only on prescription."

Sergeant O'Shea turned to me. "I take it your aunt had her Solpodol with her last night." It was a statement, not a question.

"Yes." I hesitated for a moment before plunging on. "When she woke up this morning, she discovered that several pills were missing."

Mack eyed me sharply. "How many?"

"About ten."

He whistled. "That's enough to kill a person, and fairly quickly."

"Is it feasible for Sandra to have ingested the Solpodol just before the start of the movie and to be dead by the end of the movie?" I asked the pharma-cist. "It seems fast."

"What time did you serve her the cocktail?"

"I served her two cocktails, actually. Sandra was one of the last guests to arrive. I served her the first cocktail at around eight-thirty, and she ordered a second one shortly before the movie began. That must have been nine-fifteen or thereabouts." I screwed up my forehead. "The thing is, Sandra was showing signs of being drunk after the *first* cocktail, and that was apparently unusual for her. I wonder now if she wasn't displaying a reaction to the Solpodol. Is it possible for traces of the drug to have stayed in the glass and contaminated the second cocktail enough for it to test positive for codeine?"

"The forensic toxicology lab will be able to confirm, but I'd have thought it more likely that the Solpodol was added directly to the drink I tested."

"Could it have been slipped into both cocktails?" I wondered aloud. "If so, the killer was taking a heck of a risk."

"Or Sandra was making sure she got the job done," Mack suggested gently. "She could have put the Solpodol in her own glass both times."

Sergeant O'Shea cleared his throat with theatrical exaggeration. "When did the film start?" he asked, finally showing genuine interest in the proceedings rather than expressing his annoyance at having his Saturday evening plans disrupted.

"We'd planned to start the movie at nine," I said, "but we were running late. It must have been around nine-thirty by the time we'd gotten everyone seated and the intro credits were rolling. The movie ran for an hour and forty-five minutes, assuming the information on IMDb is correct." Seeing the incredulous expressions on their faces, I added, "I checked after Sandra died."

"Interesting," Mack mused. "What time did you discover the body?"

"At eleven twenty-five," I said without hesitation.

"I glanced at my watch as I walked down the aisle toward Sandra's seat. I gave up on CPR and checked my watch, and I'd been attempting resuscitation for fifteen minutes."

"Was she cold when you found her?" Sergeant O'Shea asked.

"She felt...clammy. Yes, that's the right description."

The policeman turned to Mack. "Could Mrs. Walker have died within an hour of taking an overdose of Solpodol?"

"Honestly? I'm not sure." Mack scrunched up his forehead. "I suppose it's possible, especially if the person was in poor health and mixed the Solpodol with alcohol, but I'd have thought the timing would be more accurate if she'd been poisoned with her first cocktail, the one Maggie served her at half-past eight."

"Wait a sec," I said, reliving the events of last night in my mind. "We usually served each drink in a fresh glass, but if I recall correctly, I took Sandra's original cocktail glass without thinking and used it for her second cocktail. She ordered a Peppermint Cream cocktail on both occasions."

"Was there anything left from her first cocktail when you poured in the second?" Mack asked. "The test I ran this evening is designed to pick up any trace of codeine. It doesn't specify the amount. That requires more rigorous testing in a lab."

I pictured the scene in my mind. "Maybe a drop?

There was certainly some of the foam from the original cocktail left in the glass. I'm sorry I can't be more specific, but I was moving on autopilot by that point. We had more guests than I'd anticipated, and I was responsible for making the most popular cocktail on the menu."

"What did this cocktail contain?" Sergeant O'Shea asked.

"Apart from a lethal dose of codeine?" I quipped.

Judging by his enraged expression, the sergeant was not amused. "This isn't the moment for levity, Ms. Doyle."

I tried to look contrite. "Sure. Sorry. Just trying to lighten the mood. Ahem. Okay, Peppermint Creams contain crème de menthe, white crème de cacao, milk, Baileys Irish Cream, and hazelnut cream liqueur."

"Those sound delicious," Mack said, and then catching the sergeant's thunderous expression, he added, "The crème de menthe alone would do a good job at disguising the taste of the Solpodol."

The police officer grunted. "Looks like I'm going to miss tonight's golf club dinner."

"You guys live well," I said. "This is, what, your second night in a row out with them?"

"No," Mack said. "The golf club only meets for dinner once a week on Saturdays. My father is a member."

"Oh, but I thought…" I trailed off. My gaze met the sergeant's, and his red face turned even redder. I could have sworn he'd mentioned dining at the golf club yesterday evening when he'd been so upset to have his evening's plans disrupted by my demand that he attend to Sandra Walker's dead body. Had he lied about where he'd been? If so, why?

Sergeant O'Shea's bristly mustaches convulsed. "Seeing as Ms. Doyle is so keen to have me interview all the people with access to Sandra Walker's drink, let's start with the most obvious person." He sneered at me, and my shoulders tensed. "I suggest you get your pal, Mack McConnell, to call his barrister sister. Your aunt might have need of her services."

11

Sergeant O'Shea hauled Noreen in for questioning at seven o'clock the following morning. When it reached noon and there was still no word from her, I was becoming seriously worried. The former police officer in me knew that Noreen had to be questioned, especially if Sandra's cause of death was confirmed to be a codeine overdose, but I was uncomfortably aware that Sergeant O'Shea had latched on to Noreen as a person to bully just to annoy me. By discovering the codeine in the cocktail, I'd humiliated him, and he wasn't a man who took kindly to being shown up in public, especially by an outsider.

I removed a tray of vegan raspberry-and-coconut scones from where they'd been cooling on the kitchen counter and gave them a cautious sniff. Mmm...not bad. Once I scraped the blackened edges off them, people might even eat them.

I glanced at the clock. The café only opened for the morning crowd on Sundays, and I'd close in fifteen minutes. Until then, the demand for Noreen's baked goods was brisk. So brisk, in fact, that I'd run out of the dough she'd prepared yesterday and had to resort to making some from scratch, resulting in oatmeal muffins that were as dry as sandpaper. After I'd arranged the scones in a display basket, I turned to go back out to the café.

"Maggie?" Lenny stood in the kitchen doorway, an uncharacteristic tension in his lanky frame. "Mack says Noreen is at the garda station. What's going on?"

"The what?" I blinked in confusion before comprehension dawned. Between guards, garda, and gardaí, I could never keep the Irish terminology straight. "Oh, you mean the police station. Didn't Mack tell you the results of his tests on the cocktail glass?"

Lenny shook his head. "For a stand-up dude, Mack can be annoyingly discreet at times. He told me to ask you."

"Well, you'd have heard soon enough—I expect Sergeant O'Shea will want you to give a statement. Long story short, Sandra Walker's cocktail was laced with codeine, and Noreen discovered that her prescription medicine containing codeine was half empty after the Movie Club meeting."

Lenny let out a slow breath. "Whoa. Poor Noreen. First, Sandra pops her clogs in Noreen's movie theater, and now it turns out her meds did the job."

"We don't know that for sure yet. Sandra's body was sent to the mainland for an autopsy, but the formal toxicology results will take weeks."

"Weeks?" Lenny's eyebrows rose. "Why so long? It never takes that long on *CSI*."

I snorted. "TV and movies always get that part wrong. Toxicology test results take ages. The lab will supply a preliminary report in a couple of weeks, but the formal results will take longer. However, there's enough circumstantial evidence to indicate Sandra's death wasn't natural. Unless Sergeant O'Shea is a total fool, he has to start inquiries now." I maneuvered past Lenny and placed the sconces on the counter.

Lenny followed me and cast a surreptitious glance around the half-empty café. He dropped his voice to a whisper. "The idea of Noreen killing someone is totally out there."

"I agree, but Noreen's feud with Sandra is well known."

"Who didn't have a feud with Sandra at some point? The woman was notorious." Lenny scratched his beard. "If Sandra didn't kill herself and no one bumped her off, it's got to be the establishment, man. They're trying to cover up an alien abduction. That explains why the doctor and Sergeant O'Shea weren't keen on you wanting Sandra's body examined."

Yeah, we were back to the aliens. I suppressed a sigh. "Lenny, no aliens were involved in Sandra Walker's death."

"That sucks." Lenny looked glum. "I've never

been present at an alien abduction. It would be so cool."

"Maybe you and Mack will get lucky on your next alien spotting expedition," I said, deadpan. "In the meantime, let's focus on clearing Noreen's name. Do you have time to stick around after I lock up? I'd appreciate a sounding board while I go through the list of suspects."

"Sure." Lenny gestured behind him to the two remaining tables of customers. "Want me to start turfing the geriatrics out of here?"

"I heard that," yelled Gerry Two from his usual seat at the Cary Grant table.

"Geriatric, indeed," muttered Gerry One. "I'll have you know, young man, that I'm only eighty-five."

"As if you'd let me forget it, Granddad." Lenny grinned at my incredulous expression. "Yeah, this old codger is my grandfather. He's Gerald Logan, and his pal there is Geroid Sullivan. As you've probably gathered, everyone calls them the Two Gerries, but the geriatric description fits just as well."

"Cheeky pup." Gerry One grunted and turned his attention to me. "That scone you served me earlier wasn't half bad, Maggie. A definite improvement on yesterday's batch."

I preened in the beam of his compliment and thanked my lucky stars that he hadn't ordered an oatmeal muffin. "Why, thank you."

Lenny picked up a scone from the batch I'd just

prepared and sniffed at it cautiously. "Are you sure this is Noreen's vegan raspberry-coconut recipe?"

"Of course," I said indignantly. "I followed the recipe."

He took a bite and recoiled, gagging.

"Oh, heck." I handed him a bowl. "Don't tell me you've been poisoned as well?"

"Those," Lenny said between gasps, "are not vegan. What did you put into them, Maggie?"

I examined his discarded scone. It looked fine to me. Of course, I hadn't tasted one yet. I took a cautious bite and chewed slowly. "Tastes fine to me. That is," I amended, seeing the incredulity on his face, "it's revolting, but it's the vegan recipe. My hopes weren't high."

"Maggie," Lenny said severely, "did you mix up the almond milk with cow's milk?"

I stopped chewing. "Oops."

"Exactly." Lenny grabbed a pen and a sticky note from behind the counter and stuck an amendment onto the label of the basket of scones.

"Non-Vegan Vegan Raspberry Scones," I read aloud. "Impressive, Lenny."

"So says the woman who just tried to poison me with dairy."

I stuck my tongue out at him. "I'd better make a start on cleaning up."

In the distance, the church bells chimed the hour. As if on cue, the Spinsters and the Two Gerries bid Lenny and me a cheery farewell and shuffled off to do whatever it was that geriatrics did in Smuggler's Cove on a Sunday afternoon. Lenny helped me to clean the tables and sweep the floor. I'd just put the dishwasher on when Noreen walked in, accompanied by Bran and Sister Pauline.

"Noreen," I exclaimed. "They finally let you go. Why didn't you call me? I'd have collected you from the station."

"I know you would have, love, but I needed you here to run the café. Sister Pauline was dog-sitting Bran and she was kind enough to give me a lift."

"You look exhausted." I pulled out a chair and gestured for my aunt and Sister Pauline to take seats at the Grace Kelly table. "Can I make you a pot of tea?"

Noreen and Sister Pauline exchanged looks of alarm.

"Well, I—" Sister Pauline began.

"My tea-making abilities have improved over the last couple of days," I interjected. "Pinkie swear."

"Just don't touch the non-vegan vegan scones," Lenny drawled.

Sister Pauline patted me on the arm. "Why don't I make the tea while you finish cleaning up? And I'm sure you want to have a word with Noreen."

Noreen collapsed onto a chair, and Bran lay at her feet, clearly delighted to be reunited with his mistress. "Before you start interrogating me, could you get me a glass of water? Mack was kind enough to slip me a few extra Solpodol to replace the ones that—" her voice caught, "—went missing."

"Sure." I grabbed a clean glass from behind the counter and filled it with sparkling mineral water before giving it to my aunt. "Would Bran like to try one of my oatmeal muffins?" Maybe I could use the dog to get rid of a few of the bad batch. I put one on a plate and placed it at his feet. Bran sniffed the muffin and stared up at me balefully. I put my hands on my hips. "Seriously? Not even a lick? That's the last time I let you haul me around the countryside."

"Smart dog," Lenny said. "He has survival instincts."

I stuck my tongue out at Lenny, and then turned to my aunt. "Don't leave us in suspense. What happened at the police station?"

Noreen shook two pills onto her palm and swallowed them before she met my questioning gaze. "There's no news, love. Sergeant O'Shea asked a lot of questions that I couldn't answer. After a few hours of him asking the same questions over and over, Patricia McConnell told him to charge me or let me go home." Her smile was tight. "Given that Sandra's autopsy is being performed this afternoon, Sergeant O'Shea has nothing to charge me with."

Thank goodness he was finally moving ahead with the autopsy. Melanie would throw a fit. "I'm sorry you were dragged into this mess, Noreen. When the cocktail tested positive for codeine, I couldn't not mention your missing pills."

"I know, Maggie. You did the right thing. I just hope the district superintendent has the good sense to send someone out to Whisper Island to take over the case. O'Shea is a bumbling buffoon and far too beholden to his golf club cronies to be trustworthy."

I inclined my head in agreement. I'd surmised as much from my brief but memorable encounters with the sergeant. "Speaking of Sergeant O'Shea not being trustworthy, there's something I've been meaning to ask you. On the night Sandra died, O'Shea claimed he'd come from a golf club dinner, but Mack said they only meet on Saturdays. Why would O'Shea lie about where he was on Friday night?"

"Well…" My aunt's voice dropped to a conspiratorial whisper. "One of the blind items in Sandra's gossip column referred to a married man of influence who was having an affair with a woman half his age. Island gossip pointed the finger at O'Shea as the married man in question."

"So he might have been meeting his mistress on Friday, hence his annoyance at being disturbed?"

"It would also explain how he got to The Movie Theater Café as quickly as he did," Sister Pauline said, placing a steaming teapot and two cups on the table. "If he'd been at the golf club, he should have taken at least a quarter of an hour longer to get here."

I looked at both of them in turn. "Do either of you have any idea who his younger woman is?"

"I can't say for certain, but Sergeant O'Shea has

always been flirtatious with Mina Kelly, Brid's younger sister."

"He's been seen leaving her cottage at strange times of the day, too," Sister Pauline added.

No wonder Sergeant O'Shea hadn't been motivated to investigate Sandra's death. If she'd written about his affair in the local newspaper, he must have hated her. Had he hated her enough to want her dead? But how could he have killed her? Even if he'd lied about being at the golf club, he hadn't been here, and neither had Mina Kelly. But Mina's sister, Brid, had… I filed this information away for future reference and helped Lenny put chairs up on tables.

"When you're finished with your tea, I'll drive you home, Noreen. You look like you need some serious rest and relaxation."

"I do. I'm looking forward to curling up with an old Georgette Heyer novel." My aunt took a sip from her teacup and put it down on her saucer with a clatter. "Oh, Maggie, before I forget. Philomena says she lost the scarf she was wearing the night of the Movie Club meeting. Red tartan with a navy trim. She asked if we could check if she dropped it in the café or the movie theater."

"Sure. I'll have a look around the movie theater now."

I moved toward the back of the café and opened the doors that led to the movie theater. The hairs on my nape stood on end, and I gave myself a mental shaking. I'd avoided going into the movie theater since

Friday. Bran followed me down the steps and stopped to sniff at seats, as if hoping to find food. I checked each seat in turn, pulling it down and looking underneath, but there was no sign of Philomena's scarf. To Bran's delight, he unearthed a stale piece of popcorn. I turned to walk back up the aisle to the café when something orange caught my eye. Wedged between two seats was a screw-top medicine bottle container, identical to the one Noreen had been given at the hospital. I sucked in a breath. On autopilot, I pulled a tissue from my pocket and used it to pick up the container. On the off chance that it was relevant to Sandra's murder, I didn't want to get my fingerprints on it.

I examined the container. The label had been torn off and shed no light on its contents. My heart pounding, I poured the contents of the container into a second tissue. Four white pills gleamed back at me under the movie theater lights. Not Solpodol, thank goodness. But why had they been shoved down the side of one of the seats? Was it by accident or by design? And did their presence in the movie theater have any connection with Sandra Walker's death? After all, there was no way to know how long the container had lain concealed between the seats.

I returned the pills to the container and screwed it shut. I'd bag it as carefully as I'd preserved the cocktail glass. Once I took Noreen home, I'd call Mack and ask him to identify the pills. From my work as a cop, I was familiar with a lot of medications available in the U.S., but many had different names in Ireland.

Out in the café, Noreen and Sister Pauline drank their tea, and Lenny lounged at a neighboring table.

"No sign of Philomena's scarf." I kept my tone casual. "By the way, who sat in seats 4D and 4E? I found an old pill container stuck between the seats."

"I'm afraid we don't assign seats for the movie theater nights," Noreen said. "It's first come, first served."

"Ah. Never mind. Just thought I'd ask."

"Hang on a sec, did you say 4D and E?" Lenny asked, a line between his brows.

"Yeah. Any idea who was sitting there on Friday night?"

"Yeah." Lenny met my eye. "I was in 4D, and Julie sat in 4E."

12

The following week passed in a haze of early starts, jogs with Julie, and the occasional scorched scone. The medicine bottle I'd discovered in the movie theater was still in my purse. I wanted to show it to Mack, but he was attending a training course in Galway and wouldn't be back until Friday. Knowing Julie and Lenny had occupied the seats where I'd found the mysterious pills made my stomach cramp. I couldn't be sure they had anything to do with the pills, or that the pills had any connection with Sandra Walker's death. All the same, the pills were yet another item on my growing list of things that didn't add up.

Apart from a few stalwart regulars, business at The Movie Theater Café was down, both during the day and in the evening when the various island clubs held their meetings. From what I could glean from snatches of gossip overheard in the café, Sergeant

O'Shea had bumbled around Whisper Island, questioning the attendees of the fatal Movie Club meeting and giving the impression that Sandra took her own life, or was poisoned by Noreen, and that both eventualities were somehow my fault. I gritted my teeth. If the police officer spent less time improving his golf handicap and more attention on policing the island, he might have solved the case by now.

Just before closing time on the Thursday after Sandra's death, I glanced up from the table I was polishing. My aunt stood behind the counter, chewing her lip. Seeing her stressed from worry and lack of sleep tore me up. While I didn't believe Noreen had poisoned Sandra's cocktail, logic told me that the source of the codeine in Sandra's glass was my aunt's prescription medication.

Noreen caught my eye and forced an unconvincing smile. "Are you looking forward to playing that game with Lenny and his friends this evening?"

I made a face. "I'm not sure I'm in the mood for a game."

"It'll do you good, love. Take your mind off…" She left the sentence unfinished.

"I know." I sighed. "You know what's ironic? I came to Whisper Island to get Joe off my mind. And it worked. Unfortunately, I've replaced dwelling on my disastrous marriage with obsessing about Sandra Walker's death."

"Not the plan. Not for either of us." Aunt Noreen's lips twisted. "I'm looking forward to watching *Call the Midwife* with Sister Pauline later. I need some soothing entertainment."

"I like Sister Pauline, but she doesn't seem like a nun."

Noreen smiled. "What do you imagine a typical nun to be like?"

"More serious. And bossy. And wearing a nun's habit."

My aunt laughed. "You're behind on the times, love. Most nuns don't bother with a habit anymore. Besides, Sister Pauline had a life before she joined the order. Maybe that's what makes her different."

The bell over the café door jangled. Joan Sweetman came in, followed by Sister Pauline and my aunt Philomena. "Bliss," Joan sighed. "It's nice and warm in here."

"We've just come from the library," Philomena explained. "The heating's on the blink. I've sent John over to fix it, but we decided to decamp and come here."

"We picked up copies of the book we're reading for the next book club meeting, and we want to make sure everyone has a chance to read it." Sister Pauline pulled a dog-eared version of Josephine Tey's *Miss Pym Disposes* from her purse. "If you'd like to borrow my copy after I've finished with it, Maggie, you're more than welcome. The library only has two copies and one of them is an interlibrary loan."

"Thanks, but I have the book on my digital reader."

Philomena reared back as though I'd hit her. "You don't read those awful ebooks, do you?"

"There's nothing awful about them," Miss Murphy piped up from the table where she was playing cards with her spinster friend, Miss Flynn, and their male companions, the Two Gerries. "With my bad eyesight and arthritis in my hands, they're much better than struggling with a regular book."

Philomena pursed her lips. She was old school and didn't like change. I suspected that Whisper Island's long-overdue digital catalog was being implemented in spite of her position as head librarian rather than because of it.

"I started reading the book before all the drama," Noreen said with a bitter laugh. "I can't seem to settle back into reading about a murder mystery when I'm living one."

"It must be awful for you, Noreen." Joan's fine features settled into a frown. "And having that dreadful little man poking into everyone's business is making the situation worse. He's a menace at the golf club and utterly useless at his job."

"Perhaps they'll send over someone from the mainland," Sister Pauline said. "Surely all police officers can't be as stupid as Sergeant O'Shea."

"I'm relying on Maggie to solve the case." Noreen smiled at me. "I'm only half joking, love. If you were in charge of the investigation, I'd feel more confident that justice would be served, one way or the other."

"I can't go around Whisper Island interrogating

people," I replied gloomily. "I'd like to, but I have to watch my step. Sergeant O'Shea made that very clear."

"If it hadn't been for your quick thinking, no one would have known Sandra's cocktail contained codeine," Philomena added. "You're much smarter than O'Shea."

"My cat is smarter than O'Shea," Joan said dryly.

I bit my lip. "My drawing attention to the fact that Sandra's death might not have been natural hasn't exactly gone down well with many residents on Whisper Island."

Sister Pauline patted my hand. "Don't take it to heart. People here like a quiet life and the illusion that no violence can occur on a small island."

"If it were the summer, the word on the street would be that a tourist was responsible." Joan raised a perfectly plucked eyebrow. "Yes, many islanders are naive enough to believe that one of their own couldn't possibly poison another."

I looked around the café and took a deep breath. "Let's say Sandra's drink was deliberately spiked with Noreen's medicine. We can assume that it had to have been someone who attended the Movie Club night. Of all the people there that night, who had a reason to want Sandra Walker dead?"

The silence that descended after I voiced my question lasted for a few tense seconds. Finally, Philomena spoke. "Plenty of people disliked Sandra. Whether or not that dislike was strong enough for them to want to kill her, I can't say."

"The first day I was here, a few of you mentioned the rumor that Sandra was the pen behind a vicious blind item gossip column in the local paper. Do you have any idea who she's featured in her columns?"

"The columns didn't name anyone, but they weren't exactly subtle." Philomena grimaced. "There was that unpleasantness about Paddy Driscoll's relationship with his sheep, for example, but I never believed the rumor."

I balked at her. "Ew. Didn't Paddy Driscoll look after the animals while you were at the hospital, Noreen?"

"He did, and I wouldn't have let him near my babies if I believed that nonsense. Just because the man's a bachelor and not the most sociable of characters doesn't mean he's romantically interested in sheep." Noreen eyed me. "In fact, I'd considered setting the two of you up. He's a little long in the tooth, and an ardent nationalist, but he owns land."

"And sheep he's alleged to be more than just friends with. Sight unseen, I'm going to give the idea of a date with Paddy Driscoll a resounding no." I blew out my cheeks. "Boy, this is one conversation I never imagined I'd be having."

"Paddy's not a bad fellow," Philomena said, "but I don't see him and Maggie hitting it off."

"Was Driscoll at the movie?" I asked, keen to get

the conversation back on track and away from my aunt's matchmaking schemes.

Joan nodded. "Paddy comes to every meeting. He sat next to me last Friday."

So yet another person with a grudge against Sandra had been at the Movie Club meeting. The list kept growing.

"If you're interested in the gossip columns, we have back issues of the *Whisper Island Gazette* at the library," Philomena said. "Why don't you drop by tomorrow and I can show them to you?"

I seized on the opportunity. "That would be great. Who's the editor of the *Gazette*? I might try to track him or her down."

"Sean Clough." Philomena's lips twitched. "Sean lives and breathes the *Gazette* and writes most of the articles himself. If you want to talk to him, he has a flat above the paper. Just walk down the main street past Logan's Electronics, and you'll see a side street named Lynott Lane. The *Gazette*'s building is the second on the right. You can't miss it."

"Thanks." I had no business inserting myself into what I knew would be an official murder investigation before long. But given Sergeant O'Shea's incompetence, and his determination to pin Sandra Walker's death on Noreen if he couldn't make his suicide theory stick, I didn't feel I had a choice. I hadn't liked the woman, but if someone had murdered her, Sandra Walker deserved justice.

The door of the café crashed open, and Melanie Greer marched in, eyes blazing, fists clenched. Paul ran in behind her, out of breath. I sucked in a breath and braced myself for the onslaught. I didn't have long to wait.

Melanie turned to me. "*You.*" She drew the word out for maximum effect. I'd always felt Melanie belonged on the stage. "Why don't you go back to America where you belong and let my mother rest in peace?"

"I'm sorry that you're upset, Melanie, but I couldn't not show the test results on your mother's cocktail glass to Sergeant O'Shea."

"You had no right to perform any tests on my mother's glass. Who asked you to interfere?"

"As I'm sure you know, I was a cop. I didn't feel the sergeant was doing his job the night your mom died. In the hope that he'd display some initiative in the morning, I saved Sandra's cocktail glass." I stared at her defiantly. "And just as well I did."

"That's a matter of opinion," Melanie snapped. "Mummy is dead. No police investigation will bring her back. And now they've performed an autopsy…" She collapsed into Paul's arms, sobbing dramatically.

Over Melanie's mass of perfect black curls, Paul caught my eye. "We realize you felt you were doing the right thing, but Melanie doesn't believe the cocktail glass you tested belonged to her mother."

I placed my hands on my hips. "Are you saying I made the whole thing up? The cocktail tested positive for codeine. Ask Mack McConnell if you don't believe me."

"How do we know you didn't spike a random cocktail glass to get attention?" Melanie demanded. "It would be the type of thing you'd do. You always went in for histrionics."

I took several deep breaths. Now was not the moment to lose my cool. "Your memory of my teenage self and my own differ, but whatever. The point is that I didn't invent a story to get attention. Frankly, I came to Whisper Island for a rest. I'm sorry about your mom, Melanie, but if someone deliberately put codeine in her cocktail and caused her death, don't you think she deserves justice?"

"Justice?" Melanie sneered. "You're one to talk. You and your stoner friend broke my mother's computer. If I hadn't let Paul talk me out of it, I'd have filed a police report."

"Lenny and I didn't break Sandra's laptop. Why would we want to do that? Sandra gave it to Lenny because she wanted him to install a new RAM chip. When he tried to start it up, it didn't work." I turned to Paul. "Have you had any luck fixing it?"

He shook his head. "I gave it to our tech guy at the hotel, but he said it's toast."

I nodded, unsurprised. "That's what Lenny said."

"Sergeant O'Shea collected it yesterday to send to a computer forensics team on the mainland. Maybe they'll have better luck salvaging its content."

"If the laptop is broken, Maggie and her weirdo

friend are responsible. Everyone knows Lenny is into something dodgy. Maybe he used Mummy's computer to conduct his black market drug trade and needed to destroy the evidence. He's sly enough to do it."

"Don't be absurd. Lenny isn't a drug dealer." And yet Melanie's portrayal of Lenny bothered me, and not just because I considered him a friend. Sly? Was this a figment of Melanie's imagination, or was there a side to Lenny's character that I hadn't seen? How well did I know the guy? We'd only become reacquainted a few days ago.

Melanie glared at me, her chin at a belligerent tilt. "I saw Mummy on her laptop the evening she died, and it was working fine."

My heart rate kicked up a notch as my investigative instincts came into play. "What time was this?" I asked in as casual a tone as I could muster. "Maybe the laptop broke later that evening."

"It must have been around six o'clock." Melanie sniffed. "I called over to her house to drop off a casserole dish I'd borrowed."

Six...plenty of time for Melanie to have given her mother a fatal dose of codeine. The timing fit better with Mack's estimate of how long the drug would have taken to kill Sandra. But why would Melanie want to kill her mother? Money? Or had they had an argument? If so, over what? "Are you sure your mom's laptop was working while you were at her house?"

"Yes." Melanie's eyes filled with genuine tears, and

I felt a pang of guilt for wondering if she'd killed her only living parent. "Mummy was typing up one of her little stories for the paper, just as she always did on a Friday evening."

"Noreen mentioned Sandra wrote for the paper." I kept my tone uncharacteristically diplomatic. "I'm sure she was a great addition to their staff."

Melanie dabbed at her tears and nodded. "Mummy loved going to all the island events and writing about what people wore. She was such a sociable creature. Everyone loved her." Melanie's gaze hardened again. "Which is why your ridiculous idea about her being murdered is nonsense."

"I hope it is, Melanie," I said quietly. "I'm an ornery creature, and I like being right, but on this occasion, I'd gladly be proved wrong."

Only I wouldn't be proved wrong. Of that I was certain. Sandra Walker had been murdered, and it was up to me to find her killer.

13

The snow that had been forecast for the morning finally began to fall by late afternoon. By the time I closed the café for the day, the street was blanketed in white. After the day I'd had, I was ready for a stiff drink and a warm bath. However, I'd promised I'd stay for Lenny's Unplugged Gamers meeting, so the bath, at least, would have to wait.

I'd just finished cleaning the tables when Lenny ambled in, balancing a stack of board game boxes in his arms. He raised an eyebrow when he saw me. "Rough day?"

"That's an understatement." I grimaced. "Melanie barged in here and accused me of spiking the cocktail glass after the fact to get attention. You were also mentioned in her accusation fest."

"What did I do?" he asked, dumping the games on Bette Davis.

"Apparently, you and I broke Sandra's laptop. Melanie claims she saw Sandra using it earlier that evening and the laptop worked just fine."

Lenny shrugged. "Maybe it did. Sandra never mentioned it being busted when she roped me into collecting it. But whatever happened, that laptop was dead when I tried to start it the following day." He scratched his head. "I even checked my van for water damage, but there's no sign of a leak, and all the rest of my gear is fine."

I blew out a breath. "I wish you hadn't gotten dragged into this."

"I'd have been dragged in no matter what. If Sandra was poisoned, I had easy access to both Noreen's meds and Sandra's drink." He opened one of the game boxes and started sorting the pieces. "A game will take your mind off Sandra."

"Who all is coming to tonight's meeting? Will I know anyone?"

"It's probably just going to be you, me, and Julie."

"Wow," I said. "Does the Unplugged Gamers have so few members?"

"We have seven regulars and a few stragglers. Unfortunately, Mack's away, and Günter has the flu." Lenny shifted uncomfortably. "Some of the others don't want to come until the mystery of Sandra's death is cleared up."

I sighed. "That's what I suspected. Business has been slow at the café all week. Is Günter the disheveled guy who came to the Movie Club the night

Sandra died? Noreen described him as a weird German dude who lives on a houseboat."

"Yeah. That's him." Lenny shot me a look. "Paul Greer is also a member, but I guess he'll avoid you and the café at the moment. Melanie has him under her thumb—or so she likes to think."

"But Paul sneaks out sometimes?"

"Uh-huh." Lenny shrugged. "I know Paul's a snob, but he can be a laugh when he lightens up a little."

I remembered that side of Paul, but people changed. When I'd hung out with him during the summers I'd spent on the island, he'd been a show-off and a charmer, but quick to laugh, even at himself. My memories rewound to the evening Paul had first kissed me. We'd practiced swinging from the branches of the trees beside the lake that bordered the hotel, both dressed in our Sunday best. Determined to impress me, Paul's swings had grown ever more daring...until he'd landed with a splash in the lake, much to both our amusement. Yeah, those had been good times. It had taken me a while to realize that Paul would always put his needs and desires before anyone else, no matter what the circumstances.

A knock drew my attention to the door. Julie peered through the window, a sunny smile on her face despite a smattering of snow on her hat and scarf. I unlocked the door and let her in.

"Brr. It's freezing tonight." She removed her outdoor clothing. "Can I dry these on the radiator?"

"Sure." I took her hat, scarf, and gloves and placed them above the radiator under the front window. "Lenny says it'll be just the three of us tonight."

"So I heard." Julie examined me closely. "What's up, Maggie? You look worried. Is it Sandra Walker?"

"Yeah. Listen, do you guys mind if I bounce some ideas off you before we start the game? With Sergeant O'Shea being a moron, I feel obligated to make sure he doesn't screw up the investigation and put Noreen in handcuffs."

"Mum mentioned that business was down in the café," Julie said. "I'm happy to do anything I can to help Noreen. What do you think, Lenny? Brainstorm over a hot drink?"

Lenny gestured to the tiles on the table. "I'm game—pun intended. I like Noreen. Granddad says the rumors Sandra put around about the café being unsanitary are out in force now that Sandra died here. I'm betting that's why business is slow."

"Yeah," I said grimly. "People aren't subtle about it."

Julie moved past me and slid behind the counter. "Why don't you talk while I make us all Irish coffees?"

"Go easy on the whiskey in mine," I said. "I have to drive."

Lenny grinned. "Whereas I'm walking. Hit me with it, Julie."

The comforting whirr of the coffee machine in the background soothed me, and I was looking forward to having my first Irish coffee since I'd arrived in Ireland. I took a seat opposite Lenny and took a notebook and pen from my purse. "Okay. Until we know for sure how Sandra died, we have to assume there's a strong possibility she was poisoned. And if she was poisoned, it's highly likely that one of the other members of the Movie Club did the job."

Lenny snorted. "Not surprising. Most of them hated Sandra."

"I have the guest list from that night, but I don't know most of these people. I'd appreciate your input."

"*Sláinte,*" Julie said, placing three perfect Irish coffees on the table and collapsing onto the chair beside me.

"*Sláinte.*" I took a cautious sip from my mug and consulted my notes. "I've photocopied the guest list, complete with my notes, and I'd like you to help me go through it and figure out each person's connection with Sandra."

I handed Julie and Lenny a copy of the list and looked at my own. There were twenty-eight names on the list, including our own. I'd asked Noreen for people's ages and professions and had added my impressions of those I'd met.

- *Maggie Doyle — 29 — Yours truly. Made Sandra Walker's cocktail.*

- *Noreen Doyle — 56 — My aunt. Owner of The Movie Theater Café. Missing codeine pills. Known to have an ongoing feud with Sandra.*
- *Philomena O'Brien — 55 — My aunt. Librarian.*
- *John O'Brien — 57 — My uncle. Builder.*
- *Julie O'Brien — 28 — My cousin. Elementary school teacher.*
- *Lenny Logan — 29 — Works in electronics store. Made cocktails the night Sandra died.*
- *Sister Pauline McLoughlin — 60 — Nun. Teaches at elementary school. Knew about codeine pills.*
- *Miss Flynn — 60s — Spinster. Runs a gift shop in the summer months.*
- *Miss Murphy — 60s — Spinster. Runs a gift shop in the summer months.*
- *Gerry One aka Gerald Logan — 85 — Geriatric regular at the café.*
- *Gerry Two aka Geroid Sullivan — 82 — Geriatric regular at the café.*
- *Melanie Greer — 29 — Sandra's daughter. Owns a fish restaurant and wine bar in Smuggler's Cove. What does Melanie inherit from Sandra?*
- *Paul Greer — 31 — Sandra's son-in-law. Manager of the Whisper Island Hotel.*
- *Cormac Tate — 57 — Principal of elementary school. Acted shifty when the subject of Sandra's*

blind item gossip column came up in conversation.

- *Joan Sweetman — 53 — Widow. Owns the gallery across from The Movie Theater Café.*
- *Nick Sweetman — 37 — Joan's stepson. Owner of the Smuggler's Cove Yacht Club and sailing school.*
- *Jennifer Pearce — 30s — Nick Sweetman's girlfriend. A lawyer.*
- *Linda Logan — 54 — Lenny's mother. Runs Logan's Electronics.*
- *James Greer — 62 — Owner of the Whisper Island Hotel.*
- *Aaron Nesbitt — 55 — Partner at the law firm* Nesbitt & Son.
- *Tom Ahearn — 32 — Fireman and owns a sports store.*
- *Rita Ahearn — 31 — Tom's wife. Works in the sports store.*
- *Sandra Walker — 56 — Victim. Widow with two adult children, Melanie and Jonathan (lives in London).*
- *Thomas Reilly — 45 — Doctor. Runs the Whisper Island Medical Centre.*
- *Maria Reilly — 43 —Dr. Reilly's wife. A painter.*
- *Brid Kelly — 31 — A nurse. Works at the Whisper Island Medical Centre. Her sister, Mina,*

is suspected of having an affair with Sergeant O'Shea.

- *Paddy Driscoll — 50s — Grumpy farmer.*
Looked after Noreen's animals when she was in the hospital.
- *Günter Hauptmann — 33 — Weird German dude who lives on a houseboat.*

"Looking at this list, can you think of anyone who might have had a blind item written about them? I already know about Brid Kelly's sister and Sergeant O'Shea, and Paddy Driscoll and his sheep. Can you think of any others?"

Julie and Lenny exchanged a significant look that wasn't lost on me. They obviously knew something they were reluctant to tell me, and I'd need to tread carefully if I were to coax the information out of them.

"Most of the people on this list had reason to dislike Sandra," Julie said after a long pause. "Some of Sandra's blind items were fairly harmless and easy to guess. Others, less so—on both counts. I know Brid Kelly was upset over a blind item that implied she'd given a patient the wrong injection, but no one ever complained of feeling ill after she'd treated them, so it quickly blew over."

I made a note about Brid's blind item in my notebook. "What about Cormac Tate? He acted shifty when the topic of the gossip column came up."

Julie thought for a moment before shaking her head. "I can't think of any of the items that could refer to Cormac."

"What about anyone else on the list?" I prompted.

"Well," Julie said slowly, "there was an item about a pair of spinsters who lived and worked together and were more than 'just friends.' Everyone guessed it was about Miss Flynn and Miss Murphy, but no one cared if it was true or not."

"Were they upset?"

"Miss Flynn was," Lenny said. "My mother played golf with her soon after the column was published, and she was very embarrassed and adamant that it was all nonsense."

I took a deep breath and plunged on. "Were either of you mentioned in a blind item? Or a member of your family?"

Julie's face turned fiery red, and Lenny's pale complexion went even whiter. "No," they said in unison.

"Guys, please. You've already said most people on the island were mentioned in the column at some point. I want to eliminate you from the list of suspects."

"I didn't know I was considered a suspect," Julie said indignantly. "I didn't go anywhere near Sandra's cocktail."

"Julie, come on. If O'Shea got off his butt and conducted a proper inquiry, he'd question all of us."

"He did question me. Well," she amended, "sort

of. He just asked me to confirm I was here that night and asked if I'd seen Noreen slip something in Sandra's drink."

"Ugh. Head. Meet. Desk. He didn't ask you if anyone else had a motive to kill Sandra? Or if you saw someone apart from Lenny and me screwing around with her drink?"

"No, he didn't ask me anything like that."

Lenny guffawed. "Sure, I was standing right next to the fatal cocktail, and O'Shea didn't seem to care. All he wanted to know was if you were sane."

"Seriously?" I blew out my cheeks. "It would suit him just fine if I were proved to be a nutcase looking for attention."

"For what it's worth, he'd just come from talking to Melanie," Lenny said. "I'm sure she put the idea in his head, and he tends to latch on to stuff that might make his job easier."

"So you have nothing else to add to my notes?" I asked. "I saw the look you two exchanged when I asked if any of the blinds referred to you or your family."

My cousin flushed and fiddled with her glass. "I suppose if I don't tell you, someone else will. One of the more recent cheating items referred to someone who worked with books, and everyone assumed it meant my mother."

"Philomena, cheat on John?" I stared at her incredulously. I'd always had the impression that my aunt and uncle were crazy about one another, even after thirty years of marriage.

"It's not true, of course," Julie said quickly, and darted a glance at Lenny. "The blind said she'd been sneaking around late at night. That's ridiculous. Why would she want to go out in the dark this time of year unless she absolutely had to? It's freezing cold."

My cousin's defensiveness screamed her doubts louder than if she'd put them into words. If Philomena was having an affair, it would surprise me, but then again, how well did I know her? She and John had been together a long time. I had no idea if the united front they presented to the world was reflected behind closed doors. Julie squirmed in her seat and took a gulp of Irish coffee.

I directed my attention at Lenny. "Do you know of anyone else on this list with a serious grudge against Sandra?"

Lenny thought for a moment. "Well, it's not a blind item, but Paddy Driscoll had an argument with her over land."

I leaned forward, pen poised. "Go on."

"I don't know all the particulars." Lenny scrunched up his brow. "When Sandra's husband died, he left her a farm as well as the lease on the news agency. Sandra didn't want to keep the farm, so she arranged to sell most of the land to Paddy Driscoll. I guess a property developer came to her after she and Paddy had shaken hands on the deal and made her a better offer. Sandra left Paddy in the lurch and sold not only the farmland but the cottage she was living in at the time to a company that wanted to build holiday homes."

"I bet Paddy didn't like that," I said.

"He was livid," Julie added. "He's an organic farmer and a leading light in the detectorists' club. Paddy is dead set against greedy property developers wrecking the island and building homes that will only be occupied a few months of the year."

"Paddy had a point," I said, "but I can understand Sandra taking the more lucrative deal."

"Unfortunately, Paddy never could," Julie said. "Even three years later, he's still banging on about treasure from the old monastery buried somewhere on Sandra's land. She used to allow him and his detectorist pals to roam all over with their metal detectors —for a fee, of course. She didn't believe they'd find anything, but Sandra was always one with her eye on the money."

I ran a fingertip down the list. "You can't remember any blind items that could have been about anyone else on this list?"

"You're talking to the wrong people about the gossip column. Julie and I are in the minority of islanders who don't read the *Gazette*. Anything I know about the blind items is stuff I heard from others." Lenny leaned back in his chair and stretched his arms behind his neck. "So what's your next move? Can we help?"

"Tomorrow, I have a day free from the café. I'm

going to try to track down Sean Clough, Sandra's editor. Then I'll go to the library and take Philomena up on her offer to show me back issues of the paper. I might even pay a call to Sergeant O'Shea in the hope of persuading him to let some-thing slip."

Lenny and Julie laughed in unison. "Good luck with that," Julie said. "O'Shea won't want to tell you anything."

"Heck, no, but I have a talent for getting people to say more than they intend." I took a sip of my Irish coffee. "Now that we've done a thorough character assassination on the suspects, how about that game?"

THE FOLLOWING MORNING, I drove into Smuggler's Cove early and ate breakfast with my aunt at the café. After washing down three helpings of Noreen's divine scrambled eggs with black coffee and freshly squeezed orange juice, the zipper of my jeans groaned in protest. "So much for my vow to live healthy while I'm on the island," I said as I shrugged into my winter jacket and wrapped my scarf around my neck.

"Ah sure, the food will do you good. In this cold weather, you need to keep your strength up."

"Nothing wrong with my strength," I said with a wry smile. "It's my waistline I'm worried about." I pulled on my hat and gloves and grabbed my purse from behind the counter. "Do you need me to pick up anything for you?"

"When you're at the library, you could collect the books I reserved. Just ask Philomena."

"Okay. If you think of anything else, give me a call." I waved goodbye and stepped outside into the bitter cold.

Between working at the café and the drama over Sandra's death, this was my first opportunity to stroll through the town of Smuggler's Cove. The town ran in a semicircle around the cove that gave it its name. The main street, formally known as Greer Street after a former mayor but referred to by everyone as Main Street, ran all the way through the center of the town, following the semicircle pattern from the crossroads by the elementary school right on down to the harbor. Whisper Island had two harbors: Carraig, the harbor I'd sailed into on the ferry the night I'd arrived, and the one in Smuggler's Cove. Smuggler's Cove Harbor catered to yachts and holidaymakers. During the tourist season, the ferry stopped at both harbors, but in low season, it only went to the one nearest the mainland.

I checked my watch. Eight o'clock. Was it too early to catch Sean Clough? If I wanted to get everything done before I was due back at the café, I'd have to try. I followed the directions Philomena had given me and found Lynott Lane with no difficulty. The *Gazette*'s building was the second on the right-hand side and stood next to Nesbitt & Son Solicitors.

I pressed the bell and waited. No response. When I was about to press a second time, an elegantly dressed dark-haired woman exited the door of the legal practice. She looked me up and down. "Good morning. You work at The Movie Theater Café," she said in a matter-of-fact tone.

"That's right. I'm Noreen Doyle's niece, Maggie." I eyed her more closely. "Have we met? You look familiar."

She extended a perfectly manicured hand. "I'm Jennifer Pearce. I was at the Movie Club the night Sandra Walker died."

"Ah," I said. "I thought I'd seen you around. Nick Sweetman's girlfriend, right? The lawyer?"

"I'm a solicitor, yes." She gave a tight smile that didn't quite meet her eyes. "The sign is misleading. Old Mr. Nesbitt retired years ago. It's only me and Aaron now."

I had the impression that Jennifer would have preferred the sign to read Nesbitt & Pearce Solicitors, but hadn't gotten her way.

"I'm still in shock over what happened to Sandra," I said, dropping my voice in a confidential manner.

Jennifer's smooth forehead creased. "It was simply awful. And now Nick tells me you found codeine in her cocktail."

News traveled fast in a small town. "Yeah. Any idea who might have wanted to kill Sandra?"

Jennifer's hand fluttered to her neck, giving the

impression of a schoolgirl who'd finally won the lead role in the school play and was determined to wring every ounce of emotion out of her performance. "No, not at all," she said, eyes wide. "I'm hoping it was a horrible accident."

I treated her to my most ingratiating smile. "Is Nesbitt & Son taking care of Sandra's estate?"

Jennifer gave an elegant one-shouldered shrug. "We're the only solicitors on the island."

Which wasn't a direct answer, but was good enough.

"I suppose Sandra's children inherit everything," I mused. "Must be a decent chunk of change after she sold their land to developers."

Jennifer pursed her lips. "I can't discuss my client's private affairs."

In other words, not only was Nesbitt & Son responsible for handling Sandra's estate, but Jennifer was the solicitor in charge. Given the woman's wary expression, I decided it was time to change tack. I nodded at the *Gazette*'s offices. "I'm looking for Sean Clough, but no one is answering."

Jennifer's guarded expression softened. "Oh, Sean won't be back until tomorrow. He's covering a story on the mainland."

"Is no one else in?"

The other woman shook her head. "Apart from a few freelancers, he's a one-man show." She preened a little. "I write a monthly legal advice column."

"If you and Mr. Nesbitt are the only solicitors on the island, you must be kept busy."

"Let's just say business is brisk. Speaking of which —" she consulted her watch, "—I'd best be going. Have a good day, Maggie."

"Bye, Jennifer."

After the solicitor had left, I stared glumly at the locked door of the *Gazette*. Sergeant O'Shea must have spoken to Sean already. Maybe I could cajole him into leaking information. My mind made up, I squared my shoulders and marched back to the main street.

I didn't have to go as far as the police station before I bumped into the sergeant—literally. He was coming out of the Movie Theater Café, clutching a takeout coffee in one paw and a muffin in the other. He leaped back when he saw me, spilling hot coffee over his hand in the process.

"Ouch," I said cheerfully. "That had to hurt."

"*You.*" His mustaches did a dance of indignation.

I waited calmly for him to continue. I didn't need to wait long.

"What's all this about you poking around asking questions?" His nostrils flared. "You have no right to interrogate people."

I schooled my features into an expression of innocence. "Who, me? I can't help it if I overhear gossip in the café."

His jowls wobbled. "I don't appreciate busybodies interfering in my investigation."

"Sandra's death is big news. People talk. And the recurring topic is the gossip column Sandra is alleged to have written. A column that apparently included a blind item about you." I paused to let him digest this information. "Do you happen to know if Sandra really did write that column?"

"I do know, but I'm certainly not telling you." Sergeant O'Shea got up in my face, jabbing a chubby finger against my chest in an aggressive fashion. "I'm warning you, Ms. Doyle. Mind your own business. And don't you dare spread rumors about me."

I gave him my most serene smile. "If you don't stop poking my boobs, the next person you'll be arresting is me. Only you won't be in any position to handcuff me once I've finished with you." I hadn't decked anyone since I'd let my ex have it, and I hadn't been in the habit of hitting people before that. I was willing to make an exception for O'Shea if he didn't keep his paws to himself.

He leaped back as though I'd struck him. His fleshy lips compressed. "Are you threatening me?"

"Merely letting you know that I don't like men poking at my chest without an invitation. Stay out of my cleavage, and I'll consider staying out of your case." I winked at him and added in my best customer service voice, "You have a nice day now, Sergeant."

14

I left Sergeant O'Shca incandescent with rage and sauntered down the street to my next desti-nation. When I stepped inside McConnell's Pharmacy, Mack was behind the counter, selling an elderly lady what seemed like a crazy amount of Metamucil.

"Whoa," I said after she'd left. "Is she a Meta-mucil pusher?"

Mack gave me one of his easy smiles and ignored my dig at his customer. "Hey, Maggie. What can I do for you today? Any more tests on suspicious substances?"

"Not this time, but I do need your pharmaceutical expertise." I drew the sandwich bag containing the medicine bottle I'd found in the movie theater out of my jacket pocket and held it up to the light.

"I'm intrigued. What have you got there?"

"That's what I'm hoping you can tell me." I

handed the bag to him. "Never mind where I found it. I'd like to know what those pills are. They look like Ambien to me."

Mack donned a pair of disposable rubber gloves like a pro and unscrewed the cap. He examined a pill on his gloved palm. "Yeah, that's Stilnoct all right. It's sold as Ambien in the U.S." He fingered the ripped label. "Did you do this?"

I shook my head. "I don't know who the prescription is for, or who dropped this bottle where I found it. Do you fill many Stilnoct prescriptions in your pharmacy?"

"A few. Like all sleepers, they're highly addictive. The doctors at Whisper Island Medical Centre err on the conservative side and are cautious about prescribing Stilnoct."

"Can you tell from the leftover label if you might have filled the prescription at your pharmacy?"

"Highly unlikely." Mack opened the door to a back room and ushered me inside. He unlocked a medicine cupboard and took out a package of pills. "This is what a prescribed packet of Stilnoct looks like. The bottle you're holding might have come from a hospital dispensary, or it was obtained from a black market source."

"That's the second time you've mentioned black market prescription drugs. How common is it in Ireland?"

Mack's lips twisted into a grimace. "In the days of the internet, all too common. Black market prescription drugs are easier to come by than some of the harder stuff, and people fool themselves into thinking they'll be fine because they're taking real medicine."

"What drugs are popular on the black market?"

"Opioids like codeine, oxycodone, morphine and their friends. All kinds of sleepers and chill pills. Steroids. Viagra. Anything that'll make a person high." Mack sighed. "There's no limit to the human race's zest for self-destruction."

"I'm going to ask you a question, and I'll respect your decision not to answer it."

Mack grinned. "Sounds ominous."

"I heard a rumor that Lenny deals in prescription drugs. Is this true?"

Mack's expression darkened. "That old story again? Back when we were in school, people used to say Lenny dealt in street drugs. Absolute rubbish, then and now."

"I remember Lenny not being averse to the odd joint," I reminded him.

"But that's as far as it ever went with him. And he was never a dealer."

"Okay. I had to ask."

He inclined his head in what might have been a nod if he wasn't still irritated by my question. "Fair enough, Maggie. I know you're trying to look out for your aunt."

"But not at Lenny's expense. He's a good guy and he's been a friend to me since I arrived on the island. I hated hearing that rumor, and I'm grateful you've given me your take on the situation."

"My take is pretty succinct—there is no situation. Lenny's no saint, but has neither the inclination nor the street smarts to deal in black market product."

I eyed Mack thoughtfully. Lenny might not have the street smarts, but I'd bet good money Mack had them. And he had the expert knowledge, not to mention access to prescription drugs.

My stomach gnawed painfully. I'd defaulted into suspect-everyone mode. This had been fine back in San Francisco, where I'd never been obliged to investigate a crime that involved anyone I knew. There was no reason to suspect Mack or Lenny of dealing prescription drugs.

The pharmacist put the pill container back in the sandwich bag and handed it to me.

I slipped it into my jacket pocket. "Thanks for your help, Mack. I'll see you around."

"See you. And Maggie?"

I paused in the doorway and looked over my shoulder. Mack's expression was inscrutable.

"Be careful, okay? Word on the street is that Sergeant O'Shea isn't the only person unhappy about you asking questions."

I forced a smile, unnerved by his bland expression. "Sure. I can look after myself."

After leaving McConnell's Pharmacy, I walked down to Smuggler's Cove Harbor. Past the promenade, the library was located at the back of a small park. In summer, the park would be resplendent with flowers of all colors. In January, it appeared as bleak as the gray sky. To undo some of the damage caused by my third portion of scrambled eggs, I took the steps up to the library's entrance two at a time.

When I stepped inside, Philomena was behind the desk, her trademark horn-rimmed glasses perched on her head. She glanced up at the sound of my footsteps across the creaky wooden floor. "Hello, Maggie. Are you here to collect Noreen's books?"

"Yes, but it's not my main reason for stopping by. I decided to take you up on your offer to search back issues of the *Whisper Island Gazette* for blind gossip items. I called by the *Gazette* in the hope they'd have digital copies, but Sean Clough's away."

My aunt's eyes twinkled. "We're behind on the digitalization of our catalog, but we're not total dinosaurs. The library has digital copies of the *Gazette* going back five years. Prior to that, we only have paper editions, but you won't want to look that far back. Sandra only worked at the *Gazette* the last two years."

Philomena led me over to a table with a stack of books on each side and a computer in the center. After I'd divested myself of my jacket and other outdoor gear, I slung my bag on the floor and got to work. The digital back issues of the *Whisper Island Gazette* were stored in a folder on the library computer. There was no way to search through all the issues at once, but given that the *Gazette* was a weekly paper, and the blind gossip column appeared once a month, I only had to read through twenty-two issues to be up to date.

The gossip column was cringeworthy bad. I didn't know the residents of Whisper Island well enough to identify most of the blinds, but the heavy-handed approach of their author made me suspect that any islander with two brain cells could figure out who the item was directed at. For the next couple of hours, I noted dates and blind item topics, only pausing to drink the coffee Philomena brought me from her office.

"Only because the library is empty," she said with a wink. "I trust you not to spill. You're not clumsy."

I gave her a weak smile. Either word of my disastrous career in the café hadn't reached her, or she was choosing to ignore it. "Thanks. Hey, Philomena?"

"Hmm?" She stopped mid-stride and looked over her shoulder at me. "Have you found something interesting?"

I squinted at my notes. "I'm not sure. It's more a sense of what's not there than what is. I mean, sure, I can imagine some of the islanders were upset or embarrassed to be featured in the column. On the other hand, I don't see anything that would point to a motive for murder." I pointed to an item on my list. "Do you know who she's referring to as 'an influential man with a penchant for drink'?"

"'Influential' covers a lot of ground," Philomena said. "It could refer to any number of men."

"A doctor, a lawyer, or a politician?" I scrunched up my nose. "I don't know any of these people well enough to guess."

"Any other items you want my opinion on?"

I consulted my notes. "There's one about a baby, but it's vague. It implies that it's not its father's biological child."

My aunt smiled. "That could apply to any number of families. I'm sorry I can't be more helpful, love."

I perused my notes. "There are a couple of items about infidelity, one about a farmer and his sheep that I suspect is the Paddy Driscoll blind, and an ugly item concerning a widow having an affair with her stepson."

"The Paddy Driscoll rumor is absurd. The widow is either Joan Sweetman or Patty Davis, but I don't believe it of either of them. As for the affairs—" she shrugged, "—there are a number of contenders, unfortunately."

I chose my next words with care. "Another blind refers to someone who works with books who was having an affair."

My aunt's face stiffened and an angry flush stained her cheeks. "Absolute nonsense," she snapped, forgetting the library's rule to keep our voices down. "Yes, I know people thought it referred to me. I'd never cheat on John."

"It mentioned you sneaking around at night. What could that mean?"

The color drained from my aunt's face. "I...have no idea." She gave a weak laugh. "Why would I go out at night this time of year?"

Her denial was too hasty to be credible, but I didn't push her. If I did, she'd crawl deeper into her cave, and I'd never get the truth. Even if she wasn't cheating on her husband, she must be up to something late at night. But what?

I sighed. "Looks like I'm no closer to figuring out who killed Sandra than I was two hours ago. Anyone mentioned in the gossip column had a potential motive, depending on how upset they were over it."

"We don't know that any of the items in that column are true," Philomena said with force. "They might be all made up to sell papers."

"True. And we haven't confirmed Sandra was the pen behind the column."

My aunt pursed her lips. "We all assumed she was, and Sandra basked in the attention."

"But she never told you that she wrote it?"

"No." My aunt's expression hardened. "Very coy, she was. She loved the idea of people worrying that she'd write about them next."

I examined my aunt's face closely. "Did Sandra ever write anything about your family? Apart from the blind that appeared to refer to you?"

Philomena's neck snapped back. "No." The word was uttered too quickly to be convincing.

I sifted through the various blind items in my mind. Apart from the librarian blind item, I could think of none that could fit my aunt, her husband, or my cousin, Julie. But after so many years away, how well did I know them? In truth, how well had I ever known them? I was the American niece who came to stay summers. Of course I'd been made a fuss of. I'd seen both my relatives and the island in their summer months. If they had a dark side, I wouldn't know. Was the closeness I felt for them based on shared DNA and nostalgia?

"Are you sure you don't know more than you're saying?" I asked gently. "About the blind items referring to other people and the one about the librarian? If it's nothing relevant to the case, I promise I won't breathe a word about it outside this room."

My aunt fiddled with her rings and tugged at the cardigan that was at least two sizes too small for her round frame. "I... No. If there were anything important, I'd tell you, Maggie."

She was lying, but if I pressed her, she'd shut me out. The smart move was to give her time to think it over and hope she'd confide in me soon.

THE AFTERNOON TRADE at the café was slow as molasses. Apart from the Spinsters and the Two Gerries, no one came near the place. For a Friday afternoon, this wasn't the norm.

Noreen was visibly distressed. "Fridays are usually my best weekdays. How can the people in this town think I had anything to do with Sandra Walker's death? I couldn't stand the woman, but I wouldn't have killed her."

"Anyone who's your friend knows that."

My aunt rubbed at her eyes. "I haven't been able to sleep since it happened. Miss Flynn offered me one of her sleeping pills, and I was sorely tempted to take it. Usually, I won't touch the things."

My ears pricked up at the mention of sleeping pills. "Which ones is she on?"

"Something called Stilnoct. At any rate, I didn't want them."

So one of the Spinsters had a prescription for the same pills that I'd found wedged between Julie and Lenny's seats. Interesting. But not conclusive. As far as I knew, the sleeping pills had had nothing to do with Sandra's death and could have been in the cinema for months.

My aunt tugged at the cross she wore around her neck. "Have you heard about Sandra's body? It's been released to her family for burial. After all the drama, they're keeping the funeral to family only."

"Any news on the preliminary toxicology report?"

"Not that I've heard." She gave me a wan smile. "I feel bad worrying about my lack of customers when Sandra's moving into the graveyard. She was an awful old biddy, but she didn't deserve to die."

"Why don't we watch a movie this evening and get

an early night?" I asked. "Something silly. Maybe a romantic comedy."

"I'd like that, but I'd like my customers to come back even more."

"They'll be back once we know what happened to Sandra." I squeezed her arm. "Why don't you sit down and let me horrify you with my terrible tea-making skills?"

This remark elicited a small smile. "All right. Let's see what you can do to a cup of Earl Grey."

I performed a mock salute. "Coming right up."

"Oh, before I forget. Joan Sweetman asked me if we could drop over a smoothie and a sandwich to her before two o'clock. She's stuck in the gallery all day on her own and can't get away."

"No problem. I'll go over once I've made your tea."

Fifteen minutes later, I knocked on the door of Joan's gallery and stepped inside. The gallery special-ized in modern art and sculptures. I shuddered at a painting of boats sailing into what looked like a woman's private parts. I peered at the label. *Smuggler's Cove Harbor — Maria Reilly*. The doctor's wife had weird taste.

"Hideous, isn't it?" said a voice behind me. "But the tourists love Maria's work." Joan took the sand-wich and smoothie from my hands. "Thanks for deliv-ering, Maggie. My assistant is down with the flu and I couldn't get away."

"No problem." I hesitated a moment and then

said, "I suppose you've heard about Sandra's body being released for burial?"

"Yes." Joan shuddered. "Awful business. Many people loathed the woman, but I can't imagine who'd want to kill her."

"We're still waiting on the toxicology results," I cautioned. "We don't know if it was murder yet. And even if codeine is found in her body, we can't rule out the possibility that she took it herself."

"Suicide? Oh, no. Not Sandra."

"So everyone says. Did you know Sandra well?"

"As well as I wished to. I couldn't stand her." Joan met my gaze. "I've heard you're looking into what happened."

"Not officially, but with Noreen's café being involved, I feel obliged to make sure Sergeant O'Shea is doing his job."

Joan laughed. "He never does his job. He's far more concerned with golf, food, and—if rumors are correct—his mistress. Mark my words, if anything is found in Sandra's blood, the district superintendent will send reinforcements."

"Did you read the blind gossip column Sandra is alleged to have written?"

Joan's slim shoulders stiffened. "No. That rubbish wasn't fit to be published. Sean Clough should have had more sense, but he saw an opportunity to make money."

"Did you ever guess the identity of any of the

people mentioned in the blind items?" I asked carefully. "I mean, most seemed fairly harmless."

"Not all were harmless." Joan's voice cracked.

"I'm so sorry," I said gently. "Were you mentioned in one of them?"

Joan took a halting breath. "Yes. Total nonsense, but it caused me a lot of embarrassment."

I thought back on the list of blind items I'd read in the library. "There were a couple about widows..."

Joan touched her wedding band and twisted it. "About a year ago, the paper published a blind item that implied an island widow was having an affair with her stepson. As I have two stepsons and ticked the other checkboxes in the item, a rumor spread that the blind item was about me."

"How awful."

She smoothed the front of her pencil skirt and took a shuddery breath. "What hurt the most was seeing people I'd known for years sniggering behind my back. I don't even think they believed the blind item was true, but it was a salacious piece of gossip to amuse themselves with."

"People can be cruel," I said.

"Indeed." She pulled her shoulders back and was once again in cool and collected businesswoman mode. "Hurtful though it was, I wouldn't kill someone over a rumor. I don't know who killed Sandra, but I can't help thinking she pushed someone too far."

Joan might well be correct in her assessment, but her revelation brought me no closer to figuring out who that person was. "Thanks for sharing your story with me."

The older woman nodded. "No problem. I like Noreen, and I'm sorry she and her café are involved in this nasty business."

"Enjoy your lunch. I'd better get back to my aunt."

After I'd said goodbye to Joan, I walked back across the street to The Movie Theater Café. I'd barely had time to take off my jacket when Sergeant O'Shea barged into the café, wearing a triumphant smirk on his plump face. My heart sank. A big fish who had his small pond threatened could be vicious.

"You were right, Ms. Doyle," he said, his voice dripping smugness. "The preliminary toxicology report indicates that Sandra Walker died of a massive codeine overdose."

The words brought no comfort to me. I swore fluently.

The sergeant raised his bushy eyebrows. "Such language."

I crossed my arms over my chest and glared at him. "I guess this isn't a friendly visit to pass on the news."

"What makes you say that?"

"You have my phone number. I figure even you can figure out how to punch in a few numbers."

The smug smile vanished, replaced by the purple hue I'd grown accustomed to seeing on Sergeant O'Shea's face. His nostrils quivered, drawing my

15

Cold dread seeped through my body. "You can't be serious."

"Oh, I'm perfectly serious." Sergeant O'Shea dangled handcuffs in front of my aunt. "Now be sensible, Noreen, and let me put these on."

My aunt stared at him with a look of defiance and held out her wrists. "Go right ahead, but you're making a mistake. For heaven's sake, Colm. We've known each other for fifteen years. Do you believe I'm stupid enough to commit murder in my own café and using my prescription medicine?"

A momentary doubt flickered across the sergeant's fleshy features, but he soon had it under control. "You had the means, the opportunity, and a motive. That's good enough for me."

"Everyone at the meeting that night had the means and the opportunity," I snapped. "And from what I've heard, a number of them had a motive.

attention to a piece of snot dangling from one side. It was hard to believe that this slug had graduated from police academy and slimed his way into a comfy position on Whisper Island.

"Once again, you're right, Ms. Doyle. This isn't a social call." The smirk slid back into place, and he turned to my aunt. "Noreen Doyle, I'm here to arrest you on suspicion of murder."

Noreen's purse was on the floor by her table. It would have been easy to remove the bottle of Solpodol and steal a few pills. Sandra could have left her glass unattended, and someone spiked it."

"Did you see Sandra put her glass down somewhere?" he demanded.

"Well, no, but I was busy making cocktails, and there were a lot of people in the café that night."

"In that case, we'll be on our way." The policeman yanked my aunt to her feet and hauled her toward the café door.

"Wait a sec," I called. "Please tell me you're following other leads."

Sergeant O'Shea pulled open the door and shoved my aunt outside. "I've left no stone unturned in my inquiries, and I'm confident I've got the culprit."

I ran to the door and met my aunt's eyes as O'Shea shoved her into the back of his squad car. "I'll call a lawyer."

She opened her mouth as if to respond, but her words were lost when Sergeant O'Shea slammed the door. With a self-satisfied smirk, the policeman slid behind the wheel and took off. In a daze, I let the café door slide shut. I'd been afraid the sergeant would do something rash, but I hadn't reckoned on him acting this quickly.

"Take a seat, dear," Miss Flynn said, catching my arm. "You've had an awful shock."

"This is an outrage," thundered Gerry One. "That man is a buffoon."

"He's a buffoon with power," I said grimly, "and he intends to use it."

"We all know Noreen wouldn't hurt a fly. He'll have to let her go the moment her lawyer shows up." Miss Flynn patted my hand, while Miss Murphy fetched a clean cup and poured me tea laced with enough sugar to float a battleship.

Miss Murphy shoved the cup in front of me. "Drink up."

"Thank you." Unthinking, I took a sip and winced when the hot liquid burned my tongue.

"That man is an even bigger fool than I'd given him credit for," Miss Murphy said. "Why would Noreen put her business at risk by killing one of her customers? It makes no sense."

"Yeah, but that's because we know her." I stirred my tea on autopilot. "Movies and mystery novels love talking about motive, but regular police work is more concerned with means and opportunity. We tend to look at the motive last, and even then, it doesn't play a huge role in convicting someone."

"Surely you're not defending that fool of a policeman?" Miss Murphy demanded.

"No, but I'm saying what Noreen's lawyer will tell her once I hire one."

"Call around to Nesbitt & Son," Miss Flynn said. "If Aaron or Jennifer are in, I'm sure one of them will go with you to the station. Noreen needs a solicitor, and there's no time to wait for a specialist from the mainland to arrive."

"Doesn't she need a barrister?" I asked in confusion. "I thought they dealt with trials. Patricia McConnell went with her when she was questioned a few days ago."

"Because Patricia happened to be on the island at the time and is a trial lawyer," Gerry Two interjected. "What Noreen needs now is a solicitor who specializes in criminal law, but of course we don't have anyone like that on Whisper Island. But Aaron and Jennifer will know what to do and can represent Noreen's interests until the other solicitor gets here."

I took another sip of my tea, blowing first this time. "Thanks for the tip and the tea. I'll call Lenny and Kelly to see if one of them can look after the café. Once that's taken care of, I'll go straight over to Nesbitt & Son and get moving on finding Noreen a lawyer."

KELLY RESPONDED to my plea for help and agreed to run the café until closing time. Despite her aloof demeanor, Jennifer Pearce also came to my rescue, and she and I were soon sitting in the police station with my aunt. On the basis that it hadn't yet been established with one hundred percent certainty that Sandra had died of a codeine overdose, Jennifer persuaded O'Shea to allow me a visit alone with my aunt. I was pretty sure this was against regulations, but O'Shea was a haphazard cop at the best of times, and being confronted with a slick solicitor with killer cleavage put him at a disadvantage. I resisted the urge to stick my tongue out at him when I passed.

Noreen appeared to have shrunk in the two hours since I'd last seen her. Her shoulders were slumped in defeat, and her usually rosy cheeks held no hint of color. "Thanks for organizing Jennifer, love," she said when I sat down. "I don't know how much good she can do, but I appreciate the effort."

"She's doing an excellent job at managing O'Shea. He doesn't know where to look. And she's called a friend in Cork who specializes in criminal law. She's due to arrive later today."

My aunt's pale blue eyes filled with tears. "I never thought it would come to this. O'Shea's an eejit, but I felt sure he'd get the person who killed Sandra."

"I'm going to keep digging, Noreen. Don't give up hope."

My aunt gave me a wobbly smile. "There's something you don't know, love. It's the reason O'Shea latched onto me as the culprit."

My head snapped to attention. "What?"

My aunt nodded. "Sandra was the pen behind the gossip column. She came to me several months ago and informed me she'd found out I'd told a few white lies on my mortgage application when I wanted to buy and renovate the movie theater."

I sucked in a breath. "Is this true?"

My aunt blushed. "Yes. I'm not proud of what I did, but I knew I'd never get the loan or the planning permission if I revealed I'd already had to borrow money from your father to keep myself afloat. I convinced them that that money was earnings from my petting zoo, and I...well—" she coughed, "— might have forged a few papers."

My heart sank. This was much worse than I'd thought. It pained me to think it, but if I were in Sergeant O'Shea's position, Noreen would have moved into the position of Suspect Number One the moment I'd learned of the forgery and deceit. "How did Sandra find out about it?"

My aunt's hands curled into fists. "She brought her grandchildren to the petting zoo one day and asked me to show them around. In the meantime, she used the opportunity to have a root through my private papers, and put two and two together."

"Wow. She was that brazen?"

"Oh, yeah." Noreen's lips twisted. "She might have wondered how I convinced the bank to give me a loan, but I doubt she suspected what I'd done. She was nosy. Poking through people's stuff was what she did."

"Did Sandra threaten to write a blind item about your...deception?"

My aunt looked at me directly. "About my fraud, you mean? Yes, she did."

"But none appeared in the paper."

Noreen dropped her gaze to her fingernails. "That's correct."

I sighed. "Was Sandra Walker blackmailing you?"

"Yes." The word came out in a whisper. My aunt blinked back tears. "So you see, Maggie, it's hopeless. I'll never convince the guards I didn't do it."

I leaned back in my chair and blew out a breath. This was much worse than I'd thought. "So that's why you've been having money problems and taking on extra jobs."

"Yes. It's true that business is slower at the café during the winter, but I knew that when I opened the place, and I budgeted accordingly." A hint of bitterness entered her tone. "What I didn't budget for was blackmail. Sandra was bleeding me dry. It had gotten to the point that I was considering turning myself in and throwing myself on the bank's mercy not to press charges."

If she'd done so, she'd have risked losing the café. I squeezed my eyes shut for a moment and exhaled a sigh. "Noreen, I'm going to ask you this once, because I have to, especially given what you've just told me. Did you kill Sandra Walker?"

My aunt looked me straight in the eye. "No, I didn't."

I let out the breath I hadn't realized I was holding. "Okay. The picture is bleak, yes, but all it means is that I'm right to keep digging. We both know O'Shea won't bother."

A knock on the door made me jerk around. The reserve policeman who'd shown me in stood in the doorway. "I'll have to ask you to leave, Ms. Doyle."

"Give me two more minutes, and I'm out of here.

I need to ask my aunt some details for her solicitor." A blatant lie, but whatever worked. I batted my eyelashes, and the young man turned fiery red.

"Uh, okay." His gaze darted down the hallway. "Sergeant O'Shea will be in here any second. You'd better make it fast."

After he'd closed the door behind him, I spoke quickly. "The night of the murder, can you remember who sat near you when you were out in the café? I'm pretty sure that's when the codeine ended up in Sandra's cocktail. If someone had spiked it in the movie theater, there wouldn't have been enough time to kill her before the end of the movie."

My aunt frowned. "I've wracked my brain trying to remember all the details. I sat at Bette Davis with Sister Pauline, Philomena, and John. Brid Kelly sat with us for a while, but left to chat with Paul and Melanie after they'd arrived. I had my handbag with me the whole time."

"Did you go to the restroom at any point?"

"I can't remember. No, wait…yes, I did. I went with Philomena just before the film began."

"Did you bring your purse with you?"

She screwed up her brow. "I'm sorry, Maggie. I can't remember. I was groggy from the medication. I probably didn't bring the bag with me. Among friends, I don't think twice about leaving it at the table."

"In other words, anyone could have accessed your bag while you were gone." I frowned. "But 'just before the film began' is late in the time frame. It's more likely that Sandra's first cocktail was spiked, not her second."

A second knock sounded on the door. "The boss is on his way," the young reserve said. "Time to make tracks."

We got to our feet. I hugged my aunt, taking comfort in her familiar talcum powdery smell. "I'll get to the bottom of this, Noreen. Just hang tight."

Her smile was wobbly. "Thanks, Maggie. I'm so glad you're here."

16

After visiting my aunt, I got into the car and drove toward her cottage. I needed to track down her farmer pal, Paddy Driscoll, and ask if he'd help me look after her animals, and I was due to meet Julie for an evening run.

The views on the drive from Smuggler's Cove to my aunt's house were spectacular, but I barely noticed them today, and not merely because it was already dark. My mind mulled over what Noreen had told me. An uncomfortable weight pressed down on my shoulders. I loved my aunt, and I wanted to believe her. In my gut, I did believe she hadn't killed Sandra, but I'd been a cop too long not to have a lingering doubt. I'd seen many investigations go south because a cop was blinded by prejudice and determined to be for or against a particular suspect. If I wanted to do right by my aunt, and by the dead woman, I had to force myself to remain impartial and weigh all the evidence, however unpleasant.

The other aspect to our conversation that troubled me was the blackmail revelation. If Sandra had black-mailed Noreen, it stood to reason she had other victims. Had she pushed one of them too far until he or she had snapped?

I'd left the town by now and cruised along the winding coast road. Preoccupied with my thoughts, I saw the motorcyclist zooming toward me a second too late. I slammed on my brakes and swerved the car into the ditch. *Oh, heck.* The ditch was deep. I'd never get the car out on my own. I climbed out of the car to confront the cause of my current predicament. "Are you insane?" I yelled. "You were driving straight at me."

The motorcyclist removed his helmet, and the beam of the car lights revealed close-cropped dark blond hair and a face that would have been movie star handsome but for a nose that had been broken more than once. Despite the crazy situation, a jolt of desire fixed me to the spot.

"I was driving straight at you, all right," he said with a grin I wanted to slap off his disturbingly hand-some face. "On the left side of the road."

"Exactly. What sort of lunatic— *Oh…*" I trailed off and heat burned my cheeks.

"You were driving on the right-hand side," he said lightly. "You're not in America now."

I couldn't help but laugh. "My accent's that obvious?"

His grin spread wider, bringing a twinkle to his deep blue eyes. "Oh, yeah."

I shoved my hands in my pockets. "I'm sorry for yelling at you. And for nearly killing you," I added as an afterthought.

My companion's lips twitched. "Apology accepted." He examined the position of my car. "You're going to need help getting out of that ditch. Between the two of us, we should manage it."

"You have more faith than I do," I said glumly. "She's in pretty deep."

"Do you have cables in the boot?"

"In the what?" I met his laughing gaze and felt my cheeks grow warm again. "Oh, right. You mean the trunk. I hope so. It's not my car. I don't know where my aunt keeps stuff."

He climbed off his bike, making me instantly aware of his broad shoulders and height. I wasn't used to men who towered over me. My handsome stranger helped me open the back and soon located the cables among the debris.

I regarded his bike. It was solid, but I wasn't convinced it was up to the job. "You sure you want to try to pull a car out of a ditch with a motorbike?"

"This car is pretty light. It should work, at least to get it high enough to drive out."

"What you mean is, 'this car is a piece of excrement and is likely to fall apart at any second.'"

That wicked twinkle again. "Your words, not mine. Far be it from me to criticize a vehicle that passed the NCT. It did pass, right? Despite the rust?"

"Whatever the NCT is, the car must have passed. When I arrived, my aunt was able to put me on her car insurance."

"It's the National Car Test. We do our best to keep rust buckets off the road in Ireland." His mouth curved into a grin. "And we try to persuade drivers to obey the rules of the road."

"When you're finished insulting my driving skills and my car, let's get it out of the ditch." I regarded the motorbike dubiously. "It's a Harley, right?"

He beamed. "Correct."

"If you want to risk breaking it, it's on you."

His laughter followed me into the car.

A few minutes and several attempts later, Noreen's car was high enough that I could maneuver it out of the ditch without assistance from the motorbike. I rolled down my window. "Thanks," I said sheepishly. "And sorry again for nearly causing an accident."

"No worries. Just make sure you stay on the left side from now on."

"Okay." I eyed him more closely. "I don't think I've seen you around."

"That's because I don't live here," he said cheerfully. "I just drove off the ferry."

"Ah, that explains it." I looked at the bike and his small travel bag slung over the back. "You over for a holiday?"

"Not exactly," he replied, clearly amused by my curiosity. "Just a day trip—for now."

"Maybe I'll see you around." I cursed the hopeful note I heard in my voice. What was wrong with me? Hadn't I sworn off men for the next while, especially ones I was attracted to? I needed to break my habit of picking bad men.

My handsome stranger grinned and straddled his bike, giving me all sorts of dirty thoughts. "Have a good evening and drive carefully, or you'll have the local cops on your tail."

I snorted. "That would involve some actual work and brainpower."

He raised an eyebrow. "Not a fan of the local constabulary?"

"Let's just say the local police sergeant and I aren't on the best of terms," I said dryly. "Anyway—" I gave him a mock salute, "—enjoy your stay on the island."

My biker pal drove off in the direction of Smuggler's Cove, and I continued my journey to Noreen's cottage with a sigh. The handsome stranger was the first man who'd interested me in a long time. I'd started to think I'd gone off the opposite sex. Pity the timing and circumstances of our meeting were lousy. I shifted gears and turned my attention back to the murder investigation. I was due to meet Julie later for a run. Given that time was now of the essence, I intended to rope her and Lenny into helping me sift through the suspects and question them. Sergeant O'Shea wouldn't like it, but if it were left up to him,

Noreen would be tried and convicted, and no other potential suspect investigated. I wouldn't let that happen.

WHEN I GOT BACK to the cottage, I tried calling Paddy Driscoll but got no reply. For once, the cats were delighted to see me, and rubbed against my legs meowing in an orgy of delight when I removed several cans of cat food from the pantry. I did a quick head count and frowned. "Poly?" I called. "Where are you?" The last thing I needed right now was a missing pregnant cat. A dreadful thought struck me, and my stomach lurched. *Please don't let her be having her kittens.* What happened during a cat birth, anyway? Would I need to call a vet?

After I'd made sure the livestock was fed and watered, I changed into my running gear and went outside to look for Poly. Bran joined me, panting. I bent down to pet him. "You ate your meal in record time. Want to help me find Poly?"

He barked as if to say yes and performed an ecstatic dance around my legs.

"Hmm," I said, eyeing him warily. "This isn't a cat-hunt, you know. We want to check that Poly's okay. No funny business. Got it?"

Bran gave me a generous lick and took off in the direction of the barn. Maybe he knew something that I didn't. After all, he was the lone dog in a house full of cats. Perhaps some secret feline knowledge had rubbed off on him. Bran and I searched the barn and other outhouses, but there was no sign of Poly, and neither the goats nor the alpaca shed any light on her whereabouts. I pulled my running jacket tight around my chest in a futile effort to protect myself from the sharp sea wind. The cats all made sure to be inside before dark, and Poly was usually the first. Could she have been hit by a car? I hadn't seen any cats on the ride home, but my night vision wasn't the best.

After a last look around the barn, I gave up the search and headed for the front of the house. Bran raced ahead of me, panting, and waited impatiently at the gate. "Are you ready to go for a run?" I asked when I caught up with him.

Bran whined and pawed the gate.

I clipped his leash to his collar and looked down the road to see if there was any sign of Julie. She pulled up a few minutes later.

"I heard about Noreen," she said the moment she got out of her car. "Mum is terribly worried. That's why I'm late."

"No problem. I had to look for one of Noreen's cats. I didn't find her, unfortunately."

"Is it the pregnant one?" my cousin asked.

"Yeah." I blew out my cheeks. "I don't want to cause Noreen any more stress by telling her Poly is missing."

"She'll turn up," Julie said with more confidence than I felt. "She's probably made herself a cozy nest to have her kittens. Now back to Noreen—what's the story? Does she have a lawyer yet?"

"Jennifer Pearce is representing her until a criminal lawyer can get here."

My cousin shook her head. "How can O'Shea think Noreen had anything to do with Sandra's death? It's crazy. Why would she want to kill Sandra? Someone must have stolen her medicine and put it in Sandra's drink."

I shifted position, uncomfortably aware that I couldn't confide in my cousin without breaking my aunt's confidence. "At the moment, all O'Shea has to go on is circumstantial evidence. There's no proof that Noreen tampered with Sandra's cocktail."

"Then how can he go and arrest her? It's outrageous."

"I think he jumped the gun on the arrest, but the more time he has to gather evidence, circumstantial or concrete, the worse it'll be for Noreen. A clever prosecutor can use a mass of circumstantial evidence to convince a jury."

Julie shivered and hugged herself. "It's horrible. I've known Noreen all my life. A less violent person, you can't meet."

"We're all capable of murder, Julie," I said as we started down the path we used for our runs.

"I'm not," she said hotly, "and neither is Noreen."

"We're not all capable of the same sort of murder," I continued, "but every one of us has the capacity to kill, given the right-for-us circumstances. I can't tell if Sandra's murder was carefully planned or a spur-of-the-moment crime."

"To get the medicine into the cocktail without any of us noticing took planning," Julie said.

"But did it? Let's hash this out for a sec. How many people knew Noreen was having her wisdom teeth taken out that Friday?"

My cousin flashed me a wry smile. "Most of the island. News travels fast here, Maggie. Everyone was interested in your arrival to help out at the café."

"But who could have known for sure that Noreen would attend the Movie Club meeting that night? She might have decided to go home and get an early night."

"True. That was pure luck."

"As was her having her Solpodol medication in her bag," I continued. "She only needed to take it every four hours. She might have left it at home before coming to the café. And who knew she'd be prescribed Solpodol after her operation? A doctor, dentist, or nurse could have guessed she'd be given a painkiller of that nature."

"Anyone who'd had their wisdom teeth out with a general anesthetic must have been prescribed something similar." Julie's words came out haltingly. We'd started our first running interval, and in my preoccupation, I'd started us off at a faster pace than my cousin was used to. I forced my legs to slow down.

"My point is that the murderer either decided to kill Sandra on the spur of the moment and used what was available to them, or Sandra's death was carefully planned, and the murderer used the chance avail-ability of the Solpodol to throw suspicion onto Noreen."

"Okay, I'm confused," Julie said when we slowed to a walk. "Clearly I need to read more crime fiction. How can the murder have been carefully planned if the murderer couldn't have known Noreen would have Solpodol in her handbag?"

"Let's say the murderer planned to kill Sandra on the night of the Movie Club. Think of the scenario: a crowd of people, many of whom disliked Sandra, all drinking cocktails next to one another. Then that same group of people go into a movie theater together and sit in the dark for a couple of hours, giving Sandra plenty of time to die from whatever poison her drink had been spiked with."

"So you're saying the murderer might have intended to use a different poison?"

I nodded. "Exactly. He or she could have brought it with them, secure in the knowledge that Sandra could be relied on to drink one colorful cocktail."

"And when the murderer saw Noreen's medicine, they decided to use that instead? But why?"

"To cause confusion and throw blame away from themselves." I pointed to the stone wall up ahead. "Want to rest for a while?"

"Sounds good."

We leaned against the wall and drank from our

water bottles. "From the moment the codeine entered the story, Sergeant O'Shea assumed that the murderer was among the people closest to the Solpodol. In other words, you, me, Lenny, Noreen, Sister Pauline, and your parents. But if the murderer opted to use Solpodol instead of whatever substance they'd intended to kill Sandra with, they might have done so deliberately to cast suspicion over us and away from them."

"Meaning if we accept the premeditation theory, the murderer is more likely to be anyone *but* us."

"Right." I sighed. "Unfortunately, we can't rule out the murder being an act of momentary madness when the opportunity presented itself, so it doesn't bring us any closer to the truth."

"But it does mean Sergeant O'Shea is wrong to cling to just one group of people as potential suspects," Julie said. "That's something for Noreen's lawyer to work with. I know you won't like me saying this, but you need to leave this to the professionals, Maggie."

"If by 'the professionals' you mean Sergeant O'Shea, no way."

"I was referring to the lawyer who's arriving from Cork. I don't want you arrested for interfering with a police investigation."

"In case you've forgotten, I was a cop until a few weeks ago," I said dryly. "I might not have a legal right to investigate a case in Ireland, but I feel a moral obligation, especially when the guy in charge is more concerned with his next meal than in actual investigative work."

Julie smothered a laugh. "All the same, you're going to get into trouble if you keep butting into his case."

"Well, what do you suggest? Do you seriously want to leave Noreen to the mercy of that fool? He's not even pretending to look at anyone else for the crime, and a lawyer from Cork won't have a handle on the locals. Heck, *I* don't have a handle on them, which is why I'm relying on you and Lenny to help me."

"I'm not sure what we can do other than tell you a bit about each person," Julie said. "Frankly, I don't like the idea of interrogating someone who might be a murderer. It gives me the creeps. And speaking of people who give me the creeps, didn't you say you wanted to track down Paddy Driscoll?"

"Yeah. He's not answering his phone."

"He might now. He just pulled up in front of his house." Julie inclined her head to the left, where Paddy's land butted up against the holiday rental cottages he despised. "Do you want to see if he'll talk to you?"

"No, but I kind of have to. Why does he give you the creeps?"

"He's always grumpy and unfriendly. Plus there are those rumors about him and his sheep…"

"Rumors that we suspect Sandra started. I'm inclined to give the guy a chance."

"Good luck with that," Julie said. "Ten to one he threatens to shoot you for stepping onto his property."

"I thought firearms were rare in Ireland?"

"Driscoll is a farmer. He definitely owns a shotgun. I've seen him prowling around with it."

"Great. You're making me feel so much better about approaching him," I said dryly. "Would you be offended if I abandoned you in favor of Farmer Grumpy?"

"No. Go ahead. I won't come with you, though. If you're never seen again, at least I'll be a witness to your last known movements."

"Wow, Julie. For a woman who says she doesn't read much crime fiction, you're doing a great job at scaring the pants off me."

She grinned. "Don't say I didn't warn you."

"Come on, Bran," I said. "You'll protect me from the big, bad farmer."

Bran sniffed at the ground and pawed at my leg.

"See you later, Maggie. Give me a call when you get back to the cottage—if you survive."

"Sure, I will." I waved to Julie, and Bran and I set off toward Paddy Driscoll's house. A sense of foreboding crept under my skin. I shivered and pulled my jacket tight around me. Bran and I trudged down the trail that led from the edge of the woods past the group of holiday cottages that had been built on what was once Sandra Walker's land. The cottages were nicely spaced, allowing each house its own plot of land with a garden. Shame they were all empty. I guessed demand for holiday cottages on Whisper Island was low during the winter, especially when the ferry often didn't run due to bad weather.

Fifteen minutes later, Bran and I reached Paddy Driscoll's gate. It was unlocked, and I couldn't find a buzzer. I tried his number one last time, but he didn't pick up. After a quick scan of the terrain, I lifted the latch on the gate and urged Bran through. I didn't know what the etiquette was in Ireland regarding walking through someone else's land, but Driscoll wasn't making it easy for me to contact him. He knew my aunt. Surely he wouldn't freak when he saw me on his doorstep?

Despite Julie's warnings, we met no wild dogs on our walk up to the farmhouse, and I was starting to relax and think I'd been letting the stress and the rumors get to me. And then disaster struck.

Bran let out an excited yelp and took off like a shot. The force jerked the leash out of my hand, and he raced ahead of me. I accelerated into a sprint, but I wasn't fast enough to reach Bran before he disappeared behind the farm buildings.

I swore and pounded after him. Between the run with Julie and this exercise, I was bound to burn off that second muffin I'd eaten earlier, right? I mean, there had to be some compensation for trespassing on a man's land and losing my aunt's dog.

After I'd conducted a frantic search of my surroundings, Bran's delighted bark alerted me to his location. "Aw, man," I said and stepped into a barn full of bleating sheep. Sure enough, Bran was in there, causing mayhem. "Come on, boy. I'll feed you steak when we get back if you behave yourself."

Poor choice of words. Bran, it seemed, had lamb chops on his mind.

The sheep, terrified, bucked in their stalls. In the distance, I heard barking.

"Bran," I yelled. "We've got to get out of here."

"Who are you?" a furious voice demanded.

I turned to face an extremely disgruntled man wielding a shotgun. My heart leaped in my chest. "Whoa, easy there. I mean no harm."

"Maybe you don't," he snarled, "but what's your dog doing to my sheep?"

"Right about now, he's thinking of eating them. Help me get him out of here."

Paddy Driscoll glared at me. "You're that lunatic American who's been causing all sorts of trouble."

"I wouldn't call a few burned scones 'trouble', exactly, but yeah. That's me. Now put down the gun and help me catch Bran."

"Catch him? I'll shoot him if he touches my sheep." He did, however, deign to lower the gun.

"No shooting," I said sternly. "Noreen has enough on her plate."

"I suppose she sent you around here to get me to look after that awful alpaca she has roaming her land," Paddy grumbled. "That creature is a menace."

"Noreen wants you to look after her animals, yes."

Paddy squinted at me. "She still locked up?"

I sighed. The man was clearly a fool. "If she wasn't, I wouldn't have wasted my time hunting you down. Now are you going to stand there yapping, or are you going to help me save your sheep?"

"You're very rude," he snarled.

"So are you." I stomped into a stall past a bunch of stampeding ovines. "Come here, you silly mongrel."

"Are you referring to the dog or me?" Driscoll demanded.

I shrugged. "If the name fits…"

He gave a snort of what might have been laughter, but he covered it up with a cough.

It took me a couple of attempts to grab hold of Bran's collar and drag him out of the sheep pen. He hadn't injured any sheep, thank goodness, although he'd traumatized a few.

Driscoll glared at Bran. "Get that canine off my land. If I see him again, I'll shoot, even if he is Noreen's dog. And I'll shoot you, too, if you're stupid enough to bring him here."

"Message received." I took a deep breath. "I guess you're not in the mood to talk about Sandra Walker's murder?"

"No," he snapped. "I've heard all about your meddling. Now get your behind off my land before I set Rex and Oscar on the pair of you."

At the mere mention of Paddy Driscoll's dogs' names, Bran began to whine and tug on his leash. "I take it your dogs and Bran have history?"

Driscoll's mouth quivered. "Oh, yes. You'd better get moving."

I took the hint. "Let's go, Bran."

The dog shot off down the drive, yanking me behind him. The ominous sound of Paddy Driscoll's laughter followed us all the way to the gate.

17

Over the next few days, my opportunities to question the people who'd attended the Movie Club meeting were limited to those who visited the café. Thanks to Jacqueline Sweeney, the criminal defense lawyer who'd taken on my aunt's case, Noreen was released on bail the day after her arrest. After all the stress, she came down with a bad case of the flu that was going around the island and had to stay home in bed. I suspected that part of her bedridden state was due to her not wanting to face people, and part was because of Poly's disappearance. I couldn't blame my aunt for getting sick, but Noreen's absence from the café meant that I was left in charge. Lenny arranged his working hours at the electronics store so he could help me out over lunchtime, and Kelly offered to work a couple of extra shifts. Other than that, me and my bad cooking skills were on our own.

Once the lunch crowd dwindled on the Wednesday after Noreen's arrest, I took off my apron and stretched my sore neck. "Lenny, is it okay if I go out for a sec? I've been trying to track down Sean Clough. I'm starting to think he's avoiding me."

"Kind of weird if he is," Lenny remarked. "You'd think he'd want to talk to you about Sandra and Noreen."

"He sent one of his freelancers around to cover the story. From everything I've heard about Sean, I'm surprised he doesn't want to cover this story himself."

Lenny glanced at his watch. "I need to be back at the shop by two, so if you want to talk to Sean, better make it quick."

"Thanks. I'll be back soon." I donned my winter outdoor gear and stepped outside.

The pavement was coated in a light covering of snow, and flakes were falling fast. According to the weather forecast, we were in for several inches by nightfall. I pulled my scarf around my neck and hurried down the street.

This time, I was in luck. Through the window of the *Gazette*'s offices, I saw a red-haired man sitting hunched before a computer, frowning at the screen. In his hooded sweatshirt and baggy pants, he didn't look like a typical journalist. He was also a decade younger than I'd imagined the editor of Whisper Island's only newspaper to be. He couldn't be much older than me.

The man looked up when I knocked. "Can I help you?"

"I hope so," I said with a friendly smile. "My name's Maggie Doyle. I'd like to talk to you if you have a sec."

Was it my imagination, or did Sean Clough wince when I said my name? "Ah, sure. Come on in." He scratched his neck, and his gaze darted around the room. He leaped to his feet and cleared a stack of papers from a chair. "Take a seat." When I was seated opposite him, Sean fumbled with two cracked coffee mugs. "Want a cup of coffee? I'm afraid I only have instant."

"No, thanks. I can't stay long."

Relief flooded his face. "Oh, right. What did you want to see me about?"

"As you know, my aunt stands accused of poisoning Sandra Walker."

His Adam's apple bobbed. "I heard."

"I'm helping my aunt's lawyer prepare her defense," I lied smoothly. "With her not being able to spend a lot of time on the island, she needs someone to ask a few questions on her behalf." Sean looked doubtful at my dubious claim, but I pressed on before he could express his concerns. "I understand Sandra Walker worked for you."

Sean coughed into his fist. "Uh, yeah. She was a freelancer."

"Covering social events, fundraisers, that sort of thing?"

He nodded, but his eyes darted to the side before meeting my gaze.

"As well as the gossip column?"

Sean swallowed. "I—"

"Come on," I coaxed. "It was an open secret on Whisper Island. Everyone knew it was Sandra. And now that she's dead, there's no harm in admitting it, is there?"

The man squirmed in his seat. "I guess not."

"So it *was* Sandra?"

"Yeah." He rubbed his acne-scarred jaw. "We kept it quiet, like. It added to the mystique."

"Here's the thing, Sean. My aunt didn't kill Sandra. I need to know who had a reason to want her dead, and I suspect it was someone she targeted in her blind item column."

"I never let her publish the bad stuff," he muttered. "Just harmless gossip that could apply to any number of islanders."

My heart leaped in my chest. "Sandra had other blind items that you didn't run?"

He cleared his throat. "I didn't want to get sued, you know?"

"What was in these blind items that you refused to print?" *Material Sandra had subsequently used to blackmail people?*

"There were only two I turned down, right at the start of her time writing the column. One was about a nun who stole money from the church collection box."

I winced. "Ouch."

"We have a convent here on the island, but most

of the nuns are too old to help out at Mass. It could only refer to one of two nuns: Sister Pauline McLaughlin, or Sister Juliette O'Keefe. Without proof that the item was true, I wasn't running it."

"What about the second item you turned down?"

"Oh, that." Sean Clough sneered. "It was an unsubtle reference to Paul Greer being up to no good. I figured if Sandra had an issue with her son-in-law, she should keep it between them."

My mind went into overdrive. If there was tension between Paul and Sandra, was it serious enough for him to want her dead? What about Melanie? Had she decided to silence her mother? I focused on Sean. "What do you mean by 'up to no good'? An affair? Why would Sandra want her son-in-law's affair exposed? Surely she'd want to protect her daughter and grandkids?"

The editor screwed up his forehead. "I can't remember the exact wording. It's been a while. I know it had something to do with irregularities in the hotel's accounts."

"A hotel that Paul's parents own," I pointed out. "Wouldn't they let their son off the hook if he'd been tampering with the accounts?"

"That's just it." A sneer spread over Sean's plain face. "The Greers are only part owners in the hotel. They had financial difficulties a few years ago and were forced to seek investors. Paul's parents still own a hefty percentage of the hotel and the surrounding land, but a silent partner owns sixty percent."

I whistled. "In other words, Paul is pretty much a regular employee at the hotel?"

"Now that his father is retired, Paul is the manager. If Sandra's blind item is true, Paul embezzled money from the hotel."

"Wow." While I hadn't made a stellar choice in marrying Joe, I'd had a lucky escape from Paul.

Sean Clough gave a grim smile. "Exactly."

"I still don't understand why Sandra would threaten to expose him. He's married to her daughter and the father of her grandchildren."

Sean spread his palms wide and leaned back in his chair. "I don't know the particulars, and I don't care. I'm not interested in island gossip. I only ran the column because it sold papers."

"I don't suppose Sandra kept a backup of her files here?" I asked. "Or on a shared cloud storage service?"

He shook his head. "Sandra didn't keep anything at the *Gazette*. I guess whatever she had is on her laptop."

Yeah...a laptop that was suspiciously fried and now with computer forensics.

"Did she ever mention cloud storage?" I pushed. "Or an external hard drive?"

"Nope. We never discussed tech. We rarely spoke." His mouth twisted into a grimace. "Sandra was useful to me because her column sold papers. Other than that, I didn't like the woman."

But had that dislike extended to a motive to kill?

Had Sandra threatened to reveal something about Sean to the island?

Sean pointed at the clock on the wall. "Sorry, but I have to get back to work."

I got to my feet and held out my hand. "Thanks for your time. If you think of anything that might be useful for Noreen's defense, please let me know. I'm at The Movie Theater Café most days."

"Sure, sure." The editor accompanied me to the door, and we said a perfunctory goodbye.

As I walked down the lane to the main street, I felt Sean Clough's eyes bore into my back.

ON MY WAY home from the café that evening, I stopped by Paddy Driscoll's place for a second time. I'd made a lousy impression on him during our last meeting, and I needed to persuade him to confide in me. Apart from my aunt and the anonymous blind items targets, Paddy Driscoll was a person with a known grudge against the dead woman.

I pulled up in front of his house and killed the engine. After I got out of the car, I picked my way gingerly across the yard to the farmhouse door. I didn't fancy meeting Paddy and his shotgun again, or being confronted with his dogs.

When I reached the door, I pressed the bell and waited. After a long minute, the door opened a crack to reveal Driscoll's bulbous nose. He frowned when he registered who I was. "I thought I told you to clear off."

"We got off to a bad start the other day, Mr. Driscoll. I'm sorry." I plastered a smile across my face and shoved a basket of scones at the man. "They're made from the last of Noreen's dough, so you're less likely to die than if I'd made them from scratch."

Paddy snorted with laughter. "You'd better come in." He unlatched the chain and held open the door. After I'd shrugged off my coat, he said, "We'll talk in the living room."

Inside, Paddy Driscoll's house was a modern build and bore the hallmarks of a bachelor pad: huge reclining armchair, widescreen TV, and a stack of empty ready-meal packages in the paper recycling bin by the door. A huge Irish flag took up most of one wall, flanked by two sepia photographs of men in old-fashioned military uniforms.

"My great-uncles. Heroes from the Irish Civil War." Paddy smirked at my expression of bewilderment. "June 1922 to May 1923."

I swallowed. "Right. About my last visit—"

"I was short with you the last time we met," he muttered, scratching his grizzly beard. "I shouldn't have lost my temper."

"It's okay. I was stressed about Noreen and a missing cat. I was overly blunt, even by my low standards." I gave him a wry smile. "And I'm sorry about Bran getting in with your sheep."

"No harm done, thank goodness." He gestured at

an overstuffed armchair. "Have a seat." And then added as an afterthought, "Would you like a cup of tea?"

"No, thanks," I said, sinking into the armchair. "I can't stay long. I need to get back to Noreen with groceries."

Paddy took the armchair opposite mine. "Let's cut to the chase, Maggie. I know you've been doing some snooping on your aunt's behalf. What do you want to know? I'm not sure I have anything worth telling."

"I'm trying to find out more about these blind items Sandra is alleged to have written."

"Oh, those." He snorted. "I suppose you think I'm upset about the one implying I have an unnatural relationship with my sheep."

"Didn't it annoy you?"

"Not enough to kill Sandra." He sneered. "Why would I be stupid enough to kill the woman everyone knew I hated? And I'm not talking about some daft rumor about me and my sheep."

"You're referring to the land sale?"

He grunted his assent. "The greedy cow sold that land out from under me. A handshake isn't legally binding, but morally, it should count for something. And to sell to those developers..." His nostrils flared. "It disgusted me, I tell you. Prime farming land wasted on badly built holiday homes that stand empty half the year. It's a crying shame." Paddy sat back in his chair, as if in shock. I suspected that this speech was the most he'd spoken at once in a long time, if ever.

"I heard your detectorist club liked using the land to look for...stuff." In truth, I hadn't a clue what detectorists did, apart from wandering around with metal detectors.

He looked at me sharply. "You're not the brightest spark, are you?"

"I defer to your greater wisdom on the subject," I said, straight-faced.

Paddy narrowed his eyes, clearly unsure whether or not I was making fun of him. "We look for old metal. Coins, ring pulls, old jewelry. That sort of thing."

"Weren't you interested in more than coins on Sandra's land?"

Paddy glared at me. "The monastery buried treasure on that land. Thanks to those fools building houses, we'll never find it now."

"If there was anything to find, wouldn't you have discovered it while you were allowed on Sandra's land?" From what I'd gleaned from Philomena, the detectorists had had plenty of time to look for buried treasure.

"Nah." Paddy screwed up his forehead, adding to the series of deep furrows that plowed a path across his brow. "Sandra only let us explore certain fields. If the maps are accurate, the place most likely for the treasure was where some of them houses went up."

"Wouldn't the construction workers have found it while they were digging the foundations?"

He snorted. "Do you know anything about buried treasure?"

"Sure." I grinned. "I've watched *Pirates of the Caribbean.*"

Paddy stared at me. "You're a smart alec, aren't you?"

"So I've been told."

"If you had a clue, you'd know that sending in bulldozers and diggers is as likely to drive a buried treasure deeper underground as it is to bring it to the surface. For all I know, it's now under one of those awful new houses."

"What was the treasure you were searching for?"

A pained expression flitted across his face. "A golden chalice inlaid with semiprecious stones."

"Valuable?"

"Priceless." He enunciated both syllables, giving it a wealth of meaning.

"In my experience, everything comes with a price tag. If you'd found the chalice, who would have owned it?"

"The people of Ireland. It would have ended up in a museum. We'd probably have received some sort of monetary reward, though, and been obliged to split it with Sandra."

"Because she was the landowner?"

"Yeah. If the item discovered isn't a national treasure, the detectorist splits the proceeds with the landowner." He snorted. "This is all theoretical. We never had a chance to look for that chalice. Sandra and her greed saw to that."

"Well," I reasoned, "it was her land."

"Land she'd agreed to sell to *me*." Paddy leaned back in his chair, and the springs groaned in protest. "I don't give my word lightly, and when I do, I don't go back on it."

"You admit you hated Sandra?" I asked carefully.

"Yes, but I didn't kill her." He laughed. "If you're trying to squeeze a confession out of me, forget it."

I felt my cheeks grow warm but I kept my cool. Either Paddy genuinely had nothing to do with Sandra's death, or his direct admission that he'd hated her was a bluff designed to throw me off the scent. "Do you have any idea who did kill her?"

"No, but when you find out, I'll shake his or her hand."

I winced. "Harsh."

"But honest." Paddy Driscoll hauled himself to his feet, indicating that our interview was at an end. "You'll want to be on your way."

I took the hint and followed him into the hallway. "Enjoy the scones," I said when I'd put my winter jacket back on.

He snorted. "Is 'enjoy' the right word?"

"Maybe not." I stepped outside the house. "Try 'survive' instead."

Paddy gave a bark of laughter. Despite myself, I had a grudging liking for the man, and I suspected it was mutual. "Give my regards to Noreen," he said. "And Maggie?"

I looked over my shoulder. "Yeah?"

"You're looking in the wrong place for answers. You'd do better to look at your past."

With those cryptic words, Paddy Driscoll slammed his door in my face.

18

The next couple of days were hectic. Each day after work, I tracked down members of the Movie Club to question or re-question, but no one had anything new or interesting to add. Brid Kelly at the Whisper Island Medical Centre didn't seem concerned about the blind item Sandra had allegedly written about her. The one club member I'd been unable to talk to was Maria Reilly, the doctor's wife, who'd gone to Dublin to visit her sick mother.

By the weekend, Noreen was feeling better. I arranged for Kelly to cover my Sunday morning shift at the café while I accompanied my aunt to Mass.

"Since when are you a regular churchgoer?" Noreen demanded when we pulled into the church parking lot. "I remember you complaining every Sunday when you were a teenager."

"I've turned over a new leaf," I said primly. "I

even wore a rosary, purloined from your mantelpiece."
I unzipped the top of my jacket to reveal the butt-ugly
mother of pearl rosary underneath.

My aunt made the sign of the cross. "You don't
wear a rosary, Maggie. It's not like a crucifix."

"Why not? It fits around my neck."

"Oh, for goodness' sake. Give it here." She took
the beads off me and slipped them into her coat
pocket. "You won't have a clue when to sit, kneel, or
stand."

"No problem," I said confidently. "I'll just follow
your example."

Muttering, my aunt got out of the car, and I
followed suit. The wind was gale force and icy cold
this morning, and the stone path up to the church was
like an ice rink. I slipped twice but only landed on my
behind once. I considered that a victory.

When we reached the entrance, I could finally
take a break from concentrating on my feet and
admire my surroundings. St. Brendan's Church dated
from the twelfth century, although little remained
from the original structure. It was an imposing stone
edifice located on the edge of one of Whisper Island's
most dramatic cliffs. When I was a kid, I'd sit on one
of the benches in front of the church and stare out at
the vast expanse of the Atlantic Ocean, awed in the
certainty that if I kept going straight, I'd reach America. My enthusiasm hadn't been dampened when my
aunt had pointed out that my latitudinal calculations

weren't accurate, and that I'd actually land in Canada.

Noreen slipped her arm through mine and urged me up the steps and into the church. "Why did you want to come, Maggie? Was it to give me moral support? Because there's no need. Anyone foolish enough to believe I killed Sandra doesn't deserve to be my friend."

"I want a chance to scope out the suspects in their natural habitats. I figured some of the oldies would hang out here on a Sunday morning."

Despite her best efforts to hold it in, Noreen burst out laughing. "You're right on that score. The young people prefer to go to St. Jude's in Smuggler's Cove." She dropped her voice to a confidential whisper. "Their priest has a guitar."

"A guitar...right." I blinked, casting my mind to the church services I'd attended with my non-Catholic mother. "I guess that means we don't have one here?"

Noreen grinned. "Oh, no. Just you wait."

At that moment, bombastic organ music boomed through the building, sending my heart rate soaring.

"Whoa. That thing's loud."

My aunt dragged me to a pew where Philomena and John had saved us seats. I noted that Julie hadn't subjected herself to this morning's Organ Special.

During the ceremony, I scanned the congregation. As Noreen had said, none of the younger members of the Movie Club were present. I spotted Joan Sweetman seated on a pew with Miss Flynn, Miss

Murphy, and Cormac Tate. The Two Gerries sat beside each other, and I recalled Lenny mentioning that both men were widowers of long-standing.

When it was time to pass around the collection box, Sister Pauline supervised, reminding me about the blind item concerning a nun and stolen money. I ran through the published blind items in my head. I'd already spoken to Joan and Paddy Driscoll. Lenny, Julie, and Philomena had all denied they'd been a blind item subject, although I couldn't help feeling that Philomena was holding something back. That left the Spinsters, Sister Pauline, and Paul Greer. They'd all been implicated in blind items, either published ones or unpublished.

I didn't have long to wait for an opportunity to speak to Miss Flynn. Much to Noreen's disgust, I'd worn my running gear under my church clothes and intended to avail of the chance of a run on this side of the island. After the service had finished, we congregated on the steps outside.

"Are you sure you don't want a lift home with me?" Noreen asked, eyeing with distaste the flash of hot pink from the running shirt that my sweater didn't quite cover. "It's a cold morning to go jogging."

"I like running in the cold. I'll soon warm up." I stripped off my coat and sweater and handed them to my aunt. "Thanks for taking these."

"No problem. Will you be back in time for lunch? I'm making a roast with three veg."

I grinned. "Oh, yeah. I love your roasts. If you're cooking, I'll clean up after."

Noreen patted my arm. "We'll worry about that later. Enjoy your run."

"I will." I waved goodbye to Philomena and John and proceeded with caution down the slippery path. Once I reached the road, I'd run on the fields beside it.

I'd reached the graveyard and put music on when I chanced on Miss Flynn putting flowers on a grave. I slowed to a halt and removed my earbuds. "Morning, Miss Flynn."

"Hello, Maggie." She stood and wiped snow from her coat. "My parents," she said when she joined me at the gate. "I find it's bleak out here in the winter. I like to add a little color to their grave."

"That's a lovely idea."

We fell into step with one another, following the trail beside the winding stone wall that surrounded the graveyard.

"I like to stretch my legs after Mass," Miss Flynn explained. "Milly's rheumatism acts up this time of year, and she doesn't care to go for our usual walk."

"I can walk with you, if that's okay." Chance had offered me the perfect opportunity to speak to Miss Flynn alone, and I had no intention of wasting it.

"You're welcome to walk with me, dear." She looked me up and down. "But won't my pace be rather tame for you? You're dressed for jogging."

I laughed. "I'm not going to make you run. I'm happy for us to walk and talk."

"Ah," she said shrewdly. "You want to talk to me alone about Sandra's death."

No point in denying it. "Yeah. I'm glad to catch you away from the café."

Miss Flynn's face contorted. "How that dreadful man can think Noreen was responsible for Sandra's death is beyond me. I'm glad you're on the case, Maggie."

"Not officially," I said hastily. "Sergeant O'Shea's already warned me off more than once."

Miss Flynn waved a hand in a dismissive gesture. "That fool. Ignore him. If it were left up to O'Shea, Noreen would already be in prison, and he'd be back spending his days on the golf course."

As this was exactly my take on the situation, I nodded. "What can you tell me about Sandra?"

"Probably what you've heard from everyone else —I didn't like her." Miss Flynn frowned. "Melanie's claims that her mother was Miss Popularity are absurd. I don't for one instant think she believes it. Her relationship with Sandra wasn't always smooth sailing."

The wheels in my mind whirred. "Really? Melanie gave me the impression that she and Sandra were close."

Miss Flynn laughed. "Hardly. Melanie and Sandra presented a united front when they had a common cause, but other than that, Melanie avoided her mother. I got the impression that Melanie felt Sandra beneath her, especially once she'd married into the wealthiest family on the island."

"But Sandra had money," I pointed out. "And plenty of it from what I heard."

"Yes, but not when the children were small. She sold the land at exactly the right time and made a killing on it." Miss Flynn winced at her own words. "Well, you know what I mean. At any rate, Sandra had money in her later years, but not an ounce of class."

We walked on in silence for a couple of minutes while I weighed what she'd said. "Did Sandra do anything to you?" I asked finally. "Like, spread a nasty rumor?"

Miss Flynn raised an eyebrow. "Apart from the one about Milly and me living in sin?"

"Yes."

The older woman hunched her shoulders, and a shuttered expression came over her face. "Yes. There was a second blind item that upset me, but I'd rather not talk about it."

"I know it's hard, but I'd appreciate it if you'd tell me what was in it. I have a list of all the blind items that appeared in the *Gazette* and I'm trying to match them up with the people they referred to." This wasn't entirely true. I was ignoring the obviously petty ones that were unlikely to drive a person to murder, and two of the infidelity blinds were too obscure for me to decipher.

Miss Flynn removed a cloth handkerchief from her coat pocket and blew her nose delicately. "All right. I'll tell you, but only if you promise not to breathe a word about it to anyone else."

"If it has no bearing on Sandra's murder, sure."

She took a ragged breath. "I won the annual baking contest with—" she broke off on a sob, "—a shop-bought cake."

A gurgle of laughter surged up my throat. I coughed into my fist. "You cheated in a baking contest?"

"Yes." A fat tear rolled down her cheek. "I'm a fraud. Everyone would be disappointed in me if they knew."

"Cheating in a baking contest isn't a capital offense," I said. "People would get over it pretty quick. Besides, Whisper Island is a small community. It would be yesterday's news before long, and someone else would be in the spotlight."

Miss Flynn clutched at her pearls. I hadn't known that people did that outside of books. "Maggie, please don't tell anyone. I couldn't bear people knowing. The neighbors…"

"I won't say a word. It has nothing to do with Sandra Walker's death, and that's all I'm interested in at the moment."

"Thank you, dear. Thank you so much. If Milly knew, she'd be devastated. I've always snuck shop-bought treats into the house and claimed I'd made them."

"Miss Murphy lives with you but doesn't know you can't bake?"

"No," she whispered, biting her lip. "I've cheated for years. I know it's silly. I did it once, when we'd first gotten to know each other, and I wanted to impress her. One white lie led to two, and it went from there."

I gave a crack of laughter. "Maybe I should try that trick at the café. If I tell everyone Noreen baked everything, people might start eating the scones again."

Despite herself, Miss Flynn giggled. "Your scones are improving. It's almost a disappointment. I loved Gerry Logan's expression when he bit into one of your first attempts."

"At least no one's died," I said before I caught myself.

"Yes." Miss Flynn's tone was serious again. "Apart from Sandra. It's a dreadful thing to say of the dead, but she was an awful woman."

"Let me guess—you didn't like the woman, but…?"

The older woman nodded. "Exactly. I didn't like her, but I didn't kill her."

In other words, the same story so many others had told me up 'til now.

We reached the end of the wall and Miss Flynn slowed to a stop. "I'd better walk back. Milly is cooking Sunday lunch, and I don't want to be late. Have a nice day, Maggie."

"Same to you. And thanks again for confiding in

me." A thought struck me. "Miss Flynn? Before you go, there are two blind items about cheaters. Any idea who they might be about? I've made discreet inquiries, but no one seems to know. Or rather they could potentially apply to several people."

Miss Flynn cocked her head to the side, a pensive expression on her birdlike features. "As odd as it sounds, I'm fairly sure one of the blinds about a cheating spouse referred to Sandra's son-in-law, Paul Greer."

I stared at her, open-mouthed. Why would Sean Clough let Sandra put in a blind item about her son-in-law's infidelity when he'd already vetoed another about Paul on the grounds that he didn't want Sandra using the column to annoy her family? Unless, of course, Sean had failed to guess who the blind item was about. "What makes you think the item referred to Paul?"

"Sandra made a few snide remarks about Paul over the last few months," Miss Flynn said. "I got the impression that his marriage to Melanie wasn't the rock-solid relationship they project to the world, and Paul and Sandra never got on well. I saw them arguing outside The Movie Theater Café last month after we'd watched a film."

My ears pricked up. "Did you hear what the argument was about?"

Miss Flynn shook her head. "No. I was too far away. I knew they were arguing from their body language."

"Thanks for the info." I blew out a sigh. I had zero desire to go back to the hotel and face Paul and Melanie again, but the news that Sandra had been seen fighting with Paul was worth pursuing. I'd pay them a visit tomorrow.

AFTER I PARTED company from Miss Flynn, I took the path along the cliff and worked my way up to a fast but controlled pace. I was breathing hard and grateful for the running wrap I wore up over my mouth and nose to protect my nose and lungs from the icy air. Although we were now in February, the cold weather that had hit the island since my arrival showed no sign of giving way to warmer temperatures.

Running along the path, it felt like I was flying. I passed old beehive huts to my left. I'd explored them when I was a kid. I needed to brush up on my island history, but I remembered Noreen telling me they dated from the early Middle Ages. When I got back to the cottage, I'd dig out Noreen's copy of the island's history.

My plans for a shower and a peaceful afternoon reading were smashed to smithereens the moment I walked through the cottage door.

Noreen met me in the hallway, her face haggard. Judging by the succulent scents wafting from the kitchen, I knew it wasn't because our lunch was toast.

"What's happened?" I demanded. "Has Sergeant O'Shea done something stupid?"

"More than likely, but we can't blame this one on him." My aunt sighed. "Jennifer Pearce informed me that she could no longer act as my go-between solicitor while Jacqueline Sweeney is in Cork."

I blinked. "Why? I thought it was all arranged."

"So did I. Apparently, Paul and Melanie threatened to transfer the accounts from his hotel and her restaurant to a mainland solicitor if Jennifer didn't cut contact with me." My aunt's lips twisted into a bitter smile. "They don't want their solicitor having anything to do with Sandra's murderer."

"Oh, for heaven's sake," I snapped. "Nesbitt & Son is the only practice on the island. Where else are you supposed to go?"

"Now that Jacqueline Sweeney is representing me, I don't need Jennifer's support as much, but it was convenient to have a lawyer on the island in case I had questions."

"I'm going to have a word with Paul and Melanie," I said through gritted teeth.

"Don't bother, love. It'll only cause trouble."

I jutted my jaw. "I'd intended to call over to the hotel tomorrow anyway. I'm going to make it today instead."

Thirty minutes later, showered but still hungry, I marched into the hotel.

The same receptionist who'd greeted me the day I'd come to talk to Paul and Melanie was seated behind the reception desk. She drew back in alarm when she saw me. "Ms. Doyle, I don't think—"

"I'd like to speak to Paul," I said firmly. "And I'm not taking no for an answer. You can tell your boss that unless he wants me telling the entire hotel about his indiscretions at ninety decibels, he'd better get his butt out here and talk to me."

The woman reddened. "Just a moment." She pressed a button on her phone, either to call Paul or to contact security. With the mood I was in, either option was fine by me.

Paul appeared a moment later, looking flustered. "Maggie, this is a bad time for—"

"We'll have coffee in his office," I told the receptionist. "Make mine black with two sugars. I need something sweet to take away the sour taste of dealing with your boss." Leaving her open-mouthed, I dragged Paul in the direction of his office. When we were inside, I kicked the door shut. "So. It's time for you to talk."

"Maggie—"

"Don't 'Maggie' me. Sit your butt in that chair and start blabbing. I want to know exactly what hold Sandra had over you. And don't give me any nonsense about her being family. If you did what I think you did, family means little to you." I stood over him, hands on hips. "But here's the thing, Paul. Family means a lot to me. You shouldn't have told Jennifer Pearce to cut contact with Noreen."

"Surely you can understand that Melanie didn't

want the prime suspect in her mother's murder represented by our solicitor."

"I could understand it if Noreen did the crime, but she's innocent." I stared him down. "Which is more than I can say for you. Even if you didn't kill Sandra, I know you had plenty of reasons to want her dead."

"That's not true." Paul squirmed under my steady gaze, and his shoulders sagged. "All right, Maggie. I'd had a few disagreements with my mother-in-law, but nothing out of the ordinary."

I dropped into the chair opposite and leaned forward, pinning him in place with the intensity of my stare. "Come on, admit it. You hated Sandra."

A pained expression flitted across Paul's handsome features. "'Hate' is a harsh word."

I sat back and folded my arms across my chest. "Then how would you describe your feelings for your mother-in-law?"

Paul's face underwent a series of contortions before settling into resigned apathy. "Fine, you win. I hated Sandra. Satisfied?"

"Not yet." I whipped my notepad and pen from my purse. "Apart from the usual family bust-ups, was there a particular reason?"

Paul winced. "Is the notebook necessary?"

I raised an eyebrow. "Would you prefer me to record our conversation?" Actually, I was pretty sure audio recordings were beyond the capabilities of the half-broken cell phone Noreen had given me for my

time on the island, but I wasn't about to let
Paul know.

"Okay," he said finally. "Keep the notebook." He
picked up one of his fancy office toys—a metal take
on a Rubik's Cube—and fiddled with it before continu-
ing. "Last summer, I started a relationship with a
hotel guest."

I whistled. "Talk about pooping in your
backyard."

"You have a way with words, Maggie," he said
dryly. "I know it was stupid. I fell for her hard.
Melanie and I haven't been happy for years, but we
had the kids to consider. This was the first time I seriously thought about leaving."

"And Sandra found out?" I prompted.

He inclined his neck. "Yeah. One of the hotel
staff must have let it slip. I'm pretty sure a couple of
them guessed about the affair."

"Did Sandra confront you?"

"Yes. I told her not to bother flying into a rage. I'd
tell Melanie everything, and we'd file for a divorce."

I raised an eyebrow. "I'll bet that didn't suit
Sandra."

"No." He gave a bitter smile. "She liked having
her daughter married to the son of Whisper Island's
'wealthiest' family." He made air quotes with his
fingers. "It didn't matter to Sandra that my parents
don't have as much money as people think, at least
not anymore. She was all about keeping up
appearances."

"What hold did Sandra have over you, Paul? It can't have been revealing your affair to Melanie. If you wanted to leave your wife for another woman, she'd have found out anyway." Would he confess to the embezzlement Sean Clough had alluded to? Or something even worse?

He blew out a breath. "Sandra had a knack for ferreting out people's secrets. A nose for trouble, I guess you could say. She discovered I'd borrowed from the hotel to settle my debts."

"'Borrowed' being synonymous with 'stole,'" I said dryly.

Paul ran his hands over his slicked-back hair. "Look, I was desperate. By the time Sandra figured out what I'd done, I'd replaced a chunk of the money I'd taken."

"But you hadn't replaced *all* the money?" I prompted, leaning forward in my seat, my pen poised.

Paul stared at his manicured fingernails. "No."

I scribbled a few notes. Once I was done, I glanced at Paul. "Why didn't you ask your parents for help? It's their hotel you *borrowed* from, after all."

"If it were just my parents, the issue wouldn't be so serious." Paul didn't meet my gaze. "During the economic crisis, my father lost a lot of money and, well, he had to make changes."

"Changes that included seeking outside investors," I filled in. I smiled at his shocked expression. "It's a small island, Paul. Everyone knows a silent partner owns the majority share in the hotel. And while your parents might forgive you for taking money from the accounts, the silent partner wouldn't."

"Exactly." Paul squirmed and loosened his tie as though it were choking him. "When the other guy bought into the hotel, part of the deal was keeping me on as manager. But if he knew I'd played fast and loose with the accounts, I'd be out of a job. Despite what people on Whisper Island think, I'm paid a regular hotel manager's salary. Yes, I have a nice house on the hotel grounds and access to the hotel's fleet of cars, but they're tied to my position as manager. I don't have much money of my own."

"Sandra must have had plenty of money after she sold that land," I pointed out. "Why didn't you turn to her if you were having cash flow problems?"

He looked up and gave a bitter laugh. "Sandra was tight with her money. She'd buy nice presents for the kids, but she didn't believe in handouts."

"But now that she's dead, it's pretty convenient for you, no? Melanie will inherit half of Sandra's fortune, and you'll have every reason for sticking around."

"After probate, yes." His eyes pleaded with me. "But I didn't kill her, Maggie. I swear."

"You swore to me that you hadn't slept with Melanie. Forgive me if I don't place much faith in your word."

He sneered at me. "Are you still sore about that? That happened years ago. Time to move on."

I resisted the urge to stab the arrogant slug with my pen. "Oh, I've moved on, but I'm not going to forget. Lies come easy to you, Paul. They always did, and in a variety of situations, not just your cheating with Melanie. I know you too well to believe a word you say."

"If you're not going to believe me, why bother questioning me?" Paul's mouth formed a sulky line. "You've obviously already made up your mind what to think."

"I can learn a lot from what a person *doesn't* say." I twirled my pen between my fingers. "Saying you've been evasive is an understatement. I don't know why you took the money, but I intend to find out."

Sweat beaded on his upper lip. "Okay, wait a minute. I'll tell you. I lost money on the horses. I couldn't tell Melanie. She'd have been furious. I'd done it before, and she'd told me she'd cut me off without a euro if I did it again."

"You just said you lived off your manager's salary," I pointed out. "And Melanie runs a restaurant that apparently doesn't attract many customers. What money does she have coming in that you didn't mention?"

He squirmed in his chair. "When Sandra sold her land, she gave her son, Jonathan, a lump sum of money but insisted on setting up a trust fund—or whatever those things are called—for Melanie. Melanie received money each quarter, but she couldn't touch the capital."

I gave a crack of laughter. "Sandra didn't trust you."

He reddened but chose to ignore my jibe. "Melanie was furious. She felt Sandra was treating her like a child and playing favorites."

"With Sandra dead, does Melanie now have access to all the money in the trust?"

Paul nodded. "Yes. Plus half of Sandra's estate."

Thus giving both Melanie and Paul a strong motive for wanting Sandra out of the way. I looked him straight in the eye. "How did you react when Sandra threatened to expose your embezzlement?"

He looked startled. "I was furious, of course. My mother hasn't been in the best of health, and she'd be horrified. And I couldn't afford to let my parents' silent partner find out, or I'd lose my job and my home. She told me she'd keep silent if I stayed with Melanie and tried to make our marriage work."

"Paul, did you kill Sandra? Or ask someone to do it on your behalf? Melanie, perhaps?"

He jerked back in his chair, horror written across his face. "No, of course not. I'm a liar and a cheat, fine. But did you ever know me to be violent?"

"No, but we haven't had anything to do with one another in years. For all I know, you're a closet serial killer."

"That's absurd. I've never been in a physical fight in my life, not even at school."

All of which might be true, but it didn't rule out poison. Poison was a sneaky weapon and didn't require murderers to assault their victims, or even be near them when they died. I stared across the desk at the man who was my first love. Paul had been a fun-loving kid, if easily influenced. He'd grown into a charming but weak man. Sandra had him backed into a corner, and Paul was exactly the sort to snap when put under pressure.

I stood and slid my pen and notebook back into my purse. "Call Jennifer Pearce and tell her to represent Noreen if she needs legal representation on the island."

Paul's face underwent a series of contortions. "Fine," he muttered. "I'll call her now."

I turned on my heel and walked out of Paul's office for what I hoped would be the final time.

19

Early the following week, Noreen and Sister Pauline traveled to Cork for a couple of days to liaise with my aunt's solicitor and the barrister who'd represent her in court. I was left in charge of the café with Julie, Philomena, and Lenny pitching in to help when they had time.

Sandra's funeral was held on Monday, and both the wake and the burial were kept in a small circle.

"Sandra would have hated that," Miss Murphy said on Thursday evening, sipping her tea and scanning the latest edition of the *Whisper Island Gazette*. "Murdered or not, she'd have wanted a big affair with the whole island in attendance."

I glanced up from where I was polishing the glass display counter, behind which was an array of cakes, scones, muffins, and other sweet treats to tempt customers we didn't have. "I doubt Melanie and her brother are in the mood for crowds at the moment," I said. "And I don't blame them."

"Jonathan won't stick around long," Miss Flynn interjected. "He never does. He's some hot-shot stock-broker in London, you know." She sniffed as though this was synonymous with being a pimp or drug dealer.

Joan laughed. "Sandra always played favorites with her children. However trying Melanie can be, I always found Jonathan insufferably arrogant."

"He was Sandra's favorite?"

"Oh, yes." Joan stirred her tea before taking a delicate sip. "Jonathan was in school with Nick and bullied him rather badly."

I raised an eyebrow. "The apple didn't fall far from the tree, eh?"

"It's a dreadful thing to say," Miss Flynn said, "but Whisper Island is more peaceful without Sandra."

"I've spoken to Sean Clough," Joan added, "and I'm delighted to say he's discontinuing the blind gossip column. The item that ran last month about Philomena was outrageous."

"The one referring to her sneaking around at night with a man who wasn't her husband?" I asked. "She says it's nonsense."

"I'm sure it is." Joan wrinkled her nose. "Although I have seen her out late at night on a couple of occa-sions, both times near the school. I have no idea what she's doing, but I can't imagine it involves cheating on John. They're a devoted couple."

My stomach lurched. So my aunt truly was sneaking around after dark? What was she up to? It had to be something she wanted to conceal, or she'd have told me straight out when I'd asked her about it at the library. I sucked air through my teeth. What was I going to do? Follow her? Conduct a stakeout with my aunt as the target?

It was absurd, but I kept running into dead ends. If I'd been back in the U.S., I'd have put family considerations aside and treated everyone who had a motive or acted suspiciously as a potential suspect. Why should I act differently here? I swallowed a sigh and formulated my plan of campaign. I'd follow Philomena after work. Ten to one, she'd go straight home, or make an innocent late-night run to the ATM.

I loaded dirty cups onto a tray and took them into the kitchen. There was very little to wash up, unfortunately. Now that the initial drama surrounding Sandra's death and Noreen's arrest was dying down, I'd hoped trade would pick up, but many people were still boycotting The Movie Theater Café. Even the various clubs that used the premises in the evenings had lower-than-usual attendance, and Philomena let slip that the Historical Society had asked her permission to use the library for their meetings. I put down my polishing cloth and checked the cash register. I sighed at the figure on the display. If our takings remained this low, my aunt would be out of business long before her case came to trial.

The bell over the café door jangled. I stiffened the instant I clocked who was standing on the threshold. "Noreen's not here," I said to Sergeant O'Shea.

He muttered something under his breath and lumbered into the café.

"Is your investigation not going well?" I inquired in a sarcastic tone. "Not finding sufficient concrete evidence to convict my aunt for a crime she didn't commit?"

His eyes flashed. "I'm only doing my job. I've got nothing against Noreen personally."

"Maybe you don't have an issue with my aunt, but as for doing your job…" I let my words trail off, and noted his reddening cheeks with satisfaction.

"You don't need to worry about me doing my job anymore, Ms. Doyle. That fancy solicitor of Noreen's has been causing trouble." He grunted. "She's persuaded the district superintendent to send some young fella out to take charge of the case."

Finally. I breathed a sigh of relief. There was no guarantee that the "young fella" would prove any more competent than Sergeant O'Shea, but at least there was a chance that the police would start to take other suspects seriously.

Sergeant O'Shea must have interpreted my expression correctly, because he guffawed and treated me to a sneer. "Don't get too excited. Noreen is still charged with the murder. I don't know what the new fella is going to do, apart from causing trouble for me."

"I see." I crossed my arms over my chest and fixed him with a knowing stare. "And you're telling me this because…?"

The man sniffed, suddenly finding his polished loafers fascinating. "I'd appreciate it if you didn't bad-mouth me to him." Sergeant O'Shea looked up at me and attempted to disguise his blatant dislike of me with a rictus of a smile. "It's true that I don't have much experience of murder investigations, but I've done my best. You can't expect more than that."

I rolled my eyes. "You've *done your best* to get back to the golf course as quickly as possible each day."

Rage burned in his eyes and he opened his mouth to defend himself. Before the man could utter the blustering denial that I knew was on his tongue, the bell above the door jangled a second time, and the handsome motorcycle guy walked in.

My heart skipped a beat. And then I registered what he was wearing.

"Oh, heck," I said, raking him from head to foot. "*You're* the policeman from the mainland?"

"Indeed I am." He grinned at me and extended a hand. "Garda Sergeant Liam Reynolds."

I cringed at my fiery cheeks. Of all people to be O'Shea's replacement, did it have to be the guy I'd nearly killed and then yelled at? "Maggie Doyle," I squeaked.

Sergeant Reynolds turned to O'Shea. "Ms. Doyle and I have already met. I didn't expect to meet you in here, Colm. Are you two pals?"

Reynolds shot me a wicked grin that set my pulse racing. Oh, yeah. He remembered my offhand comment about the Whisper Island police.

"I was just, uh, ordering a cappuccino to go." O'Shea looked at me, a desperate appeal in his eyes. He knew as well as I did that his request for me not to express my opinion on his police work wasn't kosher. He'd had plenty of time to regret his decision not to bag Sandra's cocktail glass as potential evidence, or to perform even a cursory check of the movie theater for anything that could point to her death not having been natural. What he didn't know was that I'd inadvertently let slip to his replacement just what I thought of his shoddy police work.

I smothered a laugh and fixed O'Shea's cappuccino. When I handed it to him, he paid me with a comical reluctance that wasn't lost on Reynolds. I had the impression that Sergeant Hottie missed very little.

After the door had shut, I met his teasing blue eyes. "So you're in charge of the Sandra Walker murder investigation."

"That's right," he said cheerfully. "I believe you've been doing some sleuthing yourself."

I cocked my head to the side. "Did you come in here for a coffee or to warn me off?"

"Both." His lips were a straight line but his eyes twinkled with amusement. "I'd like a double espresso to go, and a quick word with you."

"Oh, yeah?" I grabbed a takeout espresso cup and ground fresh beans. "What do you want to know?"

The man laughed. "You get straight to the point, don't you, Ms. Doyle?"

"You strike me as a straight-to-the-point kind of guy, Sergeant Reynolds." I pressed the double espresso button, and delicious brown liquid dripped into the cup. "I guess you want to know what my sleuthing has unearthed."

"Exactly." He gave me a mock salute.

"Hmm…" I slid his coffee across the counter. "Can you guarantee me that you'll investigate suspects other than my aunt?"

"I can guarantee nothing, but I can promise you that I'll look at the case notes with fresh eyes and go over all the evidence. Sound fair?"

"It sounds vague," I quipped, "but I'm willing to bargain with you. I'll email you some of my notes. In return, you do what O'Shea should have done from the start."

"You do realize I'm the police, don't you?" He'd dropped his voice a notch but kept his tone playful. "I could drag you in for questioning and demand you present me with all you know."

I leaned forward on the counter, balancing on one elbow. "You could do that. Or you could play fair and give me a chance to drip-feed you information on a need-to-know basis."

Reynolds grinned and reached for his wallet. He extracted a couple of coins and dropped them into my outstretched hand. For an instant, his fingers brushed against me, sending a jolt of awareness skittering over my skin. I swallowed hard. Now wasn't the time to lose my head over a man.

"I'll play fair, as you put it, for twenty-four hours." He slid a card from his wallet and handed it to me. "Email me your notes and don't hesitate to call me if you find out anything important."

I took the card and he took the coffee. With a parting wink and a smile so wicked it made me shiver, Reynolds sauntered out of The Movie Theater Café. Somehow, I didn't think Sergeant Hottie would prove to be a lazy fool like his predecessor. I might actually have some competition in the sleuthing department. With a smile, I slipped his card into my pocket. This was going to be fun.

AFTER I'D LOCKED up the café for the night, I walked toward Noreen's car. I'd packed a thermos filled with black coffee, plus four leftover sandwiches from the café. Depending on how long Philomena kept me waiting, I might need provisions.

Lenny was waiting for me, leaning against the rusty Ford with a grin stretched across his face. "Whoa, Maggie. That's a lot of food. You throwing a party?"

I hesitated a moment before I spoke. Should I tell him? I glanced at his van, parked two in front of my vehicle. Lenny was bound to have the equipment I lacked. And then it hit me. "It's Thursday," I breathed. "You're going alien spotting with Mack."

"Yeah, dude. That's why I waited for you." He bounced on the spot and rubbed his gloved hands together. "Wanna come along?"

"Actually, I was hoping I could borrow some of your equipment. I need to do a bit of…spotting…of my own."

Lenny looked taken aback. "Uh, sure. What do you need?"

"Binoculars, preferably with night-vision capabilities. The ones I have are only suitable for daylight."

A frown etched over his forehead. "What are you up to, Maggie? I don't see you going out looking for aliens."

I opened the back door and slung my bag and provisions on the seat. "If you must know, I'm going on a stakeout."

Lenny practically danced on the spot. "Awesome, dude. Want me and Mack to come along? We love that kind of stuff."

"I think it'd be smarter if I went on my own."

"Well, that's charming." He pulled a face, but the twinkle in his eyes indicated he wasn't annoyed. "You want my gear but not my help. Come on, Maggie. Let us come along. We've never been on a stakeout before. It'll be totally happening."

I bit my lip. I trusted Mack to keep his cool, but Lenny had a tendency to get overexcited. This could go very wrong. "All right, but on one condition."

He grinned. "Name it and it's yours."

"I call the shots." I paused and added, "And the ham-and-pickle sandwich is all mine."

"Deal. And here's Mack coming down the street. Dude," Lenny yelled. "Want to go on a stakeout?"

"Shh." I held a finger to my lips. "I don't want the whole island knowing." Especially not the new cop in charge of the murder investigation. Unlike O'Shea, Reynolds didn't strike me as stupid. In fact, had the person acting furtive not been my aunt, I might have told him of my suspicions. But until I knew him better and was sure he was competent, I couldn't risk handing him one aunt on a platter in order to set the other free.

Mack reached the car, laden down with bags filled with soda and an assortment of junk food. "Hey, Maggie. What's all this about a stakeout?"

"Get in the car, and I'll tell you on the way."

"Dude," Lenny said, eyeing the bags. "Did you get fish and chips from the pub?"

"Of course." Mack held the bags aloft. "Would I let you down?"

As if on cue, my stomach rumbled loudly.

Lenny laughed. "Still want that ham-and-pickle sandwich? If you're nice to me and don't hog the night-vision binoculars, I'll share my chips. Or fries, or whatever you call them across the pond."

"Fries or chips, I'll eat both." I stuck my tongue out at him and climbed behind the wheel.

"Is that coffee?" Mack asked after he slid onto the

passenger seat, indicating the thermos flask I'd placed between the front seats.

"Yes." I suppressed a smile. "Don't you guys take hot drinks on your alien-hunting missions?"

"Nah," Lenny said from the backseat. "We stick to granddad's *poitín*."

It took me a moment to translate Lenny's Gaelic pronunciation to its English equivalent. *Cripes.* If Mack and Lenny were drinking poteen, no wonder they were spotting all sorts of weird happenings in the skies.

"So who are we following?" Mack asked. "Please tell me it's Paul Greer. I never could stand the guy."

I slid him a look and grinned. "Sorry to disappoint. It's my aunt Philomena."

Mack stared at me, jaw gaping. "The librarian? What's she done to warrant a stakeout?"

"Nothing, I hope." I sighed. "Look, you guys have to promise me you'll keep quiet about this."

"Sure," Mack said.

"Of course," Lenny yelled from the back. "Now tell us what she's done."

"She's been acting strange lately. Like, sneaking around after dark." I bit my lip. "I think she might be seeing Cormac Tate. She's been seen hanging around the school late at night."

"Seriously? You believe that blind item Sandra wrote?" Mack shook his head. "Nah. I can't see Philomena cheating. She and your uncle John are tight."

"I can't help feeling this is a bad idea, Maggie. Why not ask Philomena what she's up to?"

I drummed the wheel. "Because it might have something to do with the murder. And if it does, she's hardly likely to tell me."

"That's crazy talk," Mack said. "Philomena is no more likely to have killed Sandra than Noreen. Besides, do you want to get one aunt off the hook by incriminating the other?"

"I don't intend to incriminate anyone. Philomena's been acting weird ever since I started asking questions about the blind item column." For all I knew, the cheating blind might not be the problem. Perhaps Sandra had threatened to publish a different item, one that had the potential to do serious damage to Philomena and her family. Noreen had been on Sandra's list of blackmail victims. Why not Philomena? I didn't share this thought with the guys. How could I tell them I knew Sandra was a blackmailer without risking them finding out about Noreen's secret?

I turned the key in the ignition, and the car rumbled into life. "I'm going to drive toward the library and catch Philomena leaving work. Julie said she works late on Thursday evenings."

Mack eyed me thoughtfully. "I can't help feeling you know more than you're saying."

"I've told you everything I know." About Philomena, at least.

"Come on, Maggie," Lenny said. "If we're your partners in crime, we need all the deets."

"No crimes are going to be committed." I met Lenny's eye in the rearview mirror. "Speaking of which, isn't poteen illegal?"

Lenny and Mack exchanged a guilty look. "Well, you can buy it in the supermarket now."

"Why do I sense a 'but' coming here?"

"Yeah…Granddad's produce probably doesn't quite fit the legal status."

"Oh, fabulous," I said. "I'm stalking my aunt in a car with illegal liquor."

"Where's your sense of adventure?" Lenny beamed. "We're going on a stakeout."

I drove toward the harbor and pulled up across the road from the library just as Philomena was walking down the steps toward her car. "Duck," I said. "I can't risk her spotting us, or she'll come over to chat."

But my aunt was preoccupied and got into her car without so much as a glance in our direction. When she pulled out into the road, I waited a few seconds before following.

We drove all the way to the crossroads at the far end of town, and my aunt took the exit next to Whisper Island's elementary school. I followed at a snail's pace. When Philomena stopped in front of the school gates, I eased my car to a halt half a block farther down the street. As soon as I killed the lights, I whipped out the night-vision binoculars and peered through the lenses.

It was almost ten at night, long after school got out, and all the lights in the building were off. Cormac Tate snuck down the school steps, looking left and then right as if he was scanning the terrain for potential threats. He hurried toward my aunt's car. My aunt rolled down her window, and he spoke to her, but I couldn't hear what they were saying. Finally, she nodded and pulled her car into a side street, conveniently out of sight of the crossroads.

"What are they doing?" Lenny said. "Hey, Mack. Pass the ketchup."

"All you think of is your stomach," Mack grumbled, but he handed back a packet.

I ignored the boys and continued to peer through the binoculars. Cormac was looking about, a nervous twitch to his shoulders. When Philomena rejoined him, they hurried into the schoolhouse, careful to keep out of the path of the streetlamp.

"Is that it?" Mack asked, perplexed. "She visited Cormac?"

"But did you see how shifty he looked? And how they didn't step into the light?"

Mack stared at me, a baffled expression on his freckled face. "No."

"Seriously. Men."

We waited a full hour before Philomena reappeared. In that time, I ate two sandwiches and most of Lenny's chips. The guys consumed everything in the seemingly bottomless bags of junk food that Mack had brought along and were making inroads into my supplies.

"Want a swig of moonshine, Maggie?" Lenny asked from the backseat.

"No. I'm driving. And after the amount you've consumed, I'm taking you home."

"Philomena's coming back," Mack said, "and she's alone."

I jerked my head around and stared through the windshield. My aunt looked up and down the road before walking to her car. She got in and started the engine. After she'd pulled out into the road, we followed at a cautious distance.

"Where's she going now?" Mack asked as we followed her out the third exit at the roundabout and took the road that led toward the other side of the island. "Is she heading to Noreen's place?"

"I guess we'll find out."

Twenty minutes later, Philomena turned off the road and on to a dirt track that led through the fields near Noreen's cottage. I killed the lights and followed her. When Philomena finally parked next to the woods, I eased my car to a halt. My aunt stepped out of her car and went to the trunk. To my amazement, she removed a large garbage bag from the back before sneaking toward the woods.

"What the——" I began, but my words died in my throat when our engine backfired, making us all jump.

Philomena, alerted by the noise, whirled around

and stared directly at the car.

"Oops," Lenny said. "I guess we're busted."

I let out a groan. "Okay. Let's play it cool. Why are we in a field, cruising along? We're taking a detour to Noreen's. No, wait. We're alien spotting."

"I thought you didn't want to look for aliens," Lenny said. "You keep telling me it's ridiculous."

"I don't, and it is, but I need an excuse for us being here." I rolled down my window and plastered a smile on my face. "Hey, Philomena."

"Maggie?" My aunt squinted through the darkness. "What are you doing here this time of night?"

I switched off the engine and got out of the car. "I could ask you the same question." I looked her up and down, noting her unusual outfit for the first time. "Wow. Are you wearing running gear?"

"I… Oh, Maggie." It was too dark to see if my aunt's cheeks were red, but her embarrassment was palpable. "Promise me you won't tell anyone. Mack and Lenny, as well."

"Of course not, but why the secrecy? Isn't it a strange time to go running?"

My aunt shifted her weight from one leg to the other and clasped her hands. "On a whim, I decided to sign up for the Runathon, but I didn't want to train where everyone would see me. So I've been sneaking out at night to train while John is asleep."

"Why don't you want people knowing?" I asked, baffled.

"Because I'm *fat*, Maggie." My aunt's voice had

dropped to a whisper. "Not just a little plump, but extremely overweight. I don't want people seeing me run until I weigh less. And, well, I want to surprise John. He'll be so proud of me the day of the Runathon if I take part and complete the race."

My heart ached for her that she felt so self-conscious. Philomena was a nice-looking woman, and I suspected she would be no matter what she weighed. "That's a lovely idea, but why do you care what people think? If you're out running, you're doing something positive for your health."

"I know, but I just couldn't face kids making fun of me, or hearing snide remarks from other women." Her shoulders rounded, she stared at her running shoes. "You know how catty people can be."

"Hey," I said softly. "Julie and I go jogging a couple of times a week. Why don't you come out with us? We'll stick to the less populated routes if that'll make you feel more comfortable. And if we run across anyone, so be it."

Hope warred with indecision on Philomena's face. "Are you sure I wouldn't slow you two down? You're both a lot younger and thinner than I am."

"We'd love to have you along. Julie will be delighted when she finds out you want to participate in the Runathon. Come here." I gave my aunt a warm hug. "Keep the faith. You'll do great."

She laughed. "Thanks, Maggie. Now, whatever are you and the boys doing out here at this time of night?"

"About that…" It was my turn to resemble a beetroot. "I have a confession to make."

Philomena raised an eyebrow. "Oh?"

"We were kind of following you."

"Why?" Her tone was tinged with a mixture of embarrassment and annoyance. "I thought I noticed a car behind me earlier. Not many people are out this late on a Thursday night."

"I've been following up on those blind items."

"And you thought the one about me having an affair might be true?" Philomena sighed. "I hope you'll trust me when I say that my reason for meeting Cormac never made it into the blind gossip column. I realize you want to know why we were sneaking around the school so late, but it's not my story to tell. If you want the details, you'll have to ask Cormac. And Maggie?" She nodded to the car, where Mack and Lenny were fighting over the poteen hip flask. "Don't take those eejits with you when you do."

I laughed. "I won't, I promise."

She smiled and gave me another hug. "Now can I finish my workout in peace?"

"I get the message. Have a good run. I'll call you about setting up a time to train with me and Julie."

My aunt waved at the boys and took off into the woods.

At least, I thought as I walked back to the car, that was one mystery solved.

Unfortunately, it brought me no closer to discovering who murdered Sandra Walker.

20

On Friday morning, Noreen insisted on giving me the day free. "You've been working long hours all week, love. It's time for me to do my share."

I glanced up from the sink, where I was washing our breakfast plates. "You needed to be in Cork. I didn't have a problem running the café on my own. The Two Gerries even told me that my baking is improving."

My aunt gave a crack of laughter. "We'll make a baker out of you yet, my girl."

I grabbed a dish towel and dried the plates. "Seriously, I don't mind working today. Why don't you stay home and relax?"

"I've had enough relaxing," Noreen said. "I need the distraction. Anything to stop me from worrying all day. You said you wanted to go back and explore the beehive huts. Take the car and go play tourist for the day."

I frowned. "How will you get to the café if I have the car?"

"Paddy Driscoll is driving me as far as Smuggler's Cove. If I need a lift home, I'll give you a call later. Sound good?"

"If you're sure it's okay with you, I'd love to go exploring." Yes, I wanted to play tourist. But first, I planned to stop by the school to talk to Cormac Tate. Noreen disapproved of me asking questions, so I opted to skip that part of today's agenda. "Before I leave, I'm planning on looking for Poly again."

My aunt's face grew grave. "I'd hoped she'd show up with her kittens in tow. Maybe we have to accept that she's gone."

Perhaps we did, but I felt responsible for the cat's welfare. I'd known she was expecting, and she'd disappeared on my watch.

After Noreen had left, I put away the breakfast stuff and tidied the cottage. Roly followed my every move, meowing plaintively. I reached down to scratch under his chin. "Are you missing your mate? We'll look for her later. How does that sound?"

Apparently, Roly didn't approve of "later." My attempt to vacuum the cottage was hampered by Roly getting under my feet and between my legs. Bran appeared to have picked up on Roly's anxiety and began to whine and paw at my leg.

"Oh, for heaven's sake. What is up with you two?"

I unplugged the vacuum cleaner and hunkered down to look the animals in the eye. "What do you want me to do? You both ate a huge breakfast, and Noreen took Bran out for a walk. You can't need anything."

Roly and Bran clearly disagreed. Roly raced to the front door and sat on the mat, meowing.

I blew out my cheeks. "All right. I'll play along. Maybe you know where Poly's hiding." I bundled up for the outdoors and we stepped outside. Bran and Roly raced ahead, making straight for the barn. "I've already searched the barn," I muttered. "Several times. She's not in there."

Bran let out a bark, and I hurried my pace. In the barn, the dog was digging in straw, while Roly observed the action with pricked-up ears. After Bran had made a thorough mess, I saw what he must have smelled. "Poly," I gasped. "And...four...no, *five* kittens."

The mother cat lay in the straw, next to a wriggling pile of kittens. Far from presenting the supreme absorption I'd observed in my best friend Selena's cat when she'd had kittens, Poly was agitated. She leaped to her feet and paced before me, meowing loudly.

"Okay. Something's wrong. Can you show me what?"

Poly stopped pacing and eyed me with annoyance. Her cries for attention grew louder and more insistent. And then I noticed what lay behind the spot where she was pacing back and forth. A green drainpipe, half stuffed with straw. I kneeled down and peered inside, but it was too dark to see anything. "Hang on a sec." I leaped to my feet and found the flashlight Noreen kept hanging from a nail by the barn entrance. Armed with the flashlight, I returned to the drainpipe and aimed the light inside. A tiny kitten was in the pipe, unmoving. My heart squeezed at the sight. No wonder Roly and Poly were upset. I lay down and stretched my arm into the pipe, but it was hopeless. I couldn't reach the kitten.

"Ms. Doyle? Are you in here?" A male voice called my name, and I jerked around. My breath caught. Sergeant Hottie, aka Liam Reynolds, stood by the barn entrance, looking even more gorgeous than he had in the café. I raked him with my eyes, focusing on his arms.

"I need your help," I said without preamble. "A kitten is stuck in this drainpipe, and my arms aren't long enough to reach it."

Sergeant Reynold's cheery smile faded and his expression grew serious. Without hesitation, he shrugged off his jacket and rolled up his sleeves. A man of action—I approved. "Let's see if my arms are long enough."

He kneeled in the straw beside me. This close, I could smell his aftershave—something subtle but spicy that made my pulse race. I blinked away the X-rated scenes playing in my mind and focused on Mission Kitten Rescue. "Can you reach her?"

"Yeah, I have her." Reynolds looked up from his

position on the ground and gave me a bone-melting grin. "You sure this kitten is a she?"

"I have a feeling it's a girl." My voice caught. "I just hope she's still alive."

"Well," Reynolds said, slowly removing his arm from the pipe, "she's a wriggler. I'm taking that to be a good sign."

"Oh," I breathed in wonder when he opened his hand to reveal a squirming kitten. "She's beautiful."

"She's gorgeous, but cold and probably hungry." The police sergeant ran a finger over the tiny body. "Want to go back to your mama, little girl?" He placed the kitten onto the straw beside Poly. The mother cat licked and nuzzled her baby, and soon coaxed the adventurous kitten to nurse.

"How do I persuade Poly to bring her kittens into the house? I don't know anything about cats."

"Does your aunt have a basket you could use?" Reynolds asked. "If you make it nice and comfy and show it to Poly, she'll get the message and put her kittens into it."

"A basket… I'm sure I can rustle one up."

Ten minutes later, Poly and her kittens were back indoors, snuggling in their basket beside the fire.

"Thanks for your help, Sergeant."

He grinned at me. "All in the line of duty."

"However," I drawled, "you didn't come here to rescue kittens. Did you get my email?"

"I did, and I have a few follow-up questions."

"Hmm," I said. "Want to ask them over coffee?"

"Sounds like a plan."

We went into Noreen's cozy kitchen, and I fixed an espresso for him and a regular coffee for me. When we were seated at the table, I offered him a muffin.

"No thanks. I've just had breakfast." He cleared his throat and slipped a pen and notebook from his shirt pocket.

"So, shoot," I said. "What did you want to ask me?"

"I'm interested in your aunt's neighbor, Paddy Driscoll. Of all the people who were at the Movie Club meeting the night of the murder, he and your aunt appear to have the strongest motives for wanting Sandra dead."

"That's assuming we know all there is to know about the others," I pointed out. "If Sandra was squeezing money out of my aunt, she may have been blackmailing others."

"And given that their blind items remained unpublished, we have no idea who they might be." Reynolds took a sip of his espresso, his brow furrowed. "So far, everyone I've spoken to about Driscoll describes him as cantankerous, and fall silent when asked if he's ever displayed violent tendencies. You're not from around here and don't have the same ties. What's your opinion of Driscoll?"

I laughed. "I've only met him a couple of times. On the first occasion, he aimed a shotgun at me."

"He did what?" Reynolds's eyebrows formed twin Vs. "You know that's illegal in Ireland, right?"

I blinked. "It is? But I was trespassing on his land."

Reynolds shook his head and scribbled a note in his notebook. "That makes no difference. He's not allowed to aim a firearm at a person unless he's being attacked."

"I didn't mean to get him into trouble," I said quickly. "I didn't take him seriously. From what I could tell, Paddy Driscoll is all talk and no action."

"Do you want to file a report?" Reynolds looked me straight in the eye. "You're entitled to."

"No, of course not. Like I said, he didn't hurt me, and my aunt's dog was bothering his sheep."

At that moment, Reynolds's phone vibrated. He glanced at the display and frowned. "Sorry, but I have to take this." He pressed the phone to his ear. "Reynolds. Mmm-hmm. Okay. Sit tight. I'll be right over."

"Gotta go?" I asked as he got to his feet.

He grimaced. "Yeah. Something's come up."

"Something to do with the case?"

"I'm not at liberty to say," he said with a laugh, and drained his espresso cup. "Thanks for the coffee."

"Thanks for the use of your long arms," I returned, standing up to shake his hand. His grip was warm and firm and sent a shiver of awareness down my spine.

"I hope Poly and her kittens are okay," he said on the doorstep.

"Thanks to you, I'm sure they'll be fine. Have a good day, Sergeant."

He grinned. "You, too, Ms. Doyle."

After Liam Reynolds had left, I checked on Poly and the kittens. They were curled up in their basket, snoozing. I stifled a yawn and surveyed the cottage. I needed to finish tidying, but I'd make another coffee first.

I'd just switched on the coffee machine when the doorbell rang. I frowned. Had Reynolds forgotten something? Who would call over this time of day on a weekday? Maybe Paddy Driscoll wanted to yell at me about Bran.

I opened the door and sucked in a breath. Melanie Greer stood on the doorstep, her face pale and drawn.

"Hey," I said. "What do you want?"

"I'm not here about your aunt," she said, her tone clipped. "At least not directly. Can I come in? It's freezing out here." As if to prove her point, she tightened the belt of her cashmere coat.

"Okay." I stood back, and she stepped inside.

Melanie's gaze swept over the cottage and her lip curled. "How quaint."

"We can't all live in a twelve-room mansion," I said dryly.

Melanie sniffed the air. "Do I smell coffee?"

I sighed. Looked like I wouldn't be getting her to leave in a hurry. "Yeah. I just made a pot. Do you want some?"

"Yes, please. Black, no sugar." Melanie didn't beat around the bush.

When we were seated at the kitchen table, Roly and two of the other cats checked Melanie out.

"How many cats does your aunt have? I saw more in the living room."

"Eight," I said, deadpan, enjoying her look of horror. "Not counting the kittens. For what it's worth, I had a similar reaction my first night here." I took a sip of my coffee and regarded her over the brim of my mug. "Why are you here, Melanie? I guess it's not to catch up on old times."

Her grip on her mug faltered, and she put the mug back on the table. "No. I don't think we've ever been on chatting terms."

And whose fault is that? I pressed my lips together. "So what brings you here today? Noreen won't be back until this evening."

"I wanted to talk to you," she said, fiddling with her sleeves. "I understand you've taken it upon yourself to make inquiries into my mother's death."

"Sergeant O'Shea didn't exactly inspire confidence. I wanted to protect my aunt."

"O'Shea is an idiot." Melanie leaned forward in her chair, her expression grave. "I wanted to ask you about what you've discovered. O'Shea shared a lot with me, but this new person—Ryan or Reynolds or whatever his name is—isn't as forthcoming."

I struggled to keep a straight face. So Sergeant Reynolds was less inclined to fall for her damsel-in-distress act? My opinion of the man's intelligence rose.

"It seems O'Shea is now backtracking and harking back to the suicide theory," Melanie said. "Much as I loathe the idea of someone murdering Mummy, I know she wouldn't have killed herself."

I rolled my eyes. "Why am I not surprised? O'Shea is panicking and trying to get rid of the police officer from the mainland. He won't want a fellow policeman reporting back to the district superintendent on all the mistakes he's made, not to mention all the working hours he's spent on the golf course."

"As far as I've been able to find out, neither O'Shea nor Reynolds is making headway finding proof that your aunt killed my mother."

"They're not finding anything more than circumstantial evidence against my aunt, because there's nothing to find," I said with a sigh. "Look, Melanie, if you're hoping I have information to share with you, I'm sorry. First, I don't have a clue who killed your mother. And second, I don't trust you."

"Fair enough. You don't have to trust me. All I'm asking is if Sergeant Reynolds has confided in you at all."

Did she seriously think a police officer was going to chat with a civilian about a case? "Uh, no. Why would he?"

Melanie shrugged. "I thought he might, seeing as you used to be in the police."

"Not the Irish police," I reminded her. This

conversation was going around in circles. Why had Melanie come here? She'd made her dislike of me plain.

Melanie twisted the rings on her hands, including an ostentatious engagement ring that must be worth a fortune. She caught the direction of my gaze and gave a bitter laugh. "It's fake, Maggie. We had to sell the original years ago."

I blinked and sucked in a breath. "Your and Paul's money troubles are that bad? I knew you weren't as flush as you'd like people to think, but I didn't think you'd resorted to selling jewelry."

Melanie's jaw tightened. "Thanks to Paul, we've had to sell everything we ever owned that had any value."

In spite of myself, I felt sorry for her. "That's too bad."

"Yeah, well, it is what it is." Melanie adjusted her pashmina, and a muscle in her cheek flexed. "I should never have taken Paul back over and over. I should never have believed him when he said he'd change." Her mouth twisted. "What's that old saying about leopards not changing their spots? Believe it or not, I did you a favor, Maggie. You were lucky Paul didn't follow through on your childish engagement. Instead, I married him, and I've had ten years to regret it."

It wasn't an apology, but it was as close to one as Melanie was ever likely to get. Even if I'd never regard her as a friend, I'd had too much humiliation at Joe's hands to crow at another woman's marital woes. "If you're unhappy, why didn't you leave him years ago?"

"There were the children to consider." Melanie jutted her chin. "Besides, I don't like quitting."

"Getting out of a bad situation isn't quitting," I said gently. "Take it from one who knows."

Her eyes met mine, and we shared a wry smile. "Sounds like neither of us had much luck in the husband department," she said.

"No," I agreed. "What do you plan to do now?"

"Now that Mummy is dead, you mean?" Melanie took a sip of her coffee before answering. "Once probate is over, I'll have the financial freedom to do whatever I want. Assuming Paul doesn't try to squeeze it all out of me."

"Lawyer up, Melanie, and don't let him take advantage of you."

"That's the plan. I have an appointment to see a solicitor on the mainland next week to ensure I keep my money away from Paul. Once that's sorted, I plan to take some time to think about what to do with my future. I don't intend to jump into divorce proceedings, but I will if I have to." She grimaced. "I never should have let Paul and Mummy talk me into resigning from my job at the Whisper Island Medical Centre. I loved working as a nurse, but they didn't feel it was fancy enough for the wife of the future owner of the Whisper Island Hotel. What a joke that turned out to be."

"I didn't know you had a nursing degree," I said, filing the information away for future reference.

"I went to nursing college after my first child was born. That's why there's a five-year gap between Cian and Clodagh." Melanie shoved her coffee cup away and stood. "Thanks for the chat, Maggie. I'm glad we had a chance to clear the air."

I wasn't certain we'd cleared anything. I wasn't even sure why Melanie had sought me out. Had she wanted to apologize to me in her own weird way? Had she wanted to discuss her marriage breakup with a woman who'd just experienced a similar situation? I accompanied Melanie to the door and said goodbye.

After Melanie had driven off, I got back to the cleaning, my mind working overtime. If Melanie felt trapped in her marriage, the money she'd inherit from Sandra was a pretty powerful motive for murder. And as a trained nurse, Melanie would know how much codeine mixed with alcohol would cause a fatal overdose.

But could Melanie bring herself to kill her mother? And to turn the situation on its head, could she be throwing suspicion on Paul in order to protect herself? With these troubling thoughts, I pulled on my jacket and stepped outside into the snow to go question another potential suspect.

21

I parked in front of The Movie Theater Café and walked to the school. The fresh air and exercise would do me good, and allow me the opportunity to think, which I didn't have when I needed to concentrate on driving. I waved to the Spinsters and Sister Pauline through the café window, and to Joan Sweetman, who was across the street polishing the front window of her gallery. As I walked, I sifted through all the people who had a motive to kill Sandra Walker. The problem with this case was that there were too many suspects, all of whom had had the opportunity to commit the murder. For the first time since I'd left the police academy, I was truly stumped. If I whittled down the list of suspects, I was left with two who stood out in my mind: Paddy Driscoll and Paul Greer.

Paddy Driscoll had stated that he hated Sandra. Perhaps finding the buried chalice was more important to Paddy than he was willing to admit, but why wait years to take his revenge? My mind drifted to Paul, who had the most obvious and pressing motive. With Sandra dead, he no longer needed to worry about his embezzlement coming to light—assuming no one else at the hotel knew and ratted him out. In addition, his wife would inherit money from Sandra—money Paul could claim half of if he filed for divorce.

By the time I reached the school gates, the bitter wind had gotten into my bones. The warmth of the school building was an enticing prospect, even if my reason for being there was less than pleasant.

Julie met me at the entrance. "You sure this is wise, Maggie? I don't like the idea of ambushing Cormac. He's a good guy."

A good guy with a grudge against Sandra.

"I won't ambush him." I caught her dubious expression. "Okay, so I'm aiming for the element of surprise here, but I promise I'll play nice. He was at the Movie Club the night Sandra died, and he's one of the few people I haven't had a chance to talk to yet."

"Sergeant Reynolds was here yesterday," Julie added. "He doesn't look half the fool that O'Shea is. Can't you leave the investigation to him?"

"Maybe Reynolds knows how to do his job, but no one is going to look out for Noreen's interests like we will. And seeing as I mixed the fatal drink, it's in my interests to make sure the real killer is caught."

My cousin sighed. "Come on then. I'll walk you to

Cormac's office." She led me through school corridors that smelled of freshly applied paint. The children were on their lunch break and played outside in the yard or ate their sandwiches on benches.

"Doesn't Tate eat his lunch with the other teachers?"

"Sometimes, but he usually prefers some alone time in his office." She laughed. "Lucky sod. I'd like to be able to close the door to everyone every now and again."

The principal's office was on the second floor, beyond classrooms whose doors were decorated with colorful paintings. Julie knocked on the door, and Tate growled for us to enter. The man greeted us with a scowl. "Don't tell me that blasted guard is back already to ask me more questions."

"It's just me," I said cheerfully.

He stared at me as if he couldn't place me.

"Maggie Doyle from The Movie Theater Café."

"I know who you are, Ms. Doyle. I'm wondering why you're here."

Fabulous. First, Melanie had wanted to slime up to me, and now Cormac Tate was acting like a bear who'd been deprived of its prey.

Julie shot me an I-told-you-so look and backed out of the office. "I'll leave you two to it."

"To what?" Tate asked after my cousin had beaten a hasty retreat.

I smiled at him, hoping to soften his mood. Judging by the thunderous expression on Tate's face, my charm offensive wasn't working. "I'd like to ask you a few questions if you have the time."

"I don't have the time," he snapped. "I have a meeting in twenty minutes."

"Perfect." I dropped into the chair opposite him. "I won't take that long."

Tate grunted. "You're as bossy as your aunt."

"To be fair, Noreen is even bossier."

"I was referring to Philomena, but both sisters are terrors."

"Actually," I said, seizing on this opening, "it's Philomena that I'd like to talk to you about."

Tate's jaw hardened. "Why? What has she said?"

"Nothing. Look, you've probably heard that I've been doing a bit of sleuthing."

He gave a snort of laughter. "'Poking your nose into other people's business' is a more accurate description."

"Noreen didn't kill Sandra Walker, but someone did. And I have a feeling her murder is connected to the blind item gossip column."

Tate's shoulders hunched. "What about it?"

"I'm trying to match items with their subjects." I waited a moment to let him digest this information and then plunged on. "I heard you were featured in the column."

"You heard wrong. I was never mentioned in the column."

"Because Sandra offered to keep the item out of the paper in return for money?"

Tate slammed his fist down on the table, making the stack of papers jump. "Who told you that? Are you sure it wasn't Philomena?"

So my guess had been correct—Tate had been on Sandra's blackmail list. "Philomena was the soul of discretion. How is she mixed up in all of this?"

Tate's scowl deepened. "I wish you'd go away and leave me in peace."

"And I wish the police would get their act together and drop the charges against my aunt." I leaned forward in my seat. "If Sandra was blackmailing you, Mr. Tate, you weren't her only victim."

The man stared at his shaking hands and sighed. "I didn't think I was. That cow had a knack for finding people's weaknesses."

"What did she discover about you? And how was it linked to my aunt?"

"You're determined to keep digging, aren't you?"

"Yes," I said firmly. "So you might as well give in gracefully. I'll keep looking for answers, but I promise I won't repeat what you tell me to anyone unless it's relevant for helping clear Noreen's name."

"Fine," he muttered. "Last academic year, I was absent for three months. The official story was that I was in the hospital. This was true, but what we didn't add was that the hospital was a rehabilitation clinic."

"I see. What were you in for?"

Cormac Tate stared out the window, a bleak expression on his face. "Alcohol and prescription pills."

I released a sharp breath. If Tate had connections to black market drugs, he might have known the effects of Solpodol. "I guess that information wouldn't go down well with the parents."

"Nor with the school board." The man caught my expression. "Oh, the board knows. There was no avoiding telling them. They were surprisingly understanding and gave me the time I needed for treatment. I returned to my position as principal on the condition that I not relapse. I struck a deal with them. I promised I'd keep seeing a therapist after my release from the clinic and attend regular meetings. And, of course, I wouldn't relapse." He grimaced. "That's the part Sandra discovered. She found me drunk in a ditch one night last June." He shook his head. "Of all the people on Whisper Island to find me in that state, it had to be her."

"And she used this information to blackmail you," I finished.

"Yes. If I didn't pay her a regular monthly sum, she said she'd publish a blind item in her gossip column that everyone would know was about me." A spasm of anguish passed over his face. "I couldn't bear the thought of the kids or their parents knowing. They'd lose all respect for me."

Sandra had been a piece of work. Despite my belief in justice for all, I couldn't fault the islanders who regarded Sandra's demise as good riddance. I focused on Tate. "How does Philomena enter the picture?"

"Your aunt does a lot of volunteer work with crisis call centers. Seeing as we don't have a huge population on the island, Dr. Reilly asked her if she'd act as my sponsor."

"So *that's* why you two have been sneaking around at night."

He raised an eyebrow. "You knew about that?"

"I, uh, might have followed her."

This elicited a hint of a smile from the moody principal. "Is that so? Does our new police sergeant know you've been interrogating his suspects?"

"Oh, yeah. I'm sure Sergeant O'Shea wasted no time informing him," I said breezily. "And why shouldn't I ask a few questions? There's no harm in having a chat with my aunt's friends."

"I'm not sure Sergeant Reynolds would agree." Cormac Tate jerked a thumb at the window. "And speaking of the devil, he's walking across the schoolyard right now. You might want to make yourself scarce."

I leaped to my feet. "Thanks for talking to me, Mr. Tate. Enjoy the rest of your…what is that?" I recoiled at the sight of the hairy-looking object on his plate.

He looked bemused by my horror. "Scotch eggs. Hard boiled eggs wrapped in sausage meat and coated with breadcrumbs. You should try one sometime. For now, I suggest you run."

My efforts at evading Sergeant Reynolds were futile. I tried to dart into a classroom but bashed my shoulder against the locked door. Apparently, even small island schools kept their computer rooms under lock and key. Who knew? Rubbing my sore arm, I sidled along the corridor, hoping to find an unlocked room I could hide in until the danger had passed.

And then I careened straight into the very muscular chest of Sergeant Reynolds.

"Whoa," he said, his bright blue eyes merry and teasing. "We've got to stop bumping into one another like this."

"Ha-ha," I said, trying to block the effect he was having on my hormones. "Very funny."

He cocked his head to the side and examined me with that half-teasing, half-serious expression that was difficult to read. "Where are you off to in such a hurry?"

Once again, I disgraced myself by blushing like a preteen. "I...have to be somewhere."

"So do I," he said lightly. "Only I suspect you've beaten me to my destination."

"What are you talking about?" I tried to look innocent, but my warm cheeks weren't helping my case.

"Come on, Ms. Doyle. Confess. You've been interrogating Cormac Tate." He shook his head, but the smile didn't falter. "You've got to stop trying to do the police's job."

I batted my eyelashes at him and ended up

blinking wildly, certain my eyelashes were clumped together with mascara. Reynolds stood before me, wearing a bone-melting grin. Just my luck to get saddled with a cute policeman to interfere with my investigation. "The last policeman wasn't fit for the job," I said with dignity. "I was the one who figured out Sandra had been poisoned. O'Shea didn't even bother to save her cocktail glass."

"So I gathered," Reynolds said dryly. "But I'm here now, and the investigation into Sandra Walker's death is *my* case. Thank you for the notes you emailed me, but I'd appreciate it if you'd leave the police work to me from now on."

I put my hands on my hips and glared at him. "Are you making an effort to find the real killer, or just gathering fluff evidence for the prosecution?"

The amusement in his eyes faded. "I realize this must be hard for you, Ms. Doyle, but you're not doing your aunt any favors by questioning my witnesses."

"*Your* witnesses? You've only started talking to them. I've been gathering information for days."

"Like I said in the café, if you have anything relevant to tell me, please do. I'm not the enemy here. I want to see justice served, but I can't allow you to interfere with my case. You have no jurisdiction in Ireland and, from what I hear, none in the U.S. anymore either."

My chest swelled in indignation. "I want justice for my aunt and, believe it or not, for Sandra Walker, even if she wasn't a nice person."

"I want the same thing. And it's my job to make sure they get justice."

When he moved past me, I registered how close together we'd been standing since I'd crashed into him. I exhaled in a whoosh. This man unnerved me, and I didn't like the sensation.

Reynolds turned back to face me before he knocked on Cormac Tate's door. "See you around, Ms. Doyle. I have a feeling we'll run into each other again before long." He grinned. "And give that little kitten I took out of the drain a kiss from me."

"I will." It was unreasonable to be jealous of a kitten. I was off men, after all—especially the ones I was attracted to. Next time I dated, I was getting someone I trusted to vet men on my behalf.

Thoroughly flustered, I marched out of the school and let the wind blow me back to Main Street. When I reached Noreen's car, Lenny had parked his van behind it and was waiting for me on the pavement. He paced back and forth in a restless dance, his every movement radiating distress.

"Hey, Lenny. What's up?"

"At last." He jerked to attention when he saw me. "I thought you'd never get back, and you weren't answering your phone."

"I had it with me." I slipped my phone from my jacket pocket. Four missed calls, all from Lenny. I frowned. In my state of agitation after my encounter with Sergeant Hottie, I must have forgotten to check my messages. "What's wrong?"

Lenny darted a look up and down the street and dropped his voice to a whisper. "Remember I gave Sandra a lift the night she was murdered?"

"Yeah. She wanted you to install a new RAM chip on her laptop, and insisted you collected it that night."

"Right. And when she got it from her home office, I put it in the back of my van, on top of all the rest of my gear. I always have a ton of cables, computer parts, and accessories in there, but I had more stuff than usual that night because I was in charge of setting up the film equipment. I had to pack the car, unpack it outside the café, and then pack it up again at the end of the night."

I nodded. "Yeah. What happened?"

"A couple of laptops were among the stuff in the back of my van. I'd picked them out of the recycling bin at my parents' shop and I wanted to salvage parts. Between one thing and another, I hadn't gotten around to working on them until today."

My heart rate kicked up a notch. "Go on."

"Well, when I started working on one of the laptops, I realized it still worked. I had a bad feeling about it, so I tried out a few passwords." He turned pale. "Maggie, the laptop belonged to Sandra. When I got the laptop out of my van the night she died, I grabbed the one on top. Sandra's was the same make and model as the one I wanted to take apart, and I guess they got mixed up in the confusion of me packing and unpacking the van."

I exhaled in a whoosh. "Wow. Did—?" I clamped

down on the rest of my question when the café door opened. Joan and Sister Pauline stepped onto the pavement, Joan clutching her daily take-out bag and the nun hauling an enormous bag from which an assortment of knitting needles protruded.

"Hello." Sister Pauline looked at Lenny and me in turn. "Anything the matter? You two look worried."

"Has there been news from that new police officer who's taken over the case?" Joan asked, wide-eyed. "I hear he's less of a fool than his predecessor."

"We're fine." I forced a smile. "No news on the case, I'm afraid."

Sister Pauline tut-tutted. "A dreadful business. I can't believe poor Noreen was dragged into this."

Much as I liked both Joan and Sister Pauline, I wasn't in the mood for a chat. I forced a smile. "I'm sure it'll all turn out fine in the end. Listen, I have to go. Maybe I'll see you in the café tomorrow."

"I told Noreen I'd help her knead bread," Sister Pauline said. "I love making soda bread."

"See you soon," Joan said, and urged the nun to cross the road.

When they were out of earshot, I turned to Lenny. "Did you manage to access Sandra's files?"

He gave me a look of scorn. "What do you take me for? Of course I did. That's why I'm here." He blew out a breath. "Maggie, there's something you need to see."

22

My heart pounded against my ribs. "What did you find?"

"Not here," Lenny said. "Meet me at your aunt's cottage. We'll have privacy there."

For loud-mouthed Lenny to show discretion, the situation must be severe. "Okay. I'll drive there right away."

"I'll be right behind you."

I got into the car and started the engine. When I pulled out into the traffic, Joan and Sister Pauline were outside the gallery, staring after me. Both wore concerned expressions. I forced a smile and waved at them. I had no idea how long Lenny had been waiting for me and pacing in front of his van, but he'd aroused their curiosity and presumably the interest of the people currently inside the café. And given that everyone on Whisper Island knew I was conducting an unofficial investigation into Sandra Walker's murder, ten to one they'd guessed that Lenny had discovered something of importance.

When I pulled up in front of Aunt Noreen's cottage, Lenny was already there, clutching the laptop in his arms and bouncing on the spot. He must have put the pedal to the metal to beat me here. Bran danced around his legs, thrilled to have company.

"Easy, tiger." I inserted the key into the lock. "You're like a man walking over hot coals."

"Are you referring to me or the dog?"

When I opened the door, Bran shot inside. Lenny tumbled after him. "You're dancing on the spot like a toddler in need of a pee," I said. "Deep breaths, Lenny."

"This is important, Maggie. And I don't know what to do with this information."

When I led him into the kitchen, Bran was waiting for us, panting. I grabbed a pair of disposable rubber gloves that my aunt kept above the sink.

"What are those for?" Lenny asked, taking a seat at the table.

I quirked an eyebrow. "You have an excuse for having your fingerprints all over the laptop. I don't."

I put the gloves on and took the seat next to Lenny's. He fired up the laptop and clicked on a folder labeled *Taxes*.

"It was the only folder on Sandra's laptop that was password protected, so I got suspicious. I know I should have left it the moment I realized whose laptop I was looking at, but I couldn't help myself."

"I presume Sandra doesn't have her tax info in that folder," I said dryly.

Lenny shook his head. "She's got a bunch of unpublished blind items in there. Much worse than any that got published. Although no names are mentioned, it's easy to guess who she's referring to. I've only had time to read through a few, but that was enough to set off alarm bells."

I scanned the screen and whistled. "Twenty-four unpublished blind items hidden in a password-protected folder. That could mean twenty-four potential blackmail victims."

"Exactly." Lenny's fingers flew over the keyboard. "There's a bunch of blinds in here that could drive a person to murder. I didn't have time to take notes. I figured you'd take care of that."

My lips twitched. "Seeing how much I love my notebooks and pens?"

"Right." Lenny frowned at the screen. "There's all sorts of crazy stuff in here. Everything from a married man having a gay affair to a bigamist who cheated her late husband's family out of their rightful inheritance."

"Sounds like material for a daytime soap," I said. "Which one alarmed you?"

"This one." Lenny clicked on a file. "It's about a nun who has a secret son."

"Let me read it."

Lenny angled the screen in my direction, and I scanned the blind. *Which nun has a secret son?*

My mind instantly turned to the published blind item concerning a nun stealing from the church collection box, and then back to a conversation I'd had with Aunt Noreen when I'd first arrived on the island. What was it she'd said about Sister Pauline? Something about her having had a life before she became a nun... Could that life have included a baby?

I drummed a restless rhythm on the kitchen table. I needed to think, and I didn't want to mention my suspicions to Lenny until I was sure. With the low number of nuns living on the island, he'd probably drawn his own conclusions. "We should bring the laptop to the police."

"Yeah. But not before I make a backup copy of that folder. Actually, I'll make two." Lenny withdrew two portable flash drives from his pocket and inserted them into the laptop. "I'll leave a backup copy with you to work through, and then I'll take the laptop straight to the station. When I get home, I'll read through the rest of the items. Between the two of us, we should be able to figure out who they're referring to." A few minutes later, the backup copies were complete, and Lenny packed up the laptop. "I'd better get moving. I feel more comfortable handing the laptop over to Sergeant Reynolds than I would have if Sergeant O'Shea was still in charge of the case."

"I agree. Let me know if there's any news."

"Will do. And ditto if you discover anything interesting among those blind items."

Lenny scratched Bran behind the ears and ambled out to his van. Unburdening himself to me had restored some of his nonchalance and good humor. I wished our encounter had done the same for me.

Lenny had just gotten into his van and driven off when another vehicle pulled into the yard, triggering a series of enthusiastic barks from Bran. I bit back a curse and shoved the flash drive into my pocket. I'd wanted time to look through the blind items, but they'd have to wait.

My stomach lurched when I saw who got out of the car.

"Hello, Maggie." Sister Pauline wore a sunny smile on her craggy face, but it failed to warm the cold horror seeping through my bones.

"Uh, hi," I said and removed my hand from my pocket.

"I was wondering if I could have a word with you." The nun's serene smile was belied by a hard glint in her eyes. "And I wanted it to be away from the prying eyes at the café. People do love to gossip."

"Yes, they do." I hovered on the doorstep, running through my options. "I guess you'd better come in."

Under other circumstances, I'd be more hospitable, but I wanted Sister Pauline out of the house so I could look through the blind items on Lenny's flash drive. And given that I was pretty sure the nun was the subject of one of those items, the situation was awkward to say the least.

"Tea?" I asked on autopilot when we reached the kitchen.

"I'd love a cup," she said, "but, ah, why don't you let me make it? I'm better with tea leaves than you are."

I released a slow breath. "Sure. You know where everything is."

Sister Pauline hummed as she prepared the pot of tea, seemingly at ease in her surroundings. I glanced at the kitchen clock. The seconds ticked by at an achingly slow pace while the flash drive burned a hole in my pocket. Bran, oblivious to my stress, lay down at my feet to take a snooze. Some guard dog he'd make.

When the tea was ready, Sister Pauline placed two cups and saucers on the table and poured one for me. An icy sensation spread over my limbs. "No," I said with more force than I'd intended, causing her eyes to widen in alarm. "I, uh, prefer coffee."

"Nonsense. Green tea is good for you, especially when you've been under stress. Drink up."

Was I crazy to wonder if the tea was poisoned? Until Lenny had discovered the unpublished blind about the nun with a secret son, it had never occurred to me to regard Sister Pauline as a serious suspect.

Her eyes followed my every movement as I held the cup to my lips. I pretended to take a sip and swallow, then replaced the cup on the table. "What did you want to talk to me about, Sister Pauline?"

"About Sandra." The nun's grip on her teacup wobbled, and she replaced it on the saucer with a clatter. "I think I need to talk to the guards, but I'd like your opinion first."

I swallowed hard. "If there's something you think the police need to know, you should tell them."

"The question is what to tell them. I don't feel comfortable talking about this topic, and I'm not sure how much I can leave out."

"Go on," I urged. "What do you know that's relevant to Sandra's murder?"

"Sandra was a blackmailer." The words tumbled out in a rush, and Sister Pauline appeared shocked by her own admission. She rallied and continued with her story. "For five months before she died, Sandra blackmailed me."

"Sandra was so desperate for money that she blackmailed someone who doesn't have any? That doesn't make sense."

Sister Pauline's smile was tinged with bitterness. "There are more ways to blackmail a person than squeezing money out of them, Maggie. I paid in information. Sandra knew that people on the island confide in me, and that I hear things as part of my work at the church. In exchange for gossip she could use in her columns—or, I suspect, to blackmail people —Sandra agreed to keep silent about my theft."

My grip on the teacup tightened. "What a horrible woman. All the things I keep hearing about her make it hard to remind myself that she deserves justice."

"It's a terrible thing to say about a dead woman,

but she was evil." Sister Pauline bowed her head. "I was a fool to give in to her demands. If I'd kept my wits about me, I should have gone straight to Father Nolan and confessed everything. He's a good man. He'd have understood and helped me. Instead, I let my shame blind me into agreeing to Sandra's terms. And by doing that, I've betrayed parishioners who trust me."

"What information did you give Sandra?"

Sister Pauline's mouth formed a hard line. "I was careful to give her nothing about anyone who deserved privacy. I can't say I feel guilty about mentioning Paul Greer's overheard confession to Father Nolan. I never liked the boy, and he's grown into a weak and spineless man. Discovering he's a cheater and a thief comes as no surprise. Other pieces of gossip were mostly harmless, but Sandra had a knack for twisting the truth to make it appear worse."

"What did she know about you that enabled her to blackmail you?" I asked gently. "It must have been serious for you to agree to pass on gossip."

Sister Pauline fidgeted with her hands before placing them on her lap. "When I was a teenager, I had an affair with the married farmer who lived next door to my parents. I fell pregnant, and my family pressured me to give the baby up for adoption. I didn't want to, but the situation was hopeless. I was fifteen with no money and nowhere to go. I had no choice." Tears filled her eyes. "They didn't even let me hold him after he was born. My baby was whisked out of the room before I'd had a chance to look at him properly."

My heart ached for her. I reached across the table and squeezed her arm. "That's awful. I'm so sorry you had to go through that."

She nodded and dabbed at her eyes with a clean tissue. "It was the Sixties. That's what they did in those days."

"How did Sandra find out?"

"About a year ago, my son got in touch with me and wanted to meet up. I was delighted, of course, and had visions of grandchildren and all the things I'd never dreamed would happen to me." She grimaced. "Reality was rather different. My son, Jimmy, is a drug addict. He's had a rough life and is currently unemployed and begging on the streets of Galway."

My gut twisted and my fist itched to punch Sandra for using this information to hurt Sister Pauline. "I...don't know what to say."

"Neither did I. I've tried to help him, but my resources are limited. When he called me one day and said he owed money he didn't have to a drug dealer, I panicked." She covered her face with her hands. "In desperation, I stole cash from the church collection box and sent it to Jimmy."

That explained the published blind item about the nun who stole from the church collection box.

Sister Pauline sighed. "In hindsight, I'm not even convinced Jimmy's desperate plea was genuine. I suspect he wanted money to buy drugs."

"How did Sandra discover your secret?"

"She's the church treasurer, and she'd seen Mrs. Greer put a fifty-euro note into the collection box the Sunday I stole the money. Sandra put two and two together and realized that either me or Sister Juliette must have taken the money. When she confronted me, I cracked, and she'd soon wormed the whole sordid tale out of me. Sandra said if I told her everything, she wouldn't tell anyone about the stolen money. What she failed to add was that she'd use the information to blackmail me." Sister Pauline's eyes rested on my untouched tea. "Drink up. It'll do you good."

The uneasy sensation I'd experienced earlier returned. Sister Pauline's story was plausible. Frighteningly so. Had it driven her to kill Sandra? I picked up my cup and went through the motions of drinking it without allowing the tea to touch my tongue. "Sister Pauline—" I began, but she cut me off.

"I know what you're about to ask me, Maggie, and the answer is no. I often fantasized about strangling Sandra Walker, but I didn't poison her. I'd never have acted on my evil thoughts, and I certainly wouldn't have framed my best friend."

I wanted to believe her, but I knew she'd need to give a statement to the police and allow them to investigate.

"What do you think I should do?" Sister Pauline twisted her hands in her lap. "I don't want this story getting out, and Sergeant O'Shea has a tendency to be loose-lipped when he's with his golfing cronies."

"I have reason to know that your story will come out, Sister Pauline, and probably today." The moment the police looked at Sandra's blind items folder on the laptop Lenny was on his way to hand in, they'd follow the breadcrumb trail to Sister Pauline. "You need to talk to Sergeant Reynolds. If he's not at the station, insist on waiting until he arrives."

Sister Pauline squeezed her eyes shut. "I don't think I can face going there alone."

"I'll come with you." I stood and urged her to do the same. "We'll leave your car here and take mine."

As if on cue, Bran opened one lazy eye, assessed the situation, and realized I was going out. He raced to the door and began to whine. I stared into his large doggy eyes and exchanged an amused glance with Sister Pauline.

"When he gets like this," she said, "Noreen always takes him with her. Otherwise, he howls for hours."

"I guess it can't hurt to bring him along for the ride." I took Bran's leash off its hook and shook a finger at him. "If you behave, I'll take you for a walk in Smuggler's Cove when I'm finished at the police station. Do we have a deal?"

Bran's only response was a woof.

23

On the drive to the station, Sister Pauline was subdued, and I was deep in thought. If I ruled out Sister Pauline as the killer, I needed to sift through the other unpublished blind items and match them up to their subjects. Despite the discovery of Sandra's laptop and its secret file, Paddy Driscoll and Paul Greer were still at the top of my list of suspects. With a bit of luck, I—or Sergeant Reynolds, I conceded grudgingly—would link them to one of the unpublished blind items.

I slowed the car as we drove the winding cliff road that led past Carraig Harbour. A couple of boats dotted the harbor. In the winter, few boats docked there, and this time of day, the fishing boats were already out for the day. I scanned the water and then peered down at the pier.

And then I hit the brakes. "Whoa." My heart thumped in my chest. Someone—a woman, I thought

—was loading what looked to be a lot of luggage onto a small yacht.

"What's wrong?" Sister Pauline asked.

"Hang on a sec. I need to check something." I pulled the car over to the side of the road and retrieved my binoculars from the glove compartment.

I leaped out of the car and ran to the edge of the cliff. I peered through the binoculars. Through the powerful lenses, Joan Sweetman was clearly visible. I sucked in a breath. She threw half-closed suitcases haphazardly onto the deck of her boat. I'd have thought Joan was the type to pack everything with tissue paper. My pulse pounded.

Sister Pauline joined me at the edge of the cliff, Bran panting at her side. "Is something the matter, Maggie?" Before I could answer, the nun gasped. "Goodness, that's Joan's yacht in the harbor. What's she doing with all those suitcases?"

"That's what I want to know," I said grimly. "Did she mention she was going on a trip when you spoke to her earlier? A trip that would require a lot of suitcases?"

The nun frowned. "Why, no. She's due to call around to the convent for dinner and a game of bridge this evening. We were making the arrangement when we passed you and Lenny outside the café."

And what had Lenny been clutching outside the café? Sandra Walker's laptop. Joan must have recognized it and realized that the broken laptop that had been sent to forensics wasn't Sandra's. *Oh, heck.*

I pulled my phone from my pocket and dialed the number for the Whisper Island Garda Station. Sergeant O'Shea answered on the second ring. "This is Maggie Doyle. Could you put me through to Sergeant Reynolds?"

"Reynolds is busy at the moment," O'Shea said, clearly loving having the opportunity to yank my chain. "Can I take a message?"

"I need to speak to him now."

"And I told you he's busy. Despite what you may think, Ms. Doyle, you're not a member of the Irish police force or affiliated with this station in any way."

I bit back a scream. "Okay, pass on a message. Tell him to look for a gossip column relating to Joan Sweetman on the laptop Lenny handed in, or will hand in any second. This is urgent."

Sergeant O'Shea chuckled. "Sure it is. Anything you and your alien-obsessed stoner pal have to say is bound to be of the utmost importance."

"I'm serious, O'Shea. Get off your butt and tell him."

This proved to be an unfortunate choice of words, but it was too late to retract them. "Stick to burning scones and stop sticking your nose into police business," the man snapped before hanging up on me.

I swore and punched in Lenny's number.

"Hey, Maggie. What's up? Did you find anything in Sandra's files?"

"Are you anywhere near the station?"

"Yeah. I just left."

"I need you to go back and tell Sergeant Reynolds to get to Carraig Harbour right away."

"Maggie, Reynolds isn't there. I had to leave the laptop with O'Shea."

"I thought we agreed you'd wait for Reynolds," I exclaimed.

"I know, but according to O'Shea, Reynolds left the island earlier today. O'Shea challenged me about hanging on to the laptop, and I gave in and let him have it. When I left, he was performing a two-fingered dance across the keyboard."

I snorted. "O'Shea was lying. I ran into Reynolds up at the school just before I met you." I looked through the binoculars again. Joan was still frantically getting her boat ready to sail. "Listen up. Joan Sweetman is loading a ton of her belongings onto a yacht. Way more than anyone needs for a vacation."

"Joan can't be going away," Lenny said. "She told my mother she'd meet her for lunch tomorrow."

"And she made an arrangement with Sister Pauline for this evening. Something spooked her, and I think it was seeing you and me with Sandra's laptop."

"Are you serious? Dude, I can't see Joan killing anyone."

"Well, someone killed Sandra, and Joan's behavior is atypical. Lenny, I don't have access to a computer at the moment. I need you to look through the blind items and see if one could refer to Joan."

"Sure. I'll pull the van over and use my laptop. It's

here in the back somewhere. Wasn't there a published blind that everyone thought referred to Joan and one of her stepsons?"

"Yes. Joan told me about it. I'm wondering if there was another more serious one that was never published and that Joan failed to mention."

"Okay. I've got the laptop open and I'm looking."

"Call me when you find something. I'm going to stay here and keep an eye on Joan."

"Will do."

I disconnected and Sister Pauline and I continued to observe Joan's progress. She'd almost finished loading her stuff onto the yacht and was moving at a frenzied pace that was at odds with the cool and collected woman I knew. *Cripes.* I couldn't wait around for Lenny to get back to me. I'd have to go down to the harbor and try to delay Joan. I swallowed hard. The fastest way to get there was via the rickety elevator I'd deftly avoided on the night of my arrival. I squeezed my eyes shut and breathed deeply. I hated enclosed spaces.

My phone buzzed, ending my contemplation of elevators. I held it to my ear. "Lenny?"

"I've hit the jackpot," he said breathlessly. "Remember the unpublished blind item I mentioned about a bigamist? I went back and reread it. The blind is about a wealthy widow who inherited the bulk of her late husband's fortune. His children from his first marriage received a sizable chunk, but the widow got the lion's share of the money. What no one knows is that she's a bigamist."

My heart rate kicked up a notch. "Go on."

"Apparently, the widow married another man when she was very young and living in England. When her husband ran off with another woman, she moved back to Ireland. Even if she'd tracked down her husband, divorce wasn't recognized in Ireland at the time. When she met the wealthy islander, she edited her previous marriage from her life story and married him."

"And if her bigamy came out, the money and property she'd inherited would be forfeited and given to the man's sons," I finished.

"Exactly."

"Okay. I need you to call the police. Not that lazy lump O'Shea, but a national number. Call the coast guard and whoever else catches criminals in Ireland. I gotta go."

I disconnected the call and started to run.

24

I reached the elevator with Sister Pauline and Bran puffing behind me. "I only heard your half of the conversation with Lenny," the nun said as the elevator doors slid shut, "but you're under the impression that Joan killed Sandra?"

My teeth chattered from being inside a moving metal coffin and I struggled to breathe—the first signs of an impending panic attack. I squeezed my eyes shut and stuttered out the story as I knew it.

"Joan a bigamist? I can't believe it." Sister Pauline sounded horrified. "Mind you, the will was a scandal at the time. Niall Sweetman left Joan almost everything he had. Nick and James received very little money, but Joan promised them she'd leave them everything she had in her will, seeing as she and Niall had no children of their own."

"I suspect this news will cause more of a scandal,"

I said dryly. "The money wasn't Joan's to inherit if she'd never been legally married to Niall."

When the elevator doors opened, Joan Sweetman's yacht was heading out to sea.

"Wait," I yelled and sprinted down the pier. "Come back."

Joan turned around and saw me.

I plastered on a smile. "Are you on your way to the mainland?" I yelled. "Could you give us a ride?"

Sister Pauline and Bran joined me on the edge of the pier, and the nun waved to Joan.

Joan's expression froze as she took in the party waiting for her on the pier. She returned her attention to the controls. Suddenly, her boat sped up.

I swore under my breath. Joan Sweetman was no fool. I whipped my head around and scanned the pier. All the fishermen were out for the day, and the ferry ticket office was empty.

I clenched my fists. "I have to go after her. I'm not letting her get away with murder."

"Look," Sister Pauline cried. "Try that boat over there."

A small speedboat was docked farther down the pier. My legs were in motion before I could formulate a response. I held my phone to my ear as I ran and hit Lenny's number again. It was busy.

"There's no time to call anyone else," Sister Pauline said when we reached the speedboat. "Can you hot-wire that boat?"

"I can, but I can't do anything else with it once

I've got the engine going," I said gloomily. "I avoid boats as well as elevators."

"If you can hot-wire it, I can operate it." Sister Pauline laughed at my gaping jaw. "My father and brothers were all fishermen. I grew up around boats."

I nodded. "It's a deal, but I gotta be honest here. I don't have a plan. I have no gun and no authority. Are you sure you want to get involved?"

"I'm already involved. Noreen is my best friend. Besides, Joan is an excellent sailor. If we don't try to catch up with her now, there's no guarantee the police or the coast guard will get to her before she reaches the mainland."

I leaped onto the deck of the boat, and Sister Pauline and Bran followed suit. "I'm hoping the police on the mainland will catch her if we can't."

"If they find her in time." Sister Pauline's expression was grim. "Joan keeps a private plane at an airport on the mainland. If I were her, that's where I'd head."

I took out my Swiss Army knife and I was in the process of hot-wiring the boat when an outraged roar made me leap in my skin.

"What are you doing to my boat?" demanded a very deep and very familiar voice. *Oh, heck.* I jerked around to see Sergeant Hottie jump into the boat, wearing a thunderous expression.

"Oops," I said cheerfully. "Is it your boat I'm stealing?"

His eyes narrowed and he folded his arms across his chest. "Yes, Ms. Doyle. This is my boat."

"Excellent." I beamed at him. "Start the engine and let's get moving. We have a murderer to catch."

To his credit, Sergeant Reynolds didn't waste time arguing with me. I'd love to say it was my winning smile and credible demeanor that convinced him to play along, but I suspect it was the presence of the nun who backed up my story.

When he'd powered up the boat and we were zooming out to sea, he turned to me. "Run this by me again. Why do you think Joan Sweetman is the killer?"

I gave him the *Reader's Digest* condensed version of the mixed-up laptops story and focused on the unpublished blind item featuring the bigamist widow. "So if I'm right," I finished, "Joan's marriage to Niall Sweetman was never valid, which means she cheated Niall's sons out of their rightful inheritance."

"Wow," Reynolds said, gripping the wheel. "Your story's plausible, but I'll need to have it confirmed before I can make the charges stick."

"Sure, but the fact that Joan is clearly making a getaway should give you enough circumstantial evidence to haul her in for questioning and buy you some time until you can get the story confirmed."

"You telling me how to do my job again?" The

twinkle in his eye softened Reynolds's serious expression.

"No… Well," I conceded, "kinda. I guess old habits die hard."

"You have a nose for ferreting out the truth. Why'd you leave the San Francisco PD?"

"That's a story for another day, preferably accompanied by a good bottle of red."

His laugh sent my pulse racing. "Consider it a date."

"Gladly. But first, we have to make sure justice is served."

"Speaking of law enforcement—" Reynolds looked me up and down and frowned, "—you're not wearing a life vest."

I gestured to his bare uniform. "Neither are you."

"You didn't give me much time to prepare for launch," he said dryly. "Put on a vest and get me one, too. You'll find spares under the seats. Sister Pauline had the good sense to dig one out for herself and hook Bran up with a makeshift doggie version."

"Which he's currently eating," I said dryly, eyeing the happy dog who was making a major mess out of his life vest. I went to the side of the boat and lifted a seat. Sure enough, it contained two orange monstrosities. I shrugged into one and handed the other to Reynolds. "I don't suppose you have a spare firearm for me?"

He threw back his head and laughed. "Ah, you're an innocent at heart, Maggie Doyle. The majority of police officers in Ireland don't carry weapons. I don't have a gun for either of us."

"Well, that's just great." I glared at him in disgust. "I'm chasing a murderer with a gunless cop, a nun, and a dog whose main occupation is eating everything in sight. This is going to end well."

As if on cue, a bullet bounced off the side of the boat.

"Whoa. That's not good."

Reynolds swore. "Hit the deck, all of you."

I hurled myself on top of Bran, and Sister Pauline dropped to the deck like a pro. An instant later, a hail of bullets assailed the boat. "Well," I quipped, "sounds like Joan didn't get the Irish firearms memo."

"She's also on a boat with better cover than we are," Reynolds said grimly. "We're sitting ducks here. Stay down, Sister Pauline. Maggie, can you crawl over to the seats and check if we have anything we can use as a weapon? I'll put a call through to the coast guard. Lenny's probably already reached them, but I want to be sure they know Joan has a gun."

I crawled over to the seats at the side of the speed-boat and lifted them up. I rooted through the contents of the storage boxes beneath, finally striking gold. "Wild," I said, delighted with my find. "I have a harpoon."

"Sorry to disappoint you, but that's a speargun. It functions best underwater. It definitely doesn't have the power to stop Joan's yacht."

"So we'll improvise. What kind of firearm does

she have? She has to run out of bullets at some point."

"We don't know how much ammo she brought with her."

"So far, we know Joan is a lousy shot. All we need to do is persuade her to use up all her bullets."

Reynolds met my eye and his mouth pressed into a grim line. "Even a lousy shot gets lucky sometimes."

"That's a risk we'll have to take. Zigzag around her yacht and get her to shoot at us."

"I can't risk the lives of two civilians engaging in that sort of harebrained action."

"Fine," I muttered. "Bring us close enough for me to speargun her right arm. I've seen Joan hold her coffee cup with her right hand, so it's a safe bet to assume she's right-handed."

"Sister Pauline, you're small. Can you fit in one of the boxes under the seats?" Reynolds asked.

"I can try." The nun crawled to the edge of the boat, and I helped her into a storage box. It was a squeeze, but she fit. Before I closed the seat, she gazed up at me with an anxious expression. "What about Bran?"

I gave her a wobbly smile. "I'll look after him." I hoped I could make good on my promise. I sure intended to try.

Once Sister Pauline was in reasonable safety, Reynolds increased our speed and brought us up to the side of the yacht. His worried eyes met mine. "You sure about this, Maggie?"

I clutched the speargun in my fist. "I'm sure. I have good aim."

He nodded. "Okay. Let's do this thing."

A moment later, Joan approached, gun raised. "You shouldn't have followed me. Why couldn't you mind your own business?"

I hoisted the speargun and let loose. It hit Joan's arm, and she let the gun drop with a cry of pain.

Ignoring Reynolds's shouts of protest, I leaped onto the deck of Joan's yacht. Had the circumstances been different, I'd have stopped to admire it—sleek wooden boards with a chrome surround. The yacht hadn't come cheap. Unfortunately, the boat's psycho owner lessened its appeal as a place to hang out.

I took a step toward the now bleeding Joan. "Hit the deck—literally. I don't want to hurt you any more than I have to."

Joan snarled at me and groped for the gun with her left hand. And struck gold. She raised the weapon and took a shot at me before I could duck. A vicious sting spread through my right earlobe, and warm blood trickled down my neck. A surge of white-hot anger burned through me. She'd barely grazed me, but I knew that was only thanks to her being a terrible shot.

Joan pulled the trigger a second time and swore when she realized she needed to reload.

I seized my opportunity. I tackled her crumpled form and kicked the shotgun out of her reach. Despite her fragile appearance, Joan fought like a tiger. She yanked the spear out of her arm and tried to stab me with it. I sidestepped her in the nick of time.

"You interfering cow," Joan snapped, advancing for a second attempt. "You should have left me alone."

"*You* shouldn't have murdered Sandra Walker and let my aunt take the blame."

An emotion I couldn't pinpoint flickered across the other woman's face before her shutters slammed down. "Using Noreen's pills wasn't planned. I intended to kill Sandra with sleeping tablets, but they must have fallen out of my purse."

That explained the Stilnoct in the movie theater. "So you decided to improvise and steal my aunt's pills to do the deed?" I glared at her. "Noreen was supposed to be your friend."

"She was my friend." Joan compressed her lips. "I'm sorry she's been blamed."

"But not sorry enough to confess to the murder."

Her eyes snapped to attention. "I'm telling you what I did, aren't I?"

"Only because you have no intention of letting me leave this yacht alive." Despite my bravado, I was quaking inside. Where the heck was Reynolds? I tasted bile, but I stood my ground. No way was I letting this woman get away with murder.

Joan took another step toward me. I stiffened, my heart pounding against my ribs. When she came just a little closer, I'd take her down with a swift punch. My fingers curled into a fist, but before I could replicate the punch that had ended my marriage and my career, Bran zoomed past me with a delighted bark and hurled himself at Joan. With a screech that was worthy of a banshee, Joan dropped like a stone.

"Bran," I yelled. "Get off her. She'll hurt you."

"I don't think she will," said Reynolds's deep voice from my left. "Looks like Bran's managed to dislodge the spear from her hand."

Slack-jawed, I stared at the scene unfolding before me. Bran straddled Joan, interspersing gleeful barks with generous tongue-lashings. "Is he attacking her?"

"Licking," said Reynolds, his voice shaking with laughter. "He's licking her into submission."

"I always liked that dog," I said as Reynolds shooed Bran away and handcuffed Joan. "He's getting a steak dinner tonight."

THE MORNING after Joan's arrest, I woke to find the fields covered in a blanket of snow. Poly's kittens were thriving, and content to snuggle with their mother in front of the fireplace. Faced with an empty fridge, Noreen and I bundled up in our warmest winter clothes, and piled Bran and several empty shopping bags into the back of the car. When we reached Smuggler's Cove, my aunt parked in her usual spot in front of The Movie Theater Café.

"Hang on a sec. You said we were going shopping,

and then meeting Philomena and Julie to take Bran for a walk."

"I lied." Noreen shoved a scarf into my hands. "Put this over your eyes."

I stroked the soft wool and blinked in confusion. "You want me blindfolded?"

"Yes."

"But—"

My aunt clucked in disapproval. "No questions, Maggie. For once, do as you're told."

I hesitated for a second, and then wrapped the scarf around my head, grumbling. "All right. We'll do it your way. This tight enough?"

My aunt narrowed her eyes. "You're peeking, aren't you?"

I laughed. "Of course."

She shook her head and sighed. "Turn around and let me tie the scarf."

"Ouch," I said as my aunt pulled the scarf tight around my eyes.

"That'll do. Hang on a sec." Noreen's door slammed. A moment later, she wrenched open the passenger door and hauled me out of the car. "Take my arm. I'll guide you in."

I heard Bran's happy panting beside me. "What's going on? I don't like surprises."

"From one chocaholic to another, trust me when I say you'll like this one."

"Ooh, chocolate. Okay, I'm game." I allowed my aunt to lead me from the car to the café entrance.

When we walked into The Movie Theater Café, the familiar jangle over the door was drowned out by applause. "Whoa. What's going on?"

My aunt whipped off my scarf, and I gasped when I registered the crowd before me. Under a "Well Done, Maggie" banner stood half the population of Whisper Island. Lenny, Julie, Philomena, Sister Pauline, the Two Gerries, the Spinsters, and a sea of faces swam before me. Even Paddy Driscoll had come to congratulate me on clearing Noreen's name.

"Wow," I murmured, flustered by the crowd, yet flattered that so many people wanted to show their gratitude. "Thank you all for coming."

Bran—probably anticipating his next meal— danced around my legs. I bent to stroke his soft fur, grateful for the distraction and the chance to regain my composure.

Paul and Melanie stood grim-faced by the Bette Davis table. Melanie slid a pleading look at her husband, but he gave her a gentle shove between the shoulder blades, urging her forward.

When she stood before me, my erstwhile adversary forced a smile and looked me in the eye. "Of all the people on Whisper Island," Melanie began in a halting voice, as if feeling her way for the correct tone to use in this situation, "I'd never have guessed that Joan Sweetman was capable of murder." She took a ragged breath. "But then I had no idea Mummy was blackmailing people. Thank you for getting to the bottom of the mystery, Maggie."

"Every murder victim deserves justice. I hope Joan's arrest will help to bring you and your brother closure." I believed in the sentiment, even if Sandra Walker hadn't been the world's nicest inhabitant.

Nick Sweetman stepped forward, a shy smile on his usually dour countenance. He held Jennifer Pearce's hand. Despite the shadows beneath both their eyes that hinted of little sleep, they'd lost the stiffness I'd noticed the first time I'd met them.

"I also want to thank you," Nick said. "If it hadn't been for you, I'd never have known my step—" he broke off, and cleared his throat. "I'd never have known that *Joan* wasn't entitled to my father's money."

"I'm sorry you had to find out under these circumstances."

Nick's smile faded. "Looking back, Joan was always secretive. I don't think her marriage to my father was a happy one, yet widowhood suited her even less. Perhaps the strain of living a lie took its toll."

"Maybe." I turned to Jennifer. "What will happen now? How long will it take for Joan to come to trial?"

"That depends," the lawyer said. "Joan's been placed under psychiatric care, temporarily at least. We're not sure if she'll be deemed fit to stand trial. Either way, she's admitted everything. Trial or no trial, she'll be locked up for a very long time."

The idea of Joan being locked away afforded me no pleasure, but I was relieved that law and order had been restored to Whisper Island. If I'd helped to make that happen, maybe all the craziness in my life over the last couple of months had had a purpose after all.

"Enough of the sad stuff. Wait until you see what I've made for you, Maggie." Noreen beamed at me and bustled into the kitchen. A moment later, she emerged carrying an enormous chocolate cake, lovingly decorated with a marzipan Irish cottage, complete with a thatched roof and stacked stone wall.

"It's beautiful," I gasped. "When did you have time to make this?"

She grinned. "I snuck out during the night."

"So much for my detective skills," I said with a laugh. "I slept like a log."

"Thanks to you, Sandra Walker's murderer is behind bars. And that means everyone knows I'm innocent." Noreen placed the cake on James Cagney and squeezed me into a bear hug. "The cake is my small token of appreciation for all that you've done for me and the rest of the islanders."

My throat swelled. I liked to think I'd done good during my time as a San Francisco cop, but unless they were career criminals, I rarely got the chance to see how the people I'd interacted with on a case fared after it was solved. Having the opportunity to use my detective skills to assist people I knew and cared about was a novel experience. "I was glad to help."

"And we're glad you were here to help." Noreen's

smile broadened. "Which brings me to your real thank-you present. Philomena?"

Her sister stepped forward and pumped my hand before shoving a gold envelope at me. "On behalf of all of us, we'd like to give you this."

Curiosity burned through me. I tore open the envelope and pulled out the card within. My eyes widened when I read its contents. "Are you serious? A lease on a cottage until the end of *May*?"

"You came to Whisper Island for some rest and relaxation," Philomena said. "Instead, you were faced with a murder to solve. We think you deserve a proper extended holiday, so we all chipped in to pay three months' rent on one of the holiday cottages next to my land."

"Sorry you can't move in sooner," Noreen added, "but the owners are using the off season to paint the insides of the cottages. You're welcome to stay with me until it's ready."

Hot tears stung my eyes. "That's incredibly kind of you. The lease, the hospitality, everything."

"So you'll stay on the island?" Julie bounced in front of me, her expression eager. "You still have to help me train for the Runathon, remember?"

I laughed. "Yes, I'll stay."

The bell over the café entrance jangled, and a cool breeze swept through the room before the new arrival closed the door. "Did I hear you say you're staying on Whisper Island?" asked a deep voice behind me. "Just promise me you'll stick to mystery movies and leave the real sleuthing to me."

I whirled around to face Sergeant Liam Reynolds. He was wearing the biker leathers he'd had on the first time I'd encountered him. Under the snow-covered brim of his hat, his bright blue eyes twinkled with good humor. My treacherous heart skipped a beat.

"I'm staying until the end of May," I said stiffly, reminding myself that the last thing I needed was to get involved with someone, especially not a sexy Irish cop who'd leave the island now that the case had been wrapped up. "I'm moving into one of the holiday cottages next door to Noreen."

"Is that so?" Reynolds's teasing smile widened. "What number?"

"Uh, I don't know." I turned to Noreen. "Which cottage did you rent for me?"

"Number Eight," she said. "It's the one nearest the entrance."

Sergeant Reynolds laughed. "In that case, Maggie and I will be neighbors."

My jaw dropped. "Wait...*you're* moving to Whisper Island?"

He grinned at my horrified expression and winked. "Yeah. I've rented the cottage next to yours."

—THE END—

Thanks for reading **Dial P For Poison.** I hope you enjoyed Maggie's first adventure on Whisper Island!

Maggie and her friends are back for more movies, mayhem, and murder in **The Postman Always Dies Twice**, out 20 April. Turn the page to read an excerpt!

And if you'd like to try Maggie's favorite cocktail, I've included a recipe for Peppermint Creams on the next page.

Join my mailing list and get news, giveaways, and an exclusive FREE Movie Club Mystery serial! Join Maggie and her friends as they solve the mystery in *To Hatch a Thief*. The first episode will be sent in April 2017.
http://zarakeane.com/newsletter2

Would you like to try Maggie's signature cocktail and the murder weapon in **Dial P For Poison**? Here's the recipe—minus the fatal ingredient!

PEPPERMINT CREAM COCKTAIL

- 3/4 (20ml) oz crème de menthe
- 3/4 (20ml) white crème de cacao
- 3/4 (20ml) hazelnut liqueur
- 3/4 (20ml) Baileys Irish Cream
- 3/4 (20ml) cream
- 3/4 (20ml) milk
- Good quality cocoa powder

1. Half-fill a cocktail shaker with ice cubes.
2. Pour in all the ingredients and shake vigorously.
3. Strain into a cocktail glass and top with milk to taste.
4. Sift a light dusting of cocoa powder on the top and serve.

Maggie's tip: If you'd prefer a more subtle hint of mint, use half the recommended amount of crème de menthe and a little more Baileys.

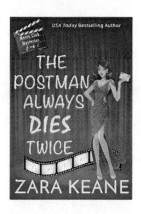

POSTMEN. POLTERGEISTS. POTEEN.

Zara's brand new cozy mystery series continues with *The Postman Always Dies Twice.*

When former San Francisco cop, Maggie Doyle, extends her stay in Ireland, dealing with more murder and mayhem isn't on her to-do list. The instant Maggie and her UFO-enthusiast friend discover the dead body of the Whisper Island postman, Maggie's plans to chill for the next two months are put on ice.

After Police Sergeant Reynolds, Maggie's handsome neighbor, arrests Lenny's brother for the murder, her friend begs her to find the real killer. Meanwhile, Maggie is hired to investigate ghostly goings on at the Whisper Island Hotel. Can she solve two crimes before St. Patrick's Day? Or will the island's annual celebrations end in a glittery flame of green, white, and orange?

EXCERPT FROM *THE POSTMAN ALWAYS DIES TWICE*

Whisper Island, Ireland

I'd encountered plenty of culture shocks since I'd swapped my cheating husband and my career in the San Francisco PD for a remote Irish island. Discovering that used car salesmen were the same slick, sons-of-guns all over the world was almost a comfort.

I fixed the proprietor of Zippy Motors with a hard stare. "I'll give you three hundred bucks, and not a penny more."

"Aw, come on, Maggie. A man's gotta eat. This little beauty will zip you around—just like our slogan." Jack Logan treated me to the killer smile that had left a trail of broken hearts across Whisper Island in the years before he'd developed a beer belly and a comb-over. I remained unmoved.

"The car's fit for scrap metal," I said. "Before I shell out any money, never mind your insane asking price, I need to know the vehicle will survive the couple of months I'm staying on the island."

"Sure it will." Jack spread his palms wide in a gesture that was presumably designed to put his customers at ease. "Would I sell you a lemon? I value my reputation."

I rolled my eyes. "Your reputation stinks. You're still in business because you get an influx of clueless tourists every summer who are willing to rent one of your wrecks for the season."

The salesman's composure faltered. "Now that's a bit harsh."

"But true. I'm Lenny's friend, remember? Your cousin's told me all about you." And the parts Lenny hadn't told me, I could guess. Jack wore designer clothes and reeked of expensive aftershave. I glanced up at Zippy Motors's battered sign. Somehow, I doubted Jack funded his flash lifestyle with the money he made from selling and renting wrecks.

I strolled around the Ford Fiesta, examining it for obvious patches of rust. "Today's your lucky day, Jack. I'm in need of a cheap ride, and your establishment is on the island if there's any trouble with my purchase." I made eye contact. "You do offer an after purchase warranty, right?"

The man's Adam's apple bobbed. "Uh, sure, but nothing will go wrong with the car."

"For your sake, I hope not." I patted the ancient vehicle and it didn't fall apart under my touch. I took this to be a good sign. "Cash, I presume?"

After I'd completed my transaction with Jack Logan, I slid behind the wheel of my new-to-me ride and drove out of Smuggler's Cove. I hung a left at the crossroads on the edge of town, and headed in the direction of my new home—a sweet little holiday cottage on the far side of Whisper Island. As a Thank You for my help in solving a murder mystery, my aunts and friends had pooled their resources to pay for two months' rent on the cottage, thus treating me to an extended vacation on their island. I'd moved in last week. After spending six weeks living with my aunt, Noreen, and her menagerie of animals, I was still getting used to the silence.

The drive across the island took thirty minutes. I took it slow, soaking in the sights. The snow we'd had earlier in the winter hadn't lasted long, and now that it was early March, the first signs of spring were starting to show. The days were growing longer, and a few flowers had begun to bloom. As the road wound around the edge of the cliffs, I passed woodland and rolling green hills before finally reaching the gates of my new residence.

My cottage was part of a complex of eight holiday homes named Shamrock Cottages—although I had yet to see any evidence that shamrocks grew in the vicinity. Built on a slope, the cottage boasted a spectacular view of the sea through my front windows. Each cottage in the complex had a fenced-in garden with just enough room for an outdoor table and chairs. There was also a communal playground, as well as a shared games room.

When I drove through the gates of Shamrock Cottages, my aunt, Noreen, was waiting on my doorstep. She wore a wide smile on her face, and balanced a tray of freshly baked scones in her arms. My mouth watered at the sight. Since moving out of her house, I'd started to skip breakfast. Not smart, but it had helped me lose a few of the pounds I'd gained while living with Noreen and eating her enormous portions. Bran, my aunt's lively Border collie-Labrador mix, danced by her side, tripping over Noreen's large bag in his excitement to see me.

The instant I stepped out of my car, Bran bounded over and treated me to an obligatory crotch sniff. "Cut that out," I said, bending down to pet his soft fur. "You gotta learn manners."

"Too late for that, I'm afraid," my aunt said with a laugh. "I've tried everything. On the plus side, he only does it to people he likes."

I scratched Bran under his chin. "While I'm honored to be liked by you, Bran, I wish you'd show your affection for me in some other way."

As if he understood my words, the dog treated my hand to a generous lick. I gave him a last pat and drew my key from my jacket pocket.

My aunt squinted at the car and then leaped back in horror. "Please don't tell me you went to Zippy Motors."

"They're cheap, and I'm low on cash." I slammed the driver's door and strode toward the cottage door, Bran at my heels. "Mmm. Those scones smell divine."

My aunt clucked with disapproval. "Don't change the subject. Jack Logan is a snake. I buy cheap cars, but even I won't go near him. I'm convinced he's laundering money at that place."

"It's a done deal now," I said cheerfully. I unlocked the door and relieved my aunt of the tray. "Want to come in for a coffee? Because I'm totally eating one of these scones."

"That would be lovely." My aunt bounded into the cottage with an agility that belied her fifty-six years. "I have some housewarming gifts for you."

I raised an eyebrow. "More? You've already given me enough towels to dry a family of six."

Noreen bounced on the spot, making her jet-black curls dance. "These gifts are of a more lively nature. Literally."

I sucked in a breath. "Oh, no. Not the pet thing again."

"Just hear me out before you object, Maggie. You could you could do with some company now that you're out here all alone. Bran can act as a guard dog."

I placed the tray on the kitchen counter and shook my head emphatically. "You're not foisting the dog onto me. No way. Besides, I live next door to a policeman. What could be safer than that?"

My aunt clucked in disapproval. "Sure, Sergeant Reynolds hasn't moved in properly yet. Even if he had, he'd hardly ever be home. He's working crazy hours in pursuit of those eejits who keep sneaking onto farms and causing havoc. Did you hear about Paddy Driscoll's sheep?"

"Clearly, I'm behind on island gossip." I switched on the coffee machine and got out plates and coffee mugs. "What happened to Paddy's sheep?"

"They were given a makeover last night,"

I looked at my aunt over my shoulder and slow-blinked. "What does a sheep makeover involve?"

"They were dressed in knitted outfits made out of acrylic yarn."

"Wow." I whistled. "An animal activist on a mission?"

"Maybe. At any rate, Paddy's chief issue was the fact that the pattern on the sheeps' outfits was the Union Jack." Noreen's lips twitched with amusement. "Not a flag likely to please a man of Paddy's political persuasions."

I recalled the huge Irish flag painted on the wall of Paddy's barn, and the various pro-I.R.A. sentiments the grumpy farmer had uttered in my presence. No, he wouldn't be pleased to find his sheep wearing the British flag.

After I'd made a cappuccino for my aunt and a double espresso for me, I placed two of the scones on plates and put everything on the table. On autopilot, I retrieved one of the doggie snacks I kept for Bran's visits from the drawer under the sink.

"I'm serious about you adopting Bran," my aunt said, watching me feed the grateful dog his treat. "You're the one taking him on most of his walks these days.

"It's not fair to the dog. I'm only on Whisper Island until May."

"Until the end of May," my aunt corrected, as though the distinction made all the difference in the world. "Why don't you take him until then? He'll be great company for you and the cats."

"Cats?" My voice rose in a crescendo. I sucked in a breath and scanned the kitchen for evidence of feline habitation. My gaze came to rest on the big carrier bag at Noreen's feet and I groaned out loud. "Oh, no."

Inside the carrier bag, six kittens snuggled against their mother, snoozing peacefully in a basket.

"Seeing as you rescued Poly's kittens, I thought you'd like to have a couple of them to keep you company. They're not ready to leave their mum permanently yet, so I brought her with them."

"A couple doesn't mean six. Besides, Sergeant Reynolds rescued one of the kittens. I just helped."

"Exactly." My aunt beamed at me. "Rosie is the one on the far left. I'm sure she'd love to come and live with you."

"Not happening, Noreen. I love you to bits, but the animals are leaving when you do."

My aunt grinned across the table and spread a generous helping of strawberry jam over her scone. "I'll wear you down, Miss Maggie. You just see if I don't."

Before I could utter another protest, the familiar splutter of an old VW van drew my attention to the kitchen window. Through the glass, I saw my friend, Lenny, park his van at the entrance to Shamrock Cottages. Like my car, the van had seen better years, and better paint jobs. Lenny's recent decision to paint it psychedelic purple hadn't enhanced the vehicle's appeal.

"Lenny just pulled up," I told my aunt. "I'll go let him in."

When I opened my front door, Lenny was ambling toward me, carrying a large plastic bag. He stopped short when he saw my new car and circled it as one would a feral beast. "Aw, Maggie. You went to Jack's place? What did I tell you about that guy?"

"That he's a crook and a swindler and to run far and fast," I replied. "And although Jack's cons list outweighs his pros, he's cheap and easily intimidated."

"I wouldn't be so sure about the easily intimidated part," Lenny said, tugging on his scraggly beard. "He's bold enough to drive a brand new Porsche around the island one minute, and plead poverty to the Inland Revenue the next."

"I take it Jack isn't keen on paying taxes?"

"That's one way of putting it. But enough about my idiot cousin. How are you doing? All settled into your new home?" My friend's easy-going smile lit up his thin face, transforming him from homely to kinda-cute-in-a-geeky-sorta-way. We'd been buddies since I'd spent my summers on Whisper Island as a child. Although we'd lost touch as adults, our friendship had picked up where we'd left off when I returned to the island in January.

"It's fab. I like it so much it'll be hard to leave when the lease is up." I nodded in the direction of the kitchen. "Want to come in for a coffee? Noreen's here and she brought scones."

"I can't stay. I have to go to Paddy Driscoll's place to fix his computer." He held up the plastic carrier bag. "I thought I'd swing by yours on the way and give you your housewarming present."

"As long as it's not a pet, we're good," I quipped, remembering the basket of kittens with a sinking sensation in my stomach. I had a feeling Noreen would wear me down.

"No worries." Lenny's bony face split into a grin that brought a twinkle to his pale blue eyes. "I thought you needed a little greenery in your new home."

He opened the bag and removed a leafy potted plant...a leafy potted cannabis plant. "I thought it'd liven up your new home."

"I can think of more legal ways to liven up my cottage." I shot him a look of exasperation. "Have you forgotten I live next door to a police officer?"

Lenny's grin faded. "Oops. I didn't think of Reynolds."

"You don't say," I said, deadpan. "Even if I was inclined to keep it, I have an unfortunate track record with plants.

Bran and my aunt emerged from the kitchen.

"She's not joking," Noreen said, pulling on her coat. "She killed a cactus while she was staying with me."

I grimaced. "Guilty as charged."

When she'd buttoned up her duffel coat, Noreen squeezed my arm. "I'd best be off, love. I need to get to the café and relieve Fiona. I'll collect you at six-thirty for the Movie Club meeting. Will that suit you?"

"Six-thirty sounds good." I noticed a conspicuous absence of kittens in her carrier bag. "Whoa. You're not leaving me with the cats and—" Bran rubbed against my legs, silencing me with the plaintive expression in his doggie eyes. I bit back a sigh. Who could resist that look? "Do you want to stay with me for a while, buddy?"

Bran's response was to lick my hand. Man, that dog knew how to pull at my heartstrings.

"If you're keeping Bran, you can hardly turf out the cats," Noreen said as if the matter was decided. She paused when she noticed the plant in my arms. "Oh, that's a beautiful bit of greenery."

I laughed. "A beautiful bit of greenery that's destined for the garbage can."

"Oh, no." My aunt looked horrified. "You can't do that. I'll take it home with me."

"Noreen, that's not a good idea."

"It'd look great in your house," Lenny said straight-faced. "It'd definitely add class to the joint."

I shot him a warning look. "Don't listen to him. Take my advice and get rid of it."

310 The Postman Always Dies Twice (Movie Club Mys...

"Nonsense," Noreen said. "I have loads of plants. It'll fit right in."

I opened my mouth to protest, but my words were drowned out by the roar of a motorcycle crunching up the gravel drive. Sergeant Liam Reynolds pulled up outside his cottage, and leaped off his bike. He pulled off his helmet to reveal close-cropped dark blond hair and a face that would have been movie star handsome but for a nose that had been broken more than once. To my annoyance, a jolt of desire set my blood humming.

"Uh, oh," Lenny whispered beside me. "Now we're for it."

The words I muttered beneath my breath were less polite. "What possessed you to show up here with a cannabis plant?" I whispered.

"I'm sorry," Lenny whispered back. "I thought it would give you a laugh."

Reynolds, also known as Sergeant Hottie—okay, known as Sergeant Hottie *by me*—pulled off his helmet and smiled at us. My heart thumped a little faster.

"Coo-ee," my aunt called. To my horror, she held up the cannabis plant for Reynolds to see. "Look what Maggie gave me. Isn't it lovely?"

Oblivious to the policeman's slack-jawed expression, my aunt got into her car, waved to us, and drove off with the cannabis plant on her passenger seat.

ALSO BY ZARA KEANE

Movie Club MYSTERIES—Cozy Mystery

BALLYBEG SERIES—Contemporary Romance

BALLYBEG BAD BOYS—Romantic Suspense

DUBLIN MAFIA—Romantic Suspense

Final Target

Kiss Shot

Bullet Point (2017)

ABOUT ZARA KEANE

USA Today bestselling author Zara Keane grew up in Dublin, Ireland, but spent her summers in a small town very similar to the fictitious Whisper Island and Ballybeg.

She currently lives in Switzerland with her family. When she's not writing or wrestling small people, she drinks far too much coffee, and tries—with occasional success—to resist the siren call of Swiss chocolate.

Zara has an active reader group, **The Ballybeg Belles**, where she chats, shares snippets of upcoming stories, and hosts members-only giveaways. She hopes to join you for a virtual pint very soon!

zarakeane.com